CW00520563

Death between the Vines

G J Bellamy

ISBN 9798432876782

SECOND EDITION

Copyright © 2021, 2022 by G J Bellamy. All rights reserved. This publication is a work of fiction. All names, characters and events in this publication, other than those clearly in the public domain, are fictitious and any resemblance to real persons, living or dead, or actual events is purely coincidental.

The moral right of the author has been asserted.

No part of this publication may be reproduced, stored in a retrieval system, or transmitted in any form or by any means, without the prior express written permission of the publisher.

G J Bellamy

gjbellamy.com

PREFACE

Dear Reader,

Here is a very brief note because I have no wish to keep you from your story.

This book might be set in a mythical and highly fictionalized US state - let's call it Transatlantica - where, and I humbly apologize for this, stories arc recorded with British spellings. Can you believe it?

So, you'll find grey instead of gray, flavour instead of flavor, and I have little to offer in defense/defence for this international outrage.

Why do this? - you might ask if you're a US reader. The answer is simple. The US is a dynamic place and is the only venue where certain elements of the story could be played out (and this goes for the rest of the series, too.) However, from my mother's knee I have learnt British English and it's the way I speak and write.

I could never pass myself off as a US national, lacking the intimate knowledge which comes from having grown up in or having travelled extensively through the US. Even if I had attempted to use US spelling and phrasing, you'd undoubtedly smell a rat and the story itself would be diminished. Neither of us would be happy with that.

Therefore, please look upon the following work of fiction as a story set in the USA but narrated and recorded by someone with a British accent.

Enough from me, I think, except to say, I hope you enjoy the story.
G J Bellamy
PS. Transatlantica is about 150 miles due East of Nantucket

Contents

1. Brent's journey begins   1

2. A tale of two cases   15

3. The police case   23

4. Taking on a gang   33

5. Snapshot of a murder   41

6. Brent comes on board   51

7. The test   57

8. Friction   65

9. No way to conduct an investigation   71

10. Plain sailing   79

11. Red, red wine   87

12. Ouch   99

13. Staff troubles   105

14. Wine industry   113

15. The old days   119

16. Things get weird   135

17. Beginning to gel   147

18. Artistic discussion   161

19. A different way   173

20. Undercurrents   183

21. Stand-off   193

22. A pleasant time   203

23. A surprising turn of events   211

24. A new friend, an old enemy   219

25. Two heads are better than one   225

26. Time for action   235

27. The big dog's house   245

28. Tea for four   261

29. All that glitters is not gold   277

30. A near miss   293

31. Journey's end   299

32. EPILOGUE   305

33. EPI-PROLOGUE   311

Also By G J Bellamy   317

Chapter One

Brent's journey begins

The late spring sun was about to rise as a swift flew low and fast over the vineyard. The bird's smooth flight against the pale grey-white sky was one long swoop. Below it, stretching into the hazy distance, were ghostly grey terraced lines, in perfectly straight order, descending a steeply sloping hill into the valley floor where the ranks of trained plants were encompassed by a fringe of dark trees, almost black in the early hour.

Grass grew between each row of double cordon grapevines in the fertile valley but further up the hill where the stony, sandy soil seemed poorer, there was only bare earth to be found. Yet here lay the terroir which produced the best pinot noir grapes and, as a result, the finest wine of its kind in the region.

The surface of the soil in this upper vineyard was damp and a light mist was rising about the vines as the dew evaporated. There was just enough moisture to form small, silver drops on the tips of the broad-lobed leaves. They looked like little jewels. One detached itself from the tip of a leaf and fell upon the sleeve of a jacket. It made a slight sound as it hit the arm, which was hung up awkwardly on the lowest of three cordon wires, but the wearer of the jacket did not hear it. She could not hear it for some vile and abominable person had put an end to her hearing, to her seeing, to her breathing, with a long kitchen knife, now buried in her heart. Only the swift and the murderer knew she was there.

Charles Babbington, widower, sat on the small, raised terrace at the rear of his house. It was 'his' house now and no longer 'their' house. His wife Sheila had been murdered, and he was alone. The sun did not warm him as he looked out over the rows of vines. He sat motionless and, though an engineer by profession, could not at that moment properly arrange two thoughts together. He remembered he needed to get butter at the store just before agonizing over why Sheila had been savagely killed. There were things he should be doing, but he could not recall what they were. Babbington guessed there were probably at least twenty tasks needing attention, but what they might be eluded him.

His sister-in-law arrived. As was usual, Nora entered the house without knocking. She called out but, receiving no response, walked to the back where the large sunroom was situated.

"I called out, but you didn't answer," said Nora.

"Hello. Uh, I didn't hear you."

"Hmm... Look, you can't let yourself go, Charles. Everything will fall to pieces around you."

"I know... Does it matter?"

"Sure it matters. You've got to move on and keep the estate running. Sheila didn't dedicate her life to this place just so you can let it fail."

"I'm still grieving, Nora."

"Aren't we all? How do you think I feel? But life goes on."

"Even when it doesn't seem worth living?"

"That's your problem, right there. You're giving up... Let me come in and manage the place. I can do it... Pay me a salary and a share of the profits. There were a lot of things Sheila should have done that needed doing - like rebranding. I've got some great ideas you should hear."

"She only died a few weeks ago... I can't think about it now."

"This is exactly when you *should* be thinking about it. The vineyard can't run itself. You need to take action."

"I don't know... We've never seen eye to eye over many things, Nora."

"This is business, and that makes it different. You have to decide. Hire me and you'll see what a difference I'll make... Sheila promised to give me a job here if the work got too much for her."

"She did? When did she say that?"

"Just after you bought the place. We had an understanding... I'm her family. Why would she not hire me? She promised me a job."

Charles sat quietly. He remembered a past conversation with Sheila but could not place the year. She had said that Nora asked for a job and that she had replied she would think about it. Privately, she had told Charles that it would be a disaster to hire Nora. Charles had agreed. Nora was the last person he would consider hiring.

"She never mentioned it to me."

"What? Are you calling me a liar?"

"Of course I'm not... but I don't think it would be a good fit if you worked here. You've never worked in the wine industry and there is so much to learn. It would take months before you were up to speed on the basics."

"So, you're saying you're not going to hire me?"

"If we hired a manager, he or she would need to be an industry professional."

"I just don't believe this. She promised me a job and you're not going to honour Sheila's promise? That's disgusting!"

Nora got up.

"You know, some of the family have been talking. They were saying how statistics show that the husband's usually the murderer. I said, no, not Charles. He hasn't got it in him. But you know what? I think they might be right."

Nora stomped off and left the house, slamming the door behind her. Charles went back to staring at the vineyard and the sky.

"You're going to close the office, then?" asked Paul Blake. The big man was sitting in a dark red, plush chair, opposite a tidy, gleaming walnut desk. He looked around the modestly sized office that was well-furnished and tastefully decorated. "That's a pity. It looks really nice... something out of the forties. I wish I could use it in my line of business. I would seriously consider taking it over from you."

"Would you? Then, go ahead. I'll give you the furniture." The good-looking man behind the desk gazed steadily and hopefully at his friend. Brent Umber had an open, friendly face, blue eyes, and thick brown hair. He looked younger than his thirty-two years.

"That's a nice thought, but who expects a plumber to have an office? C'mon, Brent, who makes an appointment with a plumber in an office? I only need a place to keep my tools, truck, and a filing cabinet for paperwork."

"Oh, I realize that. It's just that I put a lot of effort into getting the place how I wanted it and now, with the lease up, I hate the prospect of seeing it all go to pieces. I'd so much rather someone I knew would have it."

"Sorry I can't help you. But is the private investigator business that bad?"

"Not really. It's slack at the moment. Mind you, when I started a year ago, I naturally assumed, from all the hard-boiled detective stories I'd ever read, that all I had to do was open an office in a run-down neighbourhood and keep a bottle of whiskey in a filing cabinet, which two things would naturally cause adventure and success to follow. I expected sultry beauties and perspiring businessmen to be crowding through the door to hire my services. Instead, most of my business is conducted by email and phone calls. And, let me tell you, it's almost exclusively ordinary, dull matters which are not in the slightest degree stimulating. Not once has a desperate woman entered my sanctuary, fearing she was being followed."

"Ha, welcome to the real world. Plumbing has its difficulties, too. I can't tell you the number of times I've had the call, 'Save me! Save me! My house is flooding.' They're all happy and relieved to see me when I arrive at three on a Sunday afternoon. Yet, when they get the bill, they sing quite a different tune. Then it's, 'How much!? For two hours' work? I should become a plumber.'"

"Is that how it goes? I suppose your days off are not as precious to them as they are to you." Brent paused for a moment before saying, "Well, this office does not justify its continuance if it cannot generate income. I doubt I get four prospective clients a month through the door. Some of those are divorce cases which I refuse to take on."

Brent got up and went over to look out of the window. At a fraction over six feet, he was very well-dressed in casual business clothes that suited his athletic build.

"Why's that?" Paul got up and joined him. They both surveyed the street below through the Venetian blinds.

"I don't like it. Getting the dirt on cheating spouses is not for me. It's all too personal and I just don't like it."

"With divorce-work excluded, what business does that leave for you?"

"A fair bit. Thefts, a few frauds... I had an interesting embezzlement last month. And espionage, believe it or not."

"It's funny how you got into this. I mean, you really should have been a detective," said Paul.

"Well, we both know why that can't happen," said Brent.

"Yeah. S'funny... Talking of detectives, I bumped into Bennett the other day."

"To speak to?"

"Yep. We got along all right. He asked after the family and I asked after his."

"So, you don't hold a grudge against him even though he put you inside?"

"Me? No. He was only doing his job."

"A little too well, maybe," said Brent, wryly.

"True. Still, I only got a year on a minor charge. I'm respectable now. It has to stay that way, too, because the next time the judge will throw the book at me."

"It's the excitement of our former life that I miss," said Brent. "I'm not finding a satisfying replacement for it in my current occupation."

"Yeah, well, if you had been caught, you'd think differently," said Paul without humour.

"Probably. Hello, that woman across the street - she has the hallmarks of a prospective client. Yes, I do believe she's coming this way."

"How can you tell she's a client?"

"She's dressed smartly... for an appointment... it's hard to explain... she looks tense and determined... Something's bothering her and she's on a mission." Brent's gaze was fixed on the figure below as she waited at the corner for a gap in the traffic in order to cross the road. "Yes, she's coming into the building. Quick, Paul! You are now my client."

As the woman entered the outer office, the signalling bell on the door rang merrily. Brent interrupted his 'important meeting' to welcome her, with assurances that he would only be another two minutes and then would be free to see her. He closed his office door.

Once Brent was back behind his desk, Paul asked, "Did you get the passes for the Vermeer collection?" The two men had an unlikely affinity for fine art.

"My friend at the art gallery says they're in the works. We'll be masquerading as reporters because the passes are for the media reception three weeks from today. Got to dress for the part, Paul. Have you got a suit that will do?"

"I have, but whether I still fit into it is another matter. I'll find something. Just think, to see Lady with the Black Mantilla, the Butter-churner, and The Dancers all together in the same room is a once in a lifetime opportunity."

"Without question, that's true. I'm thinking that Visit to the Tomb will prove to be the most enigmatic and may well be Johannes' finest work - for me, at least, it always has been. The lighting in the foreground is astonishing."

"You're right about the light. I don't know how he did it. Anyway, how long are you going to keep the lady waiting?"

"I think this is long enough," replied Brent. Both men got up from their chairs.

Brent opened the office door to allow Paul to pass through and, as he went, Paul turned to Brent and said, "I want to thank you once more for your excellent work. We don't know what we would have done without you." Paul smiled and shook Brent's hand.

"I'm just glad I could help," replied Brent.

They said goodbye and Paul left the office, still smiling, and nodded to the potential client on his way out.

"Will you come in, please?" said Brent to the woman. "I'm sorry to have kept you waiting."

"That's perfectly fine. I'm relieved you can see me without an appointment." The pleasant-looking, well-dressed woman in her late forties attempted a smile of sorts as she entered Brent's office.

"I'm Brent Umber." He indicated for her to sit in a chair as he spoke. "How can I help you?" When she was seated he sat down himself.

"We have a difficult situation... I'm not sure where to begin, even though I can't stop thinking about it all." She looked very tense and her face had that drawn look of persistent strain.

"Let's do this, then." Brent pulled a notepad from a desk drawer and took out a pen. "What is your name?"

"Sorry, I should have said. Carol Wilson."

"Is this a family matter?"

"Yes."

"How would you describe the problem?" Brent was poised to write the word, 'divorce'.

"It's my son, Jeremy. He's twenty. Jerry's becoming a drug dealer."

"*Becoming* a drug dealer? That's an odd way of phrasing it. It sounds as though he's going through an application process or training."

"It is like training, though it's a bit of both, in a way. He's always been wild and unpredictable... He got mixed up with the wrong crowd early on, despite and no matter what his father and I said to him. We warned him repeatedly, but he would never listen. That was all in the past. Now, he's getting involved with a gang that sells drugs."

"I see. A simple progression. Does Jeremy work? Live at home?"

"He moved out when he was eighteen... I hardly ever see him and he never speaks to his father. They don't get along at all. Jerry works in construction. This is a recent photograph of him."

The added stress of unburdening her story was beginning to show on her face. Carol looked as though she might not get through the interview without tears. Brent studied the photograph. The young man was decked out in a leather jacket, a gold chain, and a baseball cap on backwards. A wannabe if ever he saw one. But he was also a seriously potential 'will be' or even an 'already is'.

"I might be able to help," said Brent. "How deeply is Jerry involved with this gang? If he is a member, it'll be much harder to extricate him than if he is, let's say, an associate."

"He's not in it... not yet. He told me he wants to join but he has to prove himself to get in."

"Is there something I'm missing? Why would he volunteer such information to you? I would have thought that you'd be the last person he'd tell."

"He takes drugs as well. Not exactly an addict... not yet, anyway. I saw him just this Saturday and he was high on something. Cocaine, I think. He didn't stop talking, and I learned a lot that I hadn't heard before."

"That was fortuitous, then. So, we have Jerry, hoping to build a career in the illegal selling of poisonous drugs and obviously fully intent upon making a mess of things. He talks to you intermittently and not at all to his dad. What is dad's name?"

"Peter. You should know that he's the Assistant Commissioner in the Belton Police Department. That's part of the problem."

"Oh, yes, I can see that it would be."

Brent put down his pen and looked over towards the window. He was silent for many seconds.

"Why did Jerry go bad? There's something you haven't told me yet."

"Peter's my second husband and Jerry's step-father," replied Carol.

"Yes, that makes sense. I believe I can fill in some blanks. I hate to ask this but it is necessary - your first husband... living or dead?"

"Living. He found somebody else and just left me and the children - Jerry has an older sister. We were all devastated - by his callousness, his lack of caring."

"Oh, I see. He was one of those types," said Brent. "Now we have to pick up the pieces. What exactly would you like me to do?"

"I thought you might get more information about Jerry's activities with the gang. Peter is in an invidious position and says that he *has* to arrest him if he sees any evidence of gang activity. I thought that if *I* could come up with some solid information, actual evidence, I could persuade Jerry to leave it all behind before Peter found out and was forced to do something. I should tell you, Peter doesn't know I'm here. Neither of them does."

"So what you are proposing is a form of blackmail. Jerry will resent you... might never talk to you again if you pursue this course."

"At least he would be alive and away from that lifestyle. I think it would be better for me to lose him as a son than he be dead or in prison for years."

"Hmm, a desperate measure for a desperate time... I think I have a better idea than yours."

"You do?"

"Yes. I'll talk to him. I will get all the information you're asking for - it's definitely needed whatever happens. But I'll do everything I can to keep your relationship with your son intact. If you give me a free hand, I think I can fix things. Would you agree to this?"

Carol paused before answering. She looked uncertain. "I suppose so, although I can't imagine what you have in mind. But I have no idea what else to do. You're my last hope."

"As you're doing me such an honour as to trust me, I shall get on with the job immediately. First, this sheet outlines my fee and expenses structure." Brent slid a single sheet of paper towards Carol. "If that is acceptable to you then we can proceed. I imagine it will take at least two days, possibly three, to get the matter resolved."

Carol studied the sheet. Then she said, "Resolved? Aren't you being a bit too optimistic?"

"I'm always optimistic, but never stupidly so. I'll report overall progress to you on a daily basis. You call me about 6 p.m. each day. I will keep the details to a minimum as a precaution against anyone suspecting there's something going on. Here's my card." Brent gave Carol a business card. "At the end, let's say in a week's time, I will present you with a detailed, written report."

"I like your confidence. I wish I had some of it."

"Well, we shall see what happens. To expedite matters, I'll need details about Jerry, as many as you can give me - phone numbers, social media accounts, current address, names of friends, where he works during the day and where he hangs out at night - all those kinds of things. You don't want to be paying me to find out things like that, things you probably already know."

For fifteen minutes, Brent took down faithfully everything Carol told him, including that Jerry's last name was Miller - Carol's family name. When they had finished, he took up the pad and, leaning back in his chair, re-read some parts, commenting on them occasionally.

"Jerry is still living in Belton but, for the last year or so, he's been coming to the city at least once a week and has never said why. That suggests he could be a courier for the gang."

Brent marked the page. "Probably one of several couriers." He paused, then added, "Does he gamble?"

"No. At least, he never did as far as I know," replied Carol.

"Belton? That rings a bell. Wasn't that where a woman was found stabbed to death in a vineyard a couple of weeks ago?"

"That's right. Her name was Sheila Babbington. She was the owner. I'd met her once, briefly... on a tour of the winery. Her murder is so awful. I don't know who could have done such a thing. I think the world's going crazy."

"Putting a face to the victim of such a crime always makes it even worse. Is Peter involved with the case?"

"Not directly, he isn't. Another department is investigating it but they're having a hard time. Peter was telling me that there are too many suspects and very little hard evidence."

"Oh, I'm sorry to hear that... Must be difficult for them if they can't narrow the field down. Anyway, I'm sure they'll catch whoever did it in the end." Brent tried to sound much more optimistic than he actually was about this prospect.

"As for us," he continued, "I think that's all at present. I'll get the investigation going and we'll see what can be done. I feel confident we can get Jerry out of this mess. Before you go, I must ask you something. What made you choose me as an investigator?"

"Um, I'm not sure, really. I was driving by and I think it was because of the way the office looked from the street. It looked like what I'd imagined a private investigator's office to be. Although, I must say, the interior is so much nicer than I expected."

"Thank you. That's kind of you to say. Look, it's nearly lunchtime, and there's a very nice restaurant within walking distance. I have to make a few phone calls first, but then we could get a bite to eat." Brent looked hopeful.

"I don't think I will. Thanks for asking, but I'm not eating or sleeping very well at the moment. Also, I have to get home. I'm a nurse and I have a night shift this evening."

"Yes, of course. I'd ask you not to worry, but it wouldn't help any. What I *will* say is this - I'll do everything I can to get Jerry away from that gang."

Carol Wilson left the office feeling a lot better than when she had arrived, proving the maxim that a problem shared is a problem halved. Brent remained at his desk and was mulling over his options as to the first steps to take in the resolution of his latest client's dilemma. Little did he know how great an impact this seemingly quite minor new case would have on his future career as an investigator. It would lead to his involvement in the case which had made the headlines and was still newsworthy after several weeks - the death that had occurred among the vines of the Songbird Estate in the outskirts of the city of Belton.

Chapter Two

A tale of two cases

The city of Belton, population one hundred and fifty thousand, was located in the centre of Belton County. The small city was its own economic hub but it was also a dormitory town for Newhampton, the very large city to the south. Commuters, by car and rail, poured forth in the morning, heading for the big smoke, and straggled back in the evening. Traffic density and rail delays turned what should have been a forty-five-minute journey into one of an hour and a half on the better days.

The very good farmland in the southern district of Belton County was, unfortunately, being gradually filled in with new housing because the prices for suburban residences there were a lot easier than closer to the city. However, the northern district was one of still relatively unspoiled countryside and contained two extensive conservation areas. The villages and small towns in this sector had not seen any significant expansion. In one northern upland area of gentle hills, eleven vineyards were to be found. It was at one of these, the Songbird Estate, that the murder of its owner had occurred.

Central offices for the various Belton police departments were housed in a recently constructed building close to the city centre. It was the dream work of an internationally renowned architect but, for many Beltonians, it was an unnecessarily expensive eyesore that strove to look sleek and sinuous but came off as raw, unfinished, and puzzling - as though not quite enough money had been thrown at it to achieve its full potential. Its entrance was palatial. The elevators were swift and excellent, and the offices to which they conveyed people thoughtfully laid out, although on the snug side. The drunk and disorderly were processed through a back entrance in the building.

In an office on the fourth floor, two detectives were eating sandwiches - their lunch - while slowly considering and purposefully discussing the Songbird Estate case, both of them still at a loss as to who might have killed Sheila Babbington.

"We're getting nowhere," said Jennifer Allen at last.

"I wouldn't say that," replied Damian Field. "We've done all the groundwork and interviewed everyone two or three times. I'd say we're doing okay."

"Yes, but we don't have a prime suspect. There are at least fifteen people who could have done it."

"Sixteen. There's the cyclist we haven't tracked down yet."

"All right, sixteen people," conceded Jennifer.

"I don't think Arlene Richards did it. She's too old to be stabbing someone in the chest. What's in your sandwich?"

"Brie, blueberries, and celery with mayonnaise."

"I was wondering why your bread had gone that colour. My sandwiches are never as interesting as yours. I suppose it's because I throw them together with whatever comes to hand at the last minute before I leave."

"Do them the night before."

"I never think of it then... Yeah, Arlene's out, as far as I'm concerned."

"I suppose she is." Jennifer drank some water. "The chief wants a report today. Fifteen days and no suspect... He's going to bring in the city boys."

"That's inevitable. Unless we pick a name at random. Hey, we get a fourteen to one chance of being right - unless, by a fluke, it's the unknown cyclist."

"You're not always as professional as you should be." Jennifer smiled.

"I bet you a sandwich...," said Damian, "- you make me one or I buy you one - that he has us go after the cyclist again."

"Probably. The public announcement last week didn't help any. I don't know what more we can do."

"Write a perfect report and hope for a break. Then he has nothing to complain about."

"Oh, he'll complain. He hates bringing in outside help. We're definitely going to hear his 'reputation of the department' speech again."

"Andy? I have a job for you - if you're interested." Brent was telephoning a close associate of his and one of his 'secret weapons'. Andy Fowler, nicknamed Deadpan, was a finder of the type of information that no one else could find. He was so completely nondescript in every respect that no one ever noticed him. He could as easily walk into a packed opera house (and find a seat!) without a ticket as walk into a supermarket. At the supermarket, any representative giving out free food samples would overlook offering the delicacy to Deadpan. Andy would have to ask for a sample and a response such as, 'I'm sorry, I didn't see you standing there in front of me', was typically returned to him. His seeming invisibility earned him a good-sized income. When he did finally attract someone's attention in the course of his inquiries, the person would invariably unburden him or herself with hardly a qualm. After all, they might think - if they thought upon the matter at all

- *it's only Deadpan* or, if they did not know him, *He looks like a harmless little man and I need to tell someone.*

"Yes, Brent," replied Deadpan. "What can I do for you?"

"I need information on one Jeremy Miller, aged twenty-two. He's known to his friends as Jerry. He's a Belton resident who is working on the fringes of a gang that distributes drugs. The gang seems to be located in Newhampton somewhere. I believe Jerry acts as a courier for them once or twice a week. He hopes to move on up and get on the inside of the operation."

"It's likely to be one of a couple of outfits I know of," said Deadpan.

"Are you busy at the moment?" asked Brent.

"Not particularly. I'll get something for you by tonight. Might be late, though."

"I'll wait for you. Anything else you need, such as a photograph?"

"Send it to me. I don't think I need any more than that."

"Thanks, Andy. Much appreciated. Photo on its way." Brent forwarded the image of a smiling Jerry that he had found and copied from that troublesome youth's social media account.

"Bye," replied Andy. He disconnected the call.

Brent looked at his phone and thought to himself, not for the first time, how he had been on friendly speaking terms with Andy for years and years, yet hardly knew anything about him. Andy, he concluded, was the most private person of his acquaintance.

Brent opened up his laptop and continued his research into Jerry Miller's life. In under an hour, he had gathered a fair amount of information - mostly Jerry's popular-culture likes and dislikes, as well as a few dated 'what I'm doing right now' posts. Nothing seemed to lead anywhere definite or give any hint of gang or drug affiliations. However, what he had seen helped to flesh out the 'portrait of a doomed young man' that Brent was slowly painting in his mind.

Further searches revealed a little about the Wilson family as a group. Brent found more on Peter Wilson because of his public duties. A career man, he had experienced a solid and respectable rise through various police departments until he had reached his current rank of Assistant Commissioner in the Belton Police. The investigator studied a photograph of the uniformed man.

Wilson certainly had been faced with a dilemma: shield a criminal in his own household or arrest his wife's son. He had made his decision and let it be known that he would indeed arrest Jerry on gang-related charges if evidence was forthcoming. Brent concluded that Wilson's stance was obviously not working as a deterrent and further believed it would have no beneficial effect if Wilson was ever obliged to carry out his threat. Jerry, he surmised, would take the consequent imprisonment and would hope thereby to rise in the gang's estimation. He thought the young man might be miscalculating the gang's reaction. The more-seasoned Brent felt it likely that, as soon as it was known Jerry had a senior police officer in the family, he would instantly become a liability and the gang would deal with him accordingly. At best, he would be let go - cut loose from the gang. At worst, he would be taught a lesson or killed. Brent thought the last to be the likeliest outcome. Of course, it was possible, too, that the gang already knew Jerry's stepfather was a policeman and had only not done anything about it up till now for its own, as yet obscure, reasons.

The homicide department of the city of Newhampton had received a request from the Belton police service for an experienced investigator to be sent to help them with the Sheila

Babbington murder case. The city's response was to assign the task to a detective sergeant named Greg Darrow.

"I've selected you for this case because you are probably - and I make no bones about saying this, Darrow - the best detective on the force. I believe you will expedite matters and bring everything to a successful conclusion." Greg's boss, seated at his desk and wearing an immaculate uniform, knew very well that Greg disliked staying away from home or travelling any distance.

"Thanks for the compliment," replied Greg. "I wish Belton had called us in earlier. Any clues at the crime scene will have gone by now."

"Yes, that is unfortunate. However, here's a copy of their summary report with a few attachments. Read it today and go to Belton tomorrow. I skimmed through the report and the work seems adequate enough. Greg, just go and show them how it's really done. I'm allowing two weeks but, if things prove difficult, you can have another detective join you and get an extension. But please don't let this drag on. The Belton police won't let us live it down if we can do no better than they did. And the case has too much media attention as it is."

"I'll do my best as I always do, sir."

"Thank you, Greg. I know I can rely on you."

At about 2:30 a.m. Brent's phone rang. When the call came in, he was lying on a couch in his apartment above an old machine shop he owned and had re-purposed into living quarters. Deadpan delivered a mass of information over the phone. Brent wrote the vital details down in a hurried scrawl. Included were a few legal names of gang members and associates, but most were nicknames such as Ice-pick, Feline, Outhouse, and Preacher. Deadpan had found out the home addresses of the gang leaders. The gang had no official name but was referred to on the street as "The Tusk" with individuals being called "Tuskers", which appellations were possibly derived from the leader's name of Toussaint - Alan Toussaint.

After the call, Brent lay down again on the couch and went over his pages of notes. Jerry Miller's part was indeed small in the gang's scheme of operations. Miller was an overnight courier and brought drugs into the gang's Belton operation. Deadpan could only guess at the quantity and estimated the 'product' value at around ten thousand a run. There were at least three couriers used for the Newhampton to Belton route and Deadpan had discovered that the pay for each run was low - under a hundred.

Brent thought about this and decided that the gang's share of the Belton market was worth something around a hundred thousand a month and supposed that other gangs must have a share in that market, too.

The classes of requirements for entry into the gang were simple. Jerry Miller would have to go to prison instead of one of the leaders - should the situation arise, or he would need to deliver a new territory to the gang, or he would have to kill someone whom the gang wished removed. Deadpan had spoken the whole time in his near monotone voice and, when he had mentioned these requirements, he sounded as though he were reading out a shopping list. It seemed to Brent to make it all the more chilling. Again, he wondered, what was Jerry Miller thinking in pursuing such a course? Circumstances of poverty or lack of opportunity did not trap him and he could easily choose to do something else with his life. Jerry Miller's career intentions were out of all proportion to his middle-class background.

Brent then asked Andy to tail Jerry Miller over the next two days. As he well knew, Andy would delegate this task to several of his associates. Although Brent had no idea who these people were, they had always given exemplary service in the past. They saved him from the mind-numbing task of waiting hours for the target to do something or go somewhere. To sit cramped or cold in a car waiting for a subject to wake up, shower, decide what to have for breakfast, choose clothes, and all the other mundane matters of his or her daily routine was beyond Brent's patience. He liked the following and the second-guessing aspects of surveillance, but detested the waiting. Once, when he was new to the investigation business, he thought he could read a book while watching a front door - if he positioned eyes just so, it took no more than a glance to see the entrance. He believed he could do both. He was mistaken. Instead, he had blown a whole day sitting, reading, and was surprised and annoyed when he saw his mark return to the building. Brent had become so engrossed in the book he had missed the man leaving his house. He had not even liked how the novel had ended.

Chapter Three

The police case

Greg Darrow entered Belton's police headquarters for his meeting with the local detectives before the appointed hour of 8:00 a.m. Waiting in the reception area to one side of the cavernous entrance, he passed some of the time by spending a few minutes talking shop with the desk sergeant and, for the rest, he looked over the items on a bulletin board. The first to arrive was Jennifer Allen, her blond hair tied back in a ponytail. She saw the heavy-set, dark-haired man in his mid-forties. He was imposing, and he looked like an old-school detective. Greg smiled when she apologized for keeping him waiting as they shook hands. Jennifer escorted him to her department section on the fourth floor. A few minutes later, Damian Field joined them. He was taller than Greg but somehow seemed less consequential.

The three detectives went into a small conference room and documents were produced from files and laid out on the glass tabletop. Greg did not interrupt the other two while they explained, in their own words, their work and findings to date. He took notes and reserved his questions for when they had finished their presentation. After half an hour, Jennifer and Damian had no more to say.

"Thank you," said Greg. "You've done a lot of work, I can see. Now, I have a few questions and observations."

"Sure," said Damian, easily, while Jennifer re-positioned herself in her chair as though she felt not quite comfortable.

"The only items of physical evidence we have," began Greg in a neutral, authoritative tone, "are the deceased's body, the clothes she was wearing at the time of her death, and the murder weapon. The deceased had no injuries, pre- or post-mortem, other than the single knife wound to the heart, which was the cause of death. There is no compelling evidence of a struggle. No DNA was found that would not have been present under normal circumstances. She had eaten lunch about 2:00 p.m. and nothing after that and the time of her death has been fixed between 5:00 and 6:30 p.m. They found a trace amount of alcohol in her blood analysis, consistent with her having drunk a glass of wine earlier in the day."

"Yeah," interjected Damian. "Probably from her own vineyard."

Greg looked at him steadily, without expression.

"What?" said Damian.

"I hadn't finished," said Greg.

"Oh, okay. Sorry. Go on," responded Damian, a little taken aback.

"No other evidence was gathered at the crime scene, even though a thorough search was carried out. One interesting fact about the position of the scene is that the lower approach to it is in full sight of the buildings below until the land curves out of view behind a screen of bushes and trees. This causes the section of the vineyard where she was killed to be hidden." This time, neither Damian nor Jennifer dared to interject a word as Greg Darrow paused slightly before continuing.

"Beyond the scant information disclosed at the crime scene, we have found no evidence of blackmail, indebtedness, or connection with any criminals. The deceased, aged 40, had no known enemies. She was faithful to her husband and an exemplary mother to her children. They are aged… 13 and 17. In other words, nothing has been found so far to provide an obvious motive for her murder."

Greg Darrow set down his notebook and clasped his hands together in front of him on the tabletop.

"From the materials I have looked through, I can see no circumstantial evidence pointing to any individual who was present on the day of the murder. The list of potential suspects runs to twenty-one persons, including an unknown cyclist and the driver of a courier truck. There could be a twenty-second person - another unknown that no one saw. The daily tour of the vineyard had ended at a little after 5:00 p.m. with twelve adults and two children present on the tour, the first of them leaving at about five-thirty. The last of them left around seven, having stayed to eat something in the small restaurant. On this particular day, only two outsiders arrived at the restaurant. They were both regulars, arriving later than six-thirty and staying until eight, when the restaurant closed. The on-site shop saw some activity as people came to purchase wine but, according to the statements provided, they all drove up to the store entrance, parked, purchased items and left again."

Greg took a photograph of a smiling Sheila Babbington from the folder in front of him and stared at it while he said, "As for the deceased, she was not seen after five until her body was found the following morning. Her husband and children had said goodbye to her because she was driving to the airport, on her way to a wine-growers convention some four hundred miles away. Yet, despite this, she seems to hide her vehicle along an overgrown track bordering the vineyard, and her body is subsequently found among the vines on her own property. The evidence suggests the only vehicle that had been on the track recently was her own." He replaced the photo in the folder.

"Considering all these things, the most likely deduction is that she feigned her setting off for the airport and returned to meet someone. That person might have been on the tour or might have been an employee. The cyclist and the courier driver are possible suspects. It is possible another person parked a vehicle on the road and walked into the top section of the vineyard. The problem with that theory is that drivers on the road could have seen this - and no one saw such a vehicle." Darrow's succinct but thorough recap of the case suitably impressed Jennifer and Damian.

"I am now at the point that you reached nearly three weeks ago," concluded Greg. "If either of you have a hunch, let me know what it is."

Damian snapped forward in his chair and said, "I think it's the husband."

"Oh, why's that?"

"No one else seems to have a motive. It must be a domestic matter."

"Any proof?"

"You asked for hunches. That's what I've got."

"Okay." Greg turned to Jennifer. "Does anyone stand out to *you* more than the rest?"

"No. I think there are a few people who *didn't* do it... the husband being one of them." She glanced at Damian.

"Okay," said Greg.

"So, how about you?" asked Damian. "Can you see a prime suspect?"

"I just got here and I'm getting up to speed. What interests me is the knife."

"The knife?" said Damian. "It's nothing special. An ordinary kitchen knife with an eight-inch blade. It could have come from the house."

"Forensics report that it had recently been cleaned with bleach and had no fingerprints on it. Looking at this photograph..." Greg opened the file again and pulled out a glossy sheet, "... we can see here that the edge has been very carefully sharpened and here, that the bleach has whitened the wooden handle and raised the grain."

Damian and Jennifer glanced at it together.

"I thought that was odd," said Jennifer. "Could it mean that this was some kind of hit?"

"Could be," said Greg. "The murderer certainly prepared the weapon in advance, not only sharpening it to perfection but also giving it a lengthy soaking in oxygen bleach so that not a chromosome remains undamaged. So assured was our assassin that the knife bore no traceable DNA, it was just left in situ; so assured of its edge, one stab and it was all over. The thrust might have been deflected by the ribcage, but it wasn't. Was the killer that good or only confident? We can't tell. What we do know is that whoever it was left no trace except for the weapon itself. Now, why would the murderer want to do that?"

"He panicked," said Damian. "Maybe saw somebody coming."

"If that's true, then surely the murderer would have been seen at the same time. Any movement disturbing those ranks of parallel vines would have been seen. There's nothing like that in the statements or in your summaries." A silence followed.

"What do we do now?" asked Jennifer.

"I'd like you to interview the Babbington family members again. Ask them to recall past events where there was a bad interaction between the deceased and another party - inside or outside the family. At the same time, try to get some information on the husband's character. Did they like him...? Had he a bad temper...? along those lines."

"Husband, see..." said Damian, nodding approvingly.

"Detective Field," said Greg, "I want you to canvas all residences, farms and businesses within a two-mile radius to see if anyone saw the cyclist or the courier van. That spreads the net a bit wider. Go back to the places you tried before and see if they saw any cyclists at all... not just the person in jeans and dark grey hoody that we know about. In addition, ask if they saw anyone who didn't belong in the area. In other words, did anyone notice anything unusual on that day at any time?"

"That'll take for-*ever*."

"Not if you get started right away. Get someone to help from another department if you can."

"What will you be doing?" asked Jennifer.

"I'm going to re-interview the people on the tour and the staff - though I see that two of the tourists live out of the area. Still, it's got to be done. I think that's all for now. We'll meet here daily, say at five, unless some additional evidence crops up - in which case, I want to know of it immediately."

Greg got up and left the room, heading to the office assigned to him.

"What do you think?" asked Damian after Greg had gone.

"I wish he would call her Sheila Babbington and not 'the deceased' all the time."

"Why'd he give me such a lousy job? We could have shared that task."

"Because you interrupted him."

"When? What, for that? Is he like a control freak or something?"

"I think it's best we just do what he asks. I find him a bit scary. Like, I know he outranks us, but he assumes he's our boss even though he's on a different force."

"That's right. We don't have to do what he says."

"Who are you going to complain to?"

"I know, I get it. What a day. He's got me knocking on about two hundred doors, maybe more."

"Like he said, you'd better get started. He looks like he's used to getting results. Remember, he'll be writing reports and we need to shine in them."

It was now evening on the following day. The sun had dipped below the horizon, but in the west there was still some light in the clear sky. Brent was in the front passenger seat of an old, dark-grey van that he owned. The van was parked on a quiet Newhampton side street. The driver, Micky, was small with a hard face. He looked perpetually annoyed about something. In the back of the van, stretched out comfortably on the carpeted floor, was a giant of a man named Ray.

They sat silently, waiting for a phone call. So far, they had been waiting for nearly two hours.

"Can we go eat after we're done?" asked the Colossus, Ray, slowly, lazily, in an amazingly deep voice.

"What? You missed your dinner or something?" asked Micky.

"No. I ate already. But I can't stop thinking about food and I don't know how long we'll be. So, I think, if we decide what we're going to eat later, I can stop thinking about it."

"Won't work," said Micky. "Once we decide where we're going and what we'll order, you'll just be thinking about getting there and eating it. That would be worse."

"I don't think so," said Ray. "We could try it, couldn't we?" There was no reply. "Well, how about this, then? Let's go and get some food now. We can order it by phone, pick it up, and we're all done in ten minutes."

"Ray," said Brent. "We're on a mission, so tighten your belt."

"I knew you'd say something like that," said Ray.

"We'll eat afterwards," said Brent. "I know a great place with good food and huge portions."

"Yeah? What kind of thing do they serve?"

"Kale soup."

"Aw, shut up, Brent. You know I hate that stuff."

Micky smiled slightly.

About fifteen minutes later, Brent received a call. He listened intently to the voice on the other end of the phone. After a few seconds, he pointed to the key and Micky started the van's engine.

"At last," said Ray, sitting up.

"He's parked his car on Wickstead," said Brent after he finished the call. "About a hundred yards in from the corner."

"Wickstead's two blocks away from the house," said Micky, putting the van into drive.

As the van pulled away, Ray leaned forward, his head level with the two seated men. "That's just what I would do. Think about it. We're watching the place. Supposin' it was the cops watching. They'd see him *and* his vehicle if he parked nearby. Once they identify his vehicle, he's done. Now, with his car a few blocks away, if there's a raid and he can get out of the house, he gets to his vehicle and he's gone."

"Makes sense," said Micky. "But I don't like walking. One block away would be good enough for me."

"So, Brent. Why's this guy Jerry so important?" asked Ray.

"I gave my word that I'd get him out of the gang. This is the quickest way I could think of."

"It's a long time since I had to kidnap anyone," said Ray. "I hope I haven't gone rusty."

"That's not what I wish to hear right now," replied Brent. "There it is."

Micky parked the van about fifty feet behind an older model black sports car. They waited once more.

"I'm not really rusty," whispered Ray after about five minutes. He was twirling a shapeless canvas sack around his finger. "I know what to do. It's just been a while. Know what I mean?"

"How many people have you kidnapped, then?" asked Micky.

"Let me see." He stopped twirling and began to count off on his fingers. "There were two businessmen who defaulted on a loan or something. I had help with those two. Then there was this guy…"

"He's coming," whispered Brent.

"Okay. I'll tell you all the rest later… Over supper, remember, Brent?" Ray laughed. "Just wait until he's gone past my door and I'll be done real quick."

Ray moved to the side door and prepared to open it and spring out. Brent moved back to join him. Micky slid down to make himself inconspicuous in the driver's seat while still able to see the target in the side mirror. It was his job to give the signal to Ray.

Jerry Miller hurried along the street. He was a little under six feet tall with brown hair, the fringe of which just showing from under his black hood. He was wearing a hoody over a t-shirt despite the warm night. It made him look suspicious rather than inconspicuous. Low-cut black jeans, white running shoes, and a heavy leather belt with large silver metal squares attached to it completed his ensemble. Over one shoulder, he carried a small pack. He had the product with him and was about to return to Belton.

Jerry had met Alan Toussaint at the house. He had not seen the gang's leader for some time. He knew him quite well because, although Toussaint was five years his senior, Jerry had been a school-friend of the leader's younger brother when the Toussaints lived in Belton. Tonight, Jerry had asked once more to be admitted to the gang. He had said he had been waiting and doing low-level grunt work long enough. Toussaint replied he would think about it. As Jerry walked along the street, his thoughts of the recent meeting were occupying his mind until he drew level with a scruffy-looking van.

The van door slid open and Ray lithely leapt out. In two simple moves, he had the sack over Jerry's head and then the massive man lifted the struggling Jerry off the ground as though he were a rag doll. He all but threw him in the open side door of their vehicle. Ray jumped in after him and closed the door.

"Wasn't more than ten seconds, was it?" he asked Micky, as he nonchalantly clamped Jerry's face into the carpeted floor and pressed a knee into the struggling young man's back, while Brent relieved the gangster of a knife, an automatic pistol, his phone, car keys, and backpack.

"No," said Micky. "I think it was about five or six."

Ray's face lit up with a smile. "See, I haven't lost my touch." Jerry was continuing to struggle and Brent was having difficulty getting a wide zip-tie around Jerry's arms until Ray held them still with a vice-like grip, saying, "Hey, hey. Don't worry, kid. This is a friendly kidnapping."

Chapter Four

Taking on a gang

"Jerry," said Brent as he removed the sack and sat back, "listen to me carefully." The van was dark inside and the light from a streetlamp illuminated one half of the captive's face with a diagonal slash. His hands and feet were tied.

"Who are you?" asked the captive who was fairly shaking with fear, or rage, or both.

"Doesn't matter. This is what is going to happen. You are leaving the gang tonight in one of two ways. Listen to me," said Brent sharply, as Jerry shook his head in a dismissive way. "We can take you to the police right now and hand you over with the drugs and you will go to prison."

"I'll do the time," said Jerry defiantly.

"Yes, you will. You will also get your sentence reduced because you will be credited with giving up your fellow gang members. We have information enough to put at least six of them away. What will you do when they find out you're a snitch?"

"What? What are you saying?"

"I'm telling you to listen carefully to your options. Option one. Do the time in prison as a snitch. That will be the word on the street."

In the silence that followed, Jerry became distraught.

"I can't leave them or betray them. If you make me do that, you might as well kill me right now."

"That's the problem, isn't it? We aren't going to kill you. Are you so foolish as to not ask about the other option?"

"Well, what is it?"

"You simply go back to Belton and leave drug trafficking and gang life to others. You go home and never do drugs again."

"Can't. Even if I wanted to, I can't."

"I can deal with Toussaint."

"How?"

"Make it worth his while to leave you alone. It's a simple, common-sense business proposition that he will accept as a businessman."

"You're going to get me killed whatever you do." He struggled violently against his bonds.

"Stop it, kid," said Ray. He reached over and gripped him by the throat - enough to immobilize without unduly cutting off Jerry's breath. "You don't want me to work you over or anything. Just sit nicely and listen to what the man has to say. That's all you gotta do." Ray released him. Jerry calmed down. "There, that's better."

"We wish you no harm," said Brent. "Option two is your only choice. Think about how you can make it work."

Jerry was morose and wretched. He was close to tears. "It's my life," he said brokenly. "They're my friends. People I care about. Besides, there's a girl I like."

"You'll have to find someone else if she's associated with the gang."

As he was saying this, Brent gave a sign to Micky, who then left the van with the pack that contained drugs having a street value of about twenty thousand.

"I... I can't do it," Jerry almost sobbed.

"Tonight. You are going to leave tonight. You are turning your back on the gang and having nothing to do with any of them ever again. I'm setting it up whether you make the choice or not. When I've finished, the gang will not want to see or hear from you again but, I promise you this, they *will* leave you alone."

Jerry shook his head. He had nothing to say in reply and looked crushed.

"You should get on board with this. I'll call Toussaint now." Brent took out a recently purchased burner phone.

"You've got his number?" asked Jerry.

"Yes. I take it you don't know it. See, you're an outsider and always will be. He knows about your step-father being a police officer."

"I never told him. I've never mentioned that to anyone except... oh."

"You really are naïve. They trust you because you are loyal and they have known you for a long time - since well before your mother remarried. But how could you expect them to do anything except keep you on the outside? If they had killed you because you were a liability, they would attract an amount of attention from the police that would be harmful to their interests."

"It's my world... all I know." He paused for a moment. "You think they would have put me down?"

"You know what they're like."

Brent took out a small notepad, found what he was looking for, and entered the number. Toussaint's phone began to ring.

"Who's this?" said Toussaint. He was alone, relaxed, and lying fully clothed on a bed, watching a favourite show on television.

"I know you. I know all about you. One of your boys is with me, as we speak."

Toussaint swung his legs off the bed and sat upright and alert. "What's this about?"

"It's about Jerry Miller. He's leaving your organization tonight."

Toussaint stood up and left the bedroom to go downstairs.

"Who? Don't know him."

"Ice Pick, alias Benny Langford, alias Marvin Shorter, real name Samuel Duggins. Phone number 439-8462, address 104 Derby street, apartment six-forty-two. As you can see, I know a lot." Brent had just given details on Toussaint's second lieutenant.

"Hmm. So this guy, Jerry, you say I know... What's the deal?" Toussaint found the man named Ice Pick in the kitchen making a sandwich for himself. He snapped his fingers to get the man's attention and pointed to the phone in his hand, waving him over to listen.

"He's out of your organization as of today, and you leave him alone."

"As I said, I don't know this Jerry you're talking about." Ice Pick now had his ear close to the phone and could just about hear Brent's voice on the other end.

"Panzer, alias Tyler Smith, alias..." Brent rattled off the details of the gang's third in command. Then he added, "You are currently present at 294 Carter Avenue. This house was rented three months ago, in the name of Alicia Higgins. Of course, that's not her real name, and she's having a baby in four months. Your baby."

Ice Pick's eyes visibly widened. Toussaint became agitated.

"That's too close to home now. You a cop?"

"Who I am does not concern you. I know you have protection... people in authority who are paid to ignore your activities. I know them, and I can bypass them and get all the information to people who will act upon it. Now, I don't have to do this, but I can if necessary. Miller goes free and you will stay out of trouble. What do you say?"

"Huh. Let me think about this." Toussaint put his hand over the microphone and looked at Ice Pick.

"This is bad, Touss," said Ice Pick. "Any ideas who this guy is?"

"None. He ain't a gangster. I don't think he's a cop, *and* he knows all about you."

"Me! Bad, that's bad. Could be some kind of vigilante. So, give him Jerry. What can we do?"

"Yeah, I think so. But Ice, how can we trust this dude?"

"Ask him for something."

"Yeah. Okay." Toussaint spoke on the phone again with Ice Pick listening in. "So, whatever your name is, I won't have anything to do with this Miller guy you're banging on about."

"That's an excellent step. But, as you can appreciate, we both have trust issues. You will be thinking that I might not have Jerry or that I will go to the police, anyway. By the same token, how do I know you won't come after him? So, you see, we have to settle a few things before we can both feel comfortable about the situation."

"Go on."

"Jerry will keep his mouth shut. I guarantee that. If he gets talkative, I will hand him over to you. Secondly, you will find your product on your front doorstep now. Send someone to bring it in."

Ice Pick pulled away from the phone and went to the front door. He returned, carrying the pack - unzipping it as he walked. "It's all here," he said.

"Okay, so far. But it's you, ain't it?" said Toussaint. "How do I know you won't make trouble?"

"You don't, except that so far I have delivered. Talk to Jerry for a moment." There was a pause while Jerry came on.

"I ain't said nothing to them," said Jerry. "They snatched me off the street..." Brent pulled the phone away.

"Loyal to the last. You really could never have him in the gang, though. He's not cut out for it and he has a serious risk factor in his background."

"I know. Okay. We're cool with the deal."

"Excellent. Now for my trust issue. As soon as you get off the phone, I'm sure you will be thinking hard about reorganizing your business. In doing so, some of the information I have will be invalidated. I get that. So, I spoke to a couple of associates earlier. They expressed much interest in my suggestions. One of them is *such* a good shot. He can hit anything he likes out to fifteen hundred yards. That's nearly a mile. The other is a demolition man. He can blow up just about anything - armoured cars, hardened bunkers, entire buildings - though I know he likes bridges the best. It must be the artist in him going for the dramatic. I don't talk to these guys often because I find them disturbing. I'd hate to have to talk to them again soon, but I would do so if I had to."

"I understand. Put Jerry back on."

When Jerry was on the phone again, Toussaint said,

"I don't want to see or hear from you again. If I hear that you've been talking, you know what we're gonna do. Put the man on."

"Yes?" said Brent.

"Are we done here?"

"I think so." Brent disconnected the call.

Micky followed the van in Jerry's car on the way to Belton. Inside the van, now driven by Ray, Brent explained a few steps necessary for Jerry to re-integrate himself into normal society. He suggested further education and learning a new trade. The young man, released from the zip-ties, was sullen and uncommunicative for the most part. As they neared the end of the journey, Brent, who was sitting in the back facing Jerry, began to lay out a few other things. They both swayed as the van went over irregular road surfaces and the intermittent, unnatural light coming in through the rear windows gave transient illumination as the van sped along.

"We're dropping you at your mother's house. You will keep in contact with her regularly and I will know if that is not happening. My friends and I will come and see you if you do not visit your mother regularly."

"You're kidding me?"

"No. Furthermore, I will dispose of your phone and weapons. Unless you can show me you have a registration for this pistol, it disappears tonight."

Jerry did not respond.

"I thought so. I'm sorry about the phone but I believe it's best that you start out this new era of your life with a set of new contacts. Here's a couple of hundred to buy yourself a new one."

"Why are you doing this?"

"To get you out of trouble. Eventually, you would have been murdered or imprisoned. You can't build any sort of life with those things facing you. You're not a thoughtful kind of guy. Do you think your pride can get you through anything? Look how Toussaint dropped you. Friendship means nothing to him. He expects your obedience and loyalty, but he behaves like he owes you nothing. He doesn't care about you and, right now, he'd kill you if he could." Brent hoped he was finally getting through to the dejected Jerry.

"I know it doesn't look like it yet, but you are a free man. You're free and with freedom comes responsibility. No one is going to do your thinking for you. It's up to you to make something of your life. You're the boss, now."

Micky parked the car in front of the Wilson's house and got out to join the others in the van across the street.

"Right. Out you get. Here are your keys and wallet." Brent handed the things back to Jerry.

"You've got a break, kid. Make good use of it," said Ray.

"Your engine needs a tune-up," said Micky.

Jerry got out. Brent stood by the van, watching him go. The younger man reluctantly took a few steps towards the house before stopping. In the half-light of the suburban street, he turned to say,

"I'll play the game and work things out."

He turned away and went to the door. Jerry rang the bell and waited. Carol Wilson opened the door and, as soon as he caught sight of her, Brent got back in the van and it sped away.

"Brent. What's this restaurant we're going to? I know you were kidding me earlier. I don't want no health food."

"No, it's good Italian cooking. And we can get there before it shuts. You'll like it."

"Italian sounds good. Say, Brent. Who are those guys you were talking about? You know, the assassins."

"Assassins?" said Micky. "Where'd they come in?"

"Yeah," said Ray. "A sniper guy and an explosives expert."

"Brent," said Micky, "I've known you for what, eleven, no, twelve years. And you are mixing with killers? That's not like you."

"It isn't like me. I made that part up."

"You bluffed them? Ha!" laughed Micky. "That's good. I wish I'd heard it."

"I completely believed it!" said Ray.

"Supposing they hadn't bought in?" Micky asked Brent.

"I had a Plan B."

"Which was?"

"A month in a remote cabin in the woods with Ray and me babysitting Jerry until things were worked out."

"That sounds kinda nice," said Ray.

"You say that now," said Micky, "but there ain't no restaurants in the woods. You'd go crazy."

"Oh, yeah. I don't think I could have gone, Brent."

"Believe me, I'm very thankful things worked out as they did." Brent liked Ray, trusted him, but to be cooped up for a month with the man would almost certainly have stretched their friendship to its breaking point.

Chapter Five

Snapshot of a murder

It was now June 25th, and the case in Belton was churning over. A week of intensive work by the three detectives had not produced anything significant. No obvious suspect or motive had emerged. The detectives felt their only progress was in their belief that the suspect list could now be pruned a little to remove those who were most unlikely to have murdered Sheila Babbington.

Greg Darrow was in the small conference room with Jennifer Allen and Damian Field for their daily five o'clock meeting. Each of them had a list of names in front of them. Greg and Damian were working together but they did not particularly like each other.

1. Arlene Richards, 78, Tour, Mother of Stuart Richards.
2. Stuart Richards, 52, Tour, Son of Arlene.
3. Margot Vaughan, 41, Tour, Office manager, friend of Sheila B.
4. Erica Stevens, 41, Tour, Hairstylist, friend of Sheila B.
5. Patricia Epstein, 32, Tour, Artist, came with McGinnis.

6. Michael McGinnis, 33, Tour, Landscape gardener, with Epstein.

7. Claude Gaudin, 38, Tour, Wine salesman for a large company.

8. Stan Forbes, 50, Tour, Wine aficionado.

9. Martha Badowski, 42, Tour, Real estate agent.

10. Stefan Badowski, 49, Tour, Real estate broker.

11. John Finch, 32, Tour, Graphic Artist.

12. Delia Finch, 32, Tour, Website designer. Finch children, aged 2 and 5.

13. Valerie Brown, 28, Employee, Tour guide.

14. Emily Harfield, 28, Employee, Senior Viticulturist.

15. Thomas Block, 26, Employee, Viticulturist.

16. Sergio Calabrese, 52, Employee, Vintner.

17. Rita Inglis, 34, Employee, Cook.

18. Janet Jones, 26, Employee, Store manager.

19. Luke Valinho, 25, Courier, in the area at 5:30.

20. Charles Babbington, 44, Husband, Engineer.

21. Cyclist, ?, ?, seen by three people.

22. Unknown person(s).

"Let's review the list and see if we can't get a little further," said Darrow.

"We've been through it ten times, already," said Field.

"What do *you* suggest we do?"

Field shrugged his shoulders. "I don't know. Maybe we'll never close the case."

"Not an option," said Darrow. "I've had cases like this before. You tread water for a while and then something comes out of the blue that hasn't been disclosed before and then everything starts falling into place. We'll continue working while waiting for that to happen."

"Shall I go first?" asked Allen.

Jennifer was getting tired of Damian's reluctance to stay focused on the case. She found Greg Darrow aloof but efficient. She had no idea what he thought of her. She imagined that he did not think so very much of Damian.

"Please do," said Greg.

"Arlene Richards is out. She is probably not physically able to have murdered Sheila. She also needs the help of her son to walk. However, Stuart Richards, left his mother sitting in the restaurant for about twenty minutes around 5:40. He could have gone out to the road and walked unseen to the top section of the vineyard. That was the only way that any employee or visitor could guarantee they were not seen by anyone on the property. He had time to go and commit the murder and return. The problem is - he had the opportunity but no motive."

"Do you think him a likely candidate?" asked Greg.

"Not really. No. It's the actions of Sheila that rule him out for me. She planned to meet someone there but, obviously, she didn't plan to be murdered. As far as I can see they have no prior connection."

"Detective Field?" said Greg.

"Like she said. They're both ruled out."

"We'll have to look into Richards again for a motive. Another background search has to be done. We'll expand it to include extended family, friends, and associates. If he is the murderer, the presence of his mother provides a useful cover." Greg Darrow sat back in his chair before continuing. "Wealthy mother, stay at home son who's waiting for her to die so he can inherit. He has a skewed outlook on life. You never know - he may have had an idea to murder just to prove to himself he could get away with it. We should get a psychological profile of him. I'll see if I can arrange that. Detective Allen, you follow up on his background and then we'll bring him in for questioning."

"Okay." Jennifer made a note before continuing with the list. "Margot Vaughan and Erica Stevens. I'm taking those two together because they're long-time school friends of Sheila's.

They vouch for each other for the whole time - unless they were in collusion, in which case one of them could have left unseen, gone by the road, and met Sheila. Again, no motive for either of them. Their grief seemed real to me."

"Did it?" said Greg. "Do you think you could get them to open up about their past a little? There might be a long-standing issue between the three of them."

"Sure, I can try. Now, Patricia Epstein and Michael McGinnis are lovers. They're both artists. She paints and he is a potter. They disappeared for fifteen minutes just after five and again for another ten minutes or so just before six, after they had eaten in the restaurant. They say they wanted to have a smoke and to be alone with each other for a while, which makes sense to me. Neither of them are handling answering questions very well. I put that down to the artistic temperament being challenged by authority."

"But they have no motive," said Damian. "It looks to me like they were just on a date. It was all rainbows and roses for them, then there's a dead body in the middle of their dream. They can't handle that reality."

"True," said Greg. "I don't see them as suspects, either. They don't seem to have the capacity for violence. Still, they had the opportunity. Detective Field, we need an exhaustive search of their backgrounds."

"I don't get this," said Damian. "I mean, I just can't see them doing the crime and then behaving normally afterwards."

"I agree. But that could apply to almost all of them. The thing is no one seems to have a motive to murder and yet somebody did. We have to investigate further and to the nth degree all those who had opportunity."

"Then why don't we just eliminate those who had no opportunity, divide up the list, and see what we find?"

"That's what we're doing."

"Oh. But we've been over all of this before."

"Unless we get a break," replied Greg Darrow sternly, "we'll be going over it again and again until we are all reassigned because the case is cold. I don't want that on my record. I take it that this would be true for both of you, too."

"Sure, I don't want that, either," said Damian.

They worked steadily through the list and, by the time they had finished, the exclusions were: Arlene Richards; Stefan Badowski who had not moved from his chair; the entire Finch family who remained together in view of others; Sergio Calabrese, who was either talking to Claude Gaudin or working in the cellars and fermentation room; Claude Gaudin, a dominant and obvious personality, who was thought to be in sight of another person all the time; Rita Inglis and Janet Jones who both never left the building that housed the restaurant, kitchen and shop; and Luke Valinho, courier, who 'hadn't seen nuthin', had been on his regular courier route and had absolutely no known connection with either the victim or the vineyard.

Nine names were stricken from the list of persons present on the day at the right time which left eleven known persons who could have committed the murder, plus the unidentified cyclist, and a hypothetical 'unknown'. No person had been seen walking on the road by the few motorists who had responded to the police appeal for witnesses.

On the property itself, Emily Harfield, the senior viticulturist, was the only one who admitted to being anywhere near the top section of the vineyard. However, she vehemently denied having entered the topmost, hidden section which could not be seen from the buildings below and was where the murder had been committed.

Greg Darrow advanced the theory that Harfield, from her vantage point, could have seen the deceased arrive further up the slope, and have decided to take advantage of her employer's solitary appearance in that remote spot. She could have crouched over and passed along rows, unseen. She could have clambered through cordon wires where necessary. She could have stabbed Sheila Babbington and returned the way she had come, crouched and hidden, till she reached the place she had been working before she seized the opportunity to kill her employer.

Damian Field intelligently argued that the well-prepared kitchen knife precluded any such spur of the moment advantage-taking. And Jennifer then suggested that Harfield may have made an appointment with Sheila, premeditating the murder and coming purposefully armed. Greg countered this by asking why, then, had Sheila hidden her vehicle, if she were just meeting one of her own employees? Jennifer said that maybe Sheila's rendezvous had been with someone else who was a no-show and Harfield had, like Greg said, just seized an opportunity. "She wouldn't have had the knife," again protested Damian. Greg Darrow smiled at his handiwork.

Brent now had everything packed up in his office because he had to be out by the last day of June. A company was coming to remove the furniture and put it into storage. His files were boxed up and he was carrying them downstairs to load into his old van which was parked at the door. On his fourth descent of the staircase he met a man coming up.

"Oh, sorry," said the man who stood to one side, allowing Brent to pass.

Brent drew level with him and came to a stop. He looked at his face and said,

"Are you Peter Wilson?" The visitor was wearing civilian clothes.

"I am. You must be Brent Umber."

"Correct. Um, as you can see, it's moving day. Go on up to the office and find yourself a chair and I'll be back in a minute when I've got rid of this box."

"Will do," said Wilson.

A few minutes later, the Assistant Commissioner and the investigator were seated together in the now completely dismantled but yet-to-be-moved office.

"I'm surprised to discover you know about me, after all," said Brent, smiling. "I thought Mrs Wilson had wanted to keep things quiet."

"Carol did. But what with Jerry coming home, saying he'd quit the gang, it became obvious that something had happened."

"So, your policeman's instincts kicked in and you began questioning all the parties involved."

"Something like that." Peter Wilson looked comfortable and relaxed. "I got your name from her. She said you had promised to get Jerry out of the situation in a few days. You delivered."

Brent was wondering where the conversation would go.

"Jerry and I are on speaking terms again. I thought that would never happen. Would you mind me asking, how did you do it?"

"No, I don't mind you asking. My apologies, though, I'm afraid I can't answer you. I will say this. A few phone calls and some very minor coercion produced the results you have seen. I'm confident you will have no repercussions over the matter."

"Very pleased to hear it. I wanted to come in person to thank you for what you've done."

Peter Wilson extended his hand which Brent took and shook heartily.

"I'm glad I could help. That's the rewarding part of this job, helping people."

"That's a good outlook to have. It's the same for me... sometimes, at least. I cannot tell you what a difference all you've done has made to me and Carol." He looked around the office. "Are you relocating?" He had a hesitant expression, as though he were concealing the thought, 'Are you going out of business?'

"No. I will work from home in future. I got to the office when I started out but very few people come here. Expenses... I've got to keep them under control and I can work just as efficiently through electronic devices."

"Ah, good, good. I had another reason to see you. Have you heard of the Sheila Babbington case?"

"I have. Carol mentioned that the detectives were having some difficulties."

"They are. A colleague of mine, he oversees the department in charge, was complaining to me about it. A Newhampton detective has been seconded to the case but we don't seem to be getting any further ahead. It's a question of too many suspects and no apparent motives."

"That's difficult. A clear target and one knows what to work towards. I sympathize with your colleagues."

"Well," Wilson cleared his throat, "would you be willing to work with my colleagues?"

"Work with them? I'm not sure I understand you."

"It's like this. You solved a problem that I could see no way around. No way. I could only deal with Jerry as a police officer. He rejected me as any type of father figure or even simply as a friend. I spoke to a couple of trusted people and they could see no solution, either. Then you come along and it's all wrapped up in a couple of days. You must be that unusual combination of ideas guy and problem-solver who comes at things from a different angle or with a fresh outlook, I don't know. Anyway, the thought occurred to me that if you reviewed the Babbington case file, you might see something that's being overlooked."

"Phew, that's very interesting. You do realize that this is completely out of my normal line of work?"

"Yes."

"What about the detectives on the case? How would they react?"

"They'd have to put up with it. I should warn you, that part might not be easy."

"I hope it won't be an issue. I'll be as charming as I can. Now, the only way I could see that my involvement would work is if I could interview witnesses and suspects."

"Yes, I'd thought of that. You see, the concern we have there is that, should an arrest be made, your involvement could injure the case against the accused."

"You said 'we'. I take that to mean you have had discussions with your peers?"

"My superior and Commander Baker who's in charge of the case. I took it to them immediately after I had the idea. I explained matters and they're willing to try you out if you accept."

"Very good," said Brent nodding. "Let me see. I think that if I declare myself to be a private investigator before speaking to any suspect or witness, then I could give testimony as a witness in a courtroom, if necessary. Would that work?"

"We were thinking along those lines. First, we thought, you would need to have a trial interview with a witness while a detective is present. We have to be sure of how you conduct yourself in an interview."

"Certainly, I have no issue with that. As you will be making the files available to me and your detectives have gathered all the information they can, the way I see it is for me to get witnesses to open up and talk freely. Hopefully, I'd find something useful or even critical to the case in what they say. In fact, that is my forte and modus operandi - I talk, I listen, and I perceive, allowing full rein to intuition and instinct. I have a network of let's call them associates who gather intel for me when necessary but I could never match the evidence-gathering abilities of your detectives."

"No, I don't suppose you could. However, you got Jerry to talk somewhere along the line. If you could only get a few witnesses to be more forthcoming it might lead somewhere."

"Then count me in," said Brent. "By the way... an awkward subject at the best of times. What would the remuneration be?"

"Your per diem plus expenses. The expenses would be restricted to only those allowed by legislation."

"So there could be no 'I had to go to a gambling den and I lost my five thousand dollar stake' - kind of expense?"

Wilson smiled. "Mileage, meal allowance, travel expenses, if pre-authorized, and things of that nature. When could you start?"

"Let's see. I have to superintend the removal of the furniture from here this afternoon and have a meeting with the landlord first thing in the morning to sign off on a few things and return the keys. I could be in Belton by about 10 a.m., though. If you prefer an earlier start, I could rearrange things."

"Ten is fine. Here's my card. Go to the front desk and they will escort you to my office. I'll introduce you to the department chief and we'll have a chat. Then we'll arrange to get a trial interview with a witness set up. While that's being done, you can review the files to get fully up to speed."

Chapter Six

Brent comes on board

"Detective Allen. We've called you in to help with a small project we're trying out." Commander Baker, the officer who was ultimately responsible for Jennifer Allen's department, was seated behind his desk. Across the desk and in front of him sat Assistant Commissioner Wilson and another man she had not seen before.

"Hello," said the stranger to her, smiling. She nodded in reply.

"This is Brent Umber. He is a private investigator and will be conducting a review of the Sheila Babbington case."

"Uh, sir?" said Jennifer.

"Yes, I know what you're thinking," interjected Baker. "Detective Darrow is already working in a similar capacity. Well, this is something we are trying because Mr Umber has a gift for problem-solving. What we shall do is allow him a trial interview with one of the witnesses. You are familiar with the case - can you suggest anyone A. who is not an actual suspect; B. who, should they take a dislike to Mr Umber or his position in relation to our department, will not cause any undue trouble; and C. who can come into the office today without any fuss?"

"Yes, sir. John Finch fits your requirements. He works from home and lives close by."

"Very good," said Baker.

Jennifer watched as Brent opened a file and, as though familiar with its contents, pulled out a summary sheet with Finch's details on it and handed it to Jennifer.

"There's his number," said Brent as he handed the sheet to her. "Would you mind giving him a call, please? Just so we can get the ball rolling."

Jennifer looked at the sheet and handed it back. She made the call and, when it connected, left the office to talk and make the arrangements.

"She's one of my best," said Baker to Brent in a confidential aside.

"Then I hope she won't be too hard on me," said Brent.

When Jennifer had finished, she returned to the office doorway to say,

"He'll be here in about half an hour, sir."

"Then I think that's all for now."

"Good luck, Brent," said Peter Wilson who patted him on the shoulder as he stood up. "Let me know how it all turns out."

When Jennifer and Brent were away from the senior officers and walking to the elevators, Brent said,

"You must be wondering what kind of idiot it is you have to babysit. First, you have a complex and sprawling case; next, you have a city detective showing you how it's done; and now, me. I'm sincerely sorry but the project was proposed to me and I accepted out of a deep interest in the kind of work being offered. I jumped at it."

"You don't have to explain anything to me." She had nearly smiled as he spoke.

"I feel, I do. Yes, I must. I'm not related to either the AC or the Commander, by the way... in case you were wondering."

They arrived at the elevators and Jennifer pressed the down button.

"Okay. Then how do you come to be here? Why did they pick you?"

"I did some work that got me noticed. That's about all. As for my ability to solve problems - it's nothing special... just a little unorthodox, sometimes."

The elevator arrived and, as it was already occupied, Jennifer and Brent descended in silence.

When they were on the fourth floor and the doors shut behind them they both tried to speak at the same time.

"Sorry," said Brent. "You go first."

"I was only going to say that I'm not really sure what I'm supposed to do in the interview. Assess you?" Now that she was facing Brent properly for the first time, she saw he was above average height, with thick brown hair, blue eyes and a lightly tanned complexion. He had an open face and seemed to be perpetually faintly amused by something. She decided it was a distinctly nice face.

"You must be severe and accurate in your assessment of what I do and say," said Brent. "If I can't cut it, let's all find out early and save embarrassment later. I have to warn you, though. I haven't read the police manual."

"Okay. We'll see what happens." Jennifer was surprised by almost everything Brent said. "What were *you* going to say?"

"Should I pass this test, I hope that any contributions I might make to furthering the case will be lumped in with those of the rest of the team. I have no desire to compete with anyone or to look better than anyone. I just want to contribute and help the team be successful. Sorry if that sounds awkward."

"No, not really. Let's go and get the files."

They began walking slowly through the fourth-floor open-plan office area.

"You'll need a desk. I'll have to find out what level of authorization has been assigned to you on the system."

"None. I'm allowed to read printouts, reports, and summaries at your discretion. You are my leader."

"Oh, I see."

"You don't sound very pleased by this state of affairs."

"No, it's not that. Doesn't matter."

"Let me guess. Mr. big city detective has taken charge and now you'll not only have to answer to him for your own actions but also for mine."

"In a way. Greg Darrow is senior in rank to me and Detective Field, Damian Field. I don't mind Darrow taking the lead because he definitely knows what he's doing but it's just…"

"It grates a little? The outsider has taken over. As I said before, now you have me, too. I swear, I'll cause no friction by word or deed. My actual presence, well, there's not much I can do about that. Besides, you can all arrest me if you like and I can't do anything except ask for a lawyer."

Jennifer laughed. "Let's hope it doesn't come to that. This is my office. I need to get a few things first."

Brent watched her from the doorway. She was nicely dressed, moved purposefully and efficiently, was five feet six in height, about the right age but, touting a black silicone ring, third finger, left hand, she was evidently married already. And he was not.

"You police make me sick! I have answered your questions ten times and given a signed statement. You want it signed in blood or something? Now leave me alone!"

Martha Badowski was in her real estate office and was getting close to screaming at Greg Darrow.

"Believe me, Mrs Badowski, if I could avoid being such a nuisance to you, I would. But you see..."

"I don't want to 'see' anything. I want you to get out. I have a *really* important deal going on here and I need to focus on that."

"I only have two questions."

"Write them down and send them to my lawyer. I'm busy." She viciously punched numbers on her desk telephone. "I'm sorry the woman died. I am. But, hey," she shrugged her shoulders, "life goes on. When this call is done I have to be somewhere else like five minutes ago."

Greg was about to speak but Martha held up a warning finger and then she began to gush into the phone.

"Thelma Andrews?" she said, with a huge smile on her face. "Oh, hi, how are you...? Now, listen, the seller is willing to drop the price by twenty thousand... Yes, I know that's not what you were hoping for but you must remember this is a tight market and the property, well, it is very, very unique and I doubt there'll be another available just like it for a long, long, long time. By then, who knows where the price will have moved... You're fine with it? Now, will Fred be okay with the price...? He left it up to you to decide? Well, that's great! I'll fix up your offer to reflect the price change. And Thelma, I want to tell you this in all sincerity, if I was not happy with my current home I would buy this one in a heartbeat. I really would... Thanks, Thelma. See you in about an hour to sign everything...? Great, just great."

Martha put the phone down and pumped the air with her fist, saying, "Yesss!" She looked at Greg. "Why are you still here?"

"I have a couple of questions," he said patiently.

"My lawyer," replied Martha. "This is his card." She pulled it out of a drawer and slapped the card on the desk in front of

Greg. Then she stood up, picked up a few papers, her jacket, and a small bag, and charged out of her office, looking for a secretary to re-jig the Andrews' offer.

Greg reached over to pick up the card which he scrutinized before putting it in his pocket. He sighed as he got up while his face provided no further clue as to his thoughts.

Chapter Seven

The test

"Mr Finch, thank you so much for coming in at such short notice," said Brent Umber. He shook hands with John Finch.

"No problem. I feel it my duty to help the police in every way I can."

"That is highly commendable. I wish more people thought the way you do. Before we proceed, I know you have met Detective Allen before..." Brent indicated Jennifer who was sitting in a chair to one side, positioned as though she were not quite a party to any conversation that would take place. "But I'm a newcomer to the case. My name is Brent Umber and I'm not a police detective. I'm a private investigator who has been asked to assist with the case."

Jennifer kept her head down but was aware when John Finch looked towards her for confirmation of this statement. Receiving no acknowledgement, he turned back to Brent.

"This is unusual, isn't it?" asked John.

"It is, rather. Please, sit down and make yourself comfortable. I'll explain why I'm involved."

There was a pause as both Brent and John took their seats on either side of the table.

"I have to say that this interview room is better-decorated than those you normally see in the movies," said Brent. "Just so you know, Mr Finch, that is a two-way mirror and we can go and look to see if anybody is occupying the room behind it if you like. I checked about five minutes ago and nobody was in there then."

"I don't mind," said John. "Although, I would think it must be nerve-wracking if a person is in here on a charge. You know, the thought you *might* be being watched but not *know* you're being watched."

"I agree. So, up until now, I have, for the most part, been engaged by private individuals and corporations who have involved me in very ordinary, run of the mill-type cases. Consequently, when this unexpected opportunity arose to assist the police in the investigation of Sheila Babbington's death, I could not help but accept. Currently, I am on probation. The police have a cautious attitude and so I am, as an outsider so to speak, under strict supervision. You have the dubious honour of being my first interviewee."

"I wish you luck," said John.

"Thanks. I'll probably need it. What I would like to say, though, before we get started, is that I hold myself to my own strict code of conduct, I strive to play fair with everyone I meet, and I would never want to see an innocent person condemned." Brent paused a moment and John Finch looked suitably impressed by his words but also a little non-plussed. Brent continued,

"You seem like a decent, upstanding man, John...May I call you John?"

"Of course," replied John.

"And you are not under any suspicion, not only because of the testimony of others but also, in part, because of the openness of your demeanour and your helpfulness in this investigation. The police have found it easy to talk to you and you have been very forthright and forthcoming. But let us suppose for a moment you were the opposite to what you are. Imagine you were uncommunicative, sullen, and obstructive. If that were the case, I would not automatically assume you were the murderer and try to pin it on you because of your evasion and lack of co-operation. I would sincerely endeavour to find out what caused you to behave in that way. I would get at the root cause before trying to find out anything about you as a murder suspect. Unless I can properly assess your character and personality, I have no basis on which to determine your potential involvement in the crime."

"Huh. That's some speech. It looks to me like you'll be okay. Detective Allen, are you going to write any of this down?"

"I'll remember it," said Jennifer.

"We have to turn to the case now," said Brent. "First, how is your family doing?"

"So far the children don't know anything about it. They pick up on the vibe in the house sometimes but they're doing well, thanks."

"And how is Delia?"

"She's not sleeping well. Bad dreams. I've had a few rough nights, too. Not at first but last week, which is weird."

"I drink teas when I can't sleep. Valerian or Chamomile."

"Delia tried Chamomile but it didn't seem to do anything."

"The brand can make a difference. Some manufacturers are a little challenged in the quality control department. Do you know the store Tea Chest Charms?"

"Yes, I know where that is."

"Try their own brand of loose tea in both those types and see if you notice a difference. Might help."

"I'll do that. Yeah, thanks."

"Coming back to the children, have you heard from them whether they noticed anything odd the day they were at the Songbird Estate?"

"I don't think so. They haven't mentioned anything. Nina is only two, so she wouldn't. Actually, now that I think about it, Kevin *did* say out of the blue that he wanted to ride a bike."

"Did he? Do you remember exactly when that was?"

"It was before the tour ended but not by much. It struck me as strange because he's never expressed an interest in bikes before. He's only just five."

"Would you say he said this before or after four o'clock?"

"It was just after we came out of the cellars and before we walked down towards the river. I'd put it at around 4:10 or so. There's a greenhouse down there and we went to see some young vines being grafted onto rootstocks. Just a demonstration kind of thing for us."

"I'm very interested in what you say about Kevin," said Brent. "You see, we have a missing and, as yet, unknown cyclist. Three witnesses had him travelling up the hill past the vineyard's entrance at about 4:45. The tour finished at five. Now we have master Kevin saying the word 'bike' earlier than that. It could mean one of three things. Kevin had a sudden thought about bikes unconnected with the cyclist the other witnesses saw. Kevin saw the same cyclist as the others which means the cyclist was hanging about the area longer than was thought before. The third possibility would be that there were two different cyclists in the vicinity."

Brent paused for a moment. Jennifer was taking notes.

"I might be going out on a limb here." Brent glanced at Jennifer but she was not looking up just then. "If I remember what the memories of small children are like, it would probably be impossible to have Kevin recall what he saw on the day through direct questioning. However, I wonder whether you'd mind doing this one little thing for me. Would you ask him to draw a picture of a bicycle or even of himself riding a bicycle and then ask dear Kevin to say where he saw such a bike?"

"I will definitely do that. Or rather, Delia can get him to do that very easily."

"Thanks. Now, if he is cooperative, could you ask him if he would like to ride the bike wearing a hoody?"

"Is that what the others saw?"

"It is. Memories are fragile. The important thing is not to lead him but patiently allow Kevin to volunteer anything he can. If he says anything more about the day or a bike, please make a note of it."

"I'll do that. Definitely - as soon as I get home, I'll tell Delia about this."

"Wonderful. Next, how are both your and Delia's reminiscences? Have either of you recalled anything that was not previously put into your statements?"

"No. We've talked about the murder until we were exhausted. When I go back to the house we'll be at it again. It's just how we are. We can't leave it alone."

"It will fade a little over time. It will fade faster if we can catch the murderer quickly. Just two more questions. The first is, would you return to the Songbird Estate?"

"Not willingly. No, never. Unless I was eighty and wanted to show the grandchildren where it all happened. Even then, no, I don't think I'll go back."

"Who do you think committed the murder?"

"Whoa, that's a shocker."

"Yes, it is. You've thought about it, though."

"I have. I don't know if it's right to say anything."

"Probably isn't. But somebody stands out in your mind."

"Well, yes. There was one guy, knew a lot about wine, who was, like, ill at ease."

"Do you mean Claude Gaudin? He's in the wine business. By all accounts, he seems to be a bit larger than life, although I haven't met him myself yet."

"I know who you mean. No, it wasn't him. It was the other guy. Kept trying to upstage the tour guide."

"Stan Forbes?"

"Yes, him."

John Finch went quiet after this.

"I want to thank you sincerely for coming in and helping the way you have. I'm anxious to hear what master Kevin has to say on life in general and bikes and their riders in particular. Here's my card. Everything you tell me I will relay to Detective Allen." Brent stood up.

"That's amazing...to think it's possible that Kevin might be an important witness."

The two men shook hands. They all three said goodbye and John Finch left the room.

When he had gone, Jennifer stretched herself in the chair before standing up.

"Very interesting," she said. "Could be productive, too. One thing I want to know. Why didn't you press him about Forbes?"

"He didn't want to say anything more. If it's important, I'll come back to John and hammer away until he tells me everything. He's not going anywhere. Besides, Kevin must speak first, then his dad can be questioned again. I'm going out for a walk and to mull over the case. You have to report to the brass on my activities. Although I'm filled with curiosity, I will refrain from asking how I did until you have delivered your assessment. Thanks for your patience and for allowing me free rein."

Brent left the room before she really had any chance to reply.

While Brent walked about outside, Jennifer went to see Commander Baker. She knocked on his door.

"Come in," called out Baker. "Detective Allen. Well?"

"I would hire him, sir."

"Really?" Baker fiddled with a pen. "What are his methods?"

"He quickly made a friend out of Finch. At the very least, he established a strong rapport. It seemed genuine to me. Finch came up with something new. It's just possible the cyclist was seen by someone else at an earlier time. It depends on what a five-year-old boy remembers. Umber played it very well. He asked questions in ways we're not trained to do. At first, it seemed off-the-wall but gradually you realize he is spinning a web. The web is not a trap. It's like a web of friendship and trust. That's it, sir."

"Hmm. Very good. I value your recommendation. We'll give him three days and see how he does. But he'll have to produce something tangible in that time. Only, don't tell him this."

"I get the impression, sir, that the more difficult the situation is made the better he would like it. Just an impression."

"Then tell him if you wish."

"Thank you, sir."

Chapter Eight

Friction

"What! They've stuck us with another guy as if Darrow isn't enough?" Damian was furious. "I'm quitting."

"No, you're not. You're a good detective... just a bit lazy. What else would you do, anyway?" Jennifer and Damian were eating in the lunchroom.

"I suppose you're right. Hey, what does Darrow make of him?"

"They haven't met yet."

"Now that should be interesting. So, what is the new guy like?"

"A bit weird. He's smart, though... totally engaged. You'll see for yourself."

"Where is he now?"

"Went to a restaurant."

"Too good to eat with the rest of us?"

"Don't be so down. He's only here for three days. Besides, he offered to buy me lunch."

They were silent for a while as they ate.

"He must be making good money," said Damian. "That's something to think about - becoming a PI after leaving the force. Is that what he did?"

"No, he's too young and has never been in law enforcement - as far as I know. Certainly doesn't act like it. It's really interesting - he was telling me just now how he became an investigator because a friend of his was murdered. Apparently, he discovered who the killers were but neither he nor the police were able to find sufficient evidence to bring them to trial. "

"Hmph. Well, all I know is that I've got to interview a whole bunch this afternoon. I get the feeling the witnesses are getting tired with the questioning. I know I am."

"Same here. Be professional and get the job done, whether you like it or not."

"Jen, *that* is straight out of training school."

"I suppose it sounds like it. You know, I wouldn't mind applying to become an instructor. You can do it part-time with your other duties."

"I think you'd be good at it. You're always telling me how to do things properly."

"Somebody has to look out for you so you don't get in trouble."

"I'll tell you something. I like working with you better than anyone else I've worked with. I mean it."

"That's nice of you to say. You're okay, too."

Brent returned from a hurried lunch to get down to some work. He found his way to the fourth floor and firstly went to his desk where he gathered up some files. He had decided he needed more space and headed towards the small conference room where he could lay things out and work up a plan of action.

As he approached, he saw a man inside the room with his own papers spread out. Brent knocked on the glass door.

"Excuse me," said Brent. "Is there anywhere else that I can do what you're doing? I need to spread things out a bit and my desk is too small."

The man turned slowly from his work. He looked Brent in the eye, having noticed the visitor-pass around his neck and the Sheila Babbington-related files he was carrying.

"Who are you?" asked the man, his face impassive.

"I'm Brent Umber. Who might you be?"

"My name's Darrow. What are you doing with those files?"

"I'm a private investigator and I've been asked in to review the case. I should…"

"Hold it. You're a civilian? And you're working on a case?"

"Yes, you see…"

"Why was I not informed about this?"

"I don't know. Perhaps you were out. It all happened this morning. I hope…"

"This makes no sense. Did Baker bring you in?"

"It's Greg, right? Listen, Greg. I'm here and you have to put up with me."

"Are you being funny?"

"I don't think so. I prefer to use first names. You can call me Brent."

"I'm going to see Baker and straighten this out."

"No one's stopping you. I should imagine he is expecting a visit from an irritated city detective about now. What do you think he'll tell you?"

For the first time, Greg Darrow hesitated. He stared at Brent.

"Okay," he said quietly. "Explain to me how you come to be here."

Brent did so in a few sentences, staying on point for the most part. When he had finished, Greg said,

"So, you are only here for three or four days. Look, Umber, I don't like this set-up for many reasons. My biggest concern is that you will upset the witnesses. You may have talked a good talk to Baker but I'm not buying it. This is so unprofessional."

"Maybe it is. I have a code of conduct that I abide by. It is doubtlessly different to yours but it's no less stringent. My oversight is my own conscience. I'm not here because of the money, which isn't that great. I'm certainly not here to be berated by people I've just met. I'm here to catch a murderer. I presume you are, too. So, setting aside all other considerations, my original question to you was - is there some open space I can use that doesn't disturb anyone?"

"Use the other side of this table. You've already disturbed me."

"Thanks, Greg. I'll try not to do it again."

Brent began to lay out files, open them up, and arrange sheets of paper and photographs into coherent sections. Greg watched him for some seconds before returning to his own work. They both worked in silence for some minutes.

"Greg? Excuse me for interrupting you. I wondered what you make of the knife?"

"It would be more interesting to hear what you make of it."

"Okay. I think this murder was committed by an assassin or a serial killer. The knife tells me that extreme care was taken over its preparation. The thorough cleansing shows the killer was mindful of consequences. The sharp, polished edge is only achieved with Japanese water stones or other expensive or laborious means. That speaks of ritual: one that has been done before or one that will be the first in a series. Leaving the knife in the wound shows a level of confidence or pride that an average person, even an average murderer, would not possess. Whoever killed Sheila was very self-assured. It could be extrapolated that the knife was deliberately left as a taunt or calling card for the police investigators."

"How sure are you about this?" asked Greg.

"About ninety per cent. It's just possible the knife already had an edge on it and the murderer acquired it and only cleaned it up. The knife is old and relatively cheap. So, if an average murderer did the deed, it would have been very easy to remove the knife from the wound and pop it in a bag for disposal. Cleaning *and* removal would have been the safest way for the murderer to reduce his or her risk of being caught. I don't see him panicking all of a sudden and forgetting to pull it out. The whole scenario looks too carefully crafted, despite its simplicity. The proof of my theory is that we're standing here agonizing over the details of an old kitchen knife while somewhere out there is a person smiling, thinking that you and I are doing just what he intended."

"I see," said Greg. "I came to a similar conclusion. The problem I have with the theory is that the location is all wrong. If the deceased was deliberately targeted it would surely have been planned to be done where there were no witnesses around."

"True. Perhaps the killer liked the thrill of nearby witnesses. It could be he subconsciously wanted to make it a public event and this was as close as he could get to achieving that. You never know - some people are very strange. But, really, I find these explanations too loose to be viable. I think the location had to be where it was for a specific reason: the reason being the vineyard was the *only* place the murder *could* be carried out and the time was the *only* time it *could* be worked. If what I said is true, then the field of suspects narrows to just those on the tour, the cyclist, or an as yet unknown person."

"An interesting angle." Greg Darrow looked at Brent. "Seeing as we have to work together and there is plenty for all of us to do, I wonder if you might do me a favour?"

"If I can."

"Thanks. I'd like you to interview someone who was on the tour. It would give you a start on substantiating your theory. Her name is Martha Badowski. She's a nice lady and a busy real estate agent, though I understand she's in the office most of the time. It's best not to call ahead. I find the spontaneity of a visit can be rewarding in and of itself. Just drop in and see her. It's not far from here so you could talk to her this afternoon. If you would work in the couple of questions I need answers to - apart from that, she's all yours."

"Sure. I'd be happy to get started. Thanks."

"No problem. Sorry if I was a little rude earlier. Being from out of town and not on my own turf, as it were, I probably got a bit defensive. I'll write the questions down for you."

"Not to worry. You know, I've already worked out the type of questions I want to ask. I'll go and see her right away."

"That's good. The sooner the better."

Brent tidied up his paperwork while Greg wrote out his questions accompanied by a few subsidiary follow-ups. When Brent left the conference room with the notes in his pocket and a file folder in his bag, Greg smiled for the first time since he had arrived in Belton.

Chapter Nine

No way to conduct an investigation

B rent opened the door of the Rising Star Realty office.
"Hi. How may I help you?" asked the receptionist.

Brent was standing at the front desk. A small waiting area lay behind him. His extended view was of a line of private offices that led away into a labyrinth of rooms and passages knit together by the same blue carpet and subdued lighting. Smaller offices were situated towards the back with larger, more imposing ones nearer the front. The tenants of this latter group could easily spring out and engage any potential client because they could hear the enquirer before seeing them.

"Good afternoon. Is Martha Badowski in the office at the moment?"

"I believe so. Let me call her and find out if she is available."

The receptionist dialled an extension and, looking away from Brent, said,

"Hi, Martha. There's someone at the front to see you." She looked up at Brent. "She'll be with you in a moment."

"Thanks."

Brent thought about sitting down but decided to stand and wait. As he stood, he noticed the name plaque on the first and largest office. It read 'Stefan Badowski, Broker.' He looked to the second office. The name was 'Martha Badowski, Vice-President, Agent.' Brent guessed that Martha, if she were in her office, had heard him when he came in because her door was open.

After five minutes, Brent began to get the impression that the delay might be deliberate. He began to walk about the room and, when the receptionist had become acclimatized to his movement, he abruptly walked into Martha's office.

Martha jumped when she saw him appear so suddenly. She was in the middle of typing a text message. She was smartly dressed, well-coiffed, had long, bright red fingernails and plenty of gold jewellery with gemstones hanging from her person in all the traditional places.

"Sorry about that," said Brent. "I thought I would wait in your office until you returned. I didn't know you were here. I'll just sit in this chair quietly until you finish."

"I've finished," she said. She looked uncomfortable.

"Ah, good. My name's Brent Umber. I'm a private investigator but I'm working with the Belton police on the Sheila Babbington case."

"You're what?" she asked, scrunching up her face at Brent's paradoxical introduction of himself.

"Well, you are Martha - I recognize you from the photographs and I need your help on the Babbington case."

"I know about that. You're a *private* investigator?"

"That's right."

"Working for the police?"

"Yes."

"Then get out. Go on, out." When Brent didn't move, she added, "Like *now!*"

"I get it. Let me guess. Have you seen Greg Darrow recently?"

"That idiot was in here this morning. Now you're here and you're not even a real cop. Are you going to leave?"

"Ah, no. Don't hold my not being a cop against me. Darrow set me up. You, too, I suspect."

"What do you mean?"

"Did you throw him out of the office?"

"I did. You can ask questions through my lawyer. That idiot has the number."

"Doesn't surprise me. I can see you detest him. I'm not exactly friendly towards him myself at the moment. You don't want him to win, do you?"

"I don't really care. Just leave." Her long red nails tapped an irritated tattoo on the desk.

"You know that a woman, about your age, was brutally murdered. Don't you want the killer to be found? He or she might strike again."

"I know all of that. I don't like it. I hope you catch the creep. My answering the same questions over and over is not going to do it."

"In the time we've spent so far we could have got some points cleared up. No matter. I have all day."

"Look, funny man, go and catch the guy who did it."

"How do you know it was a man? Did you see something?"

"No, I didn't. But it's always a man who does it."

"Not all of the time. Most of the time. Would you go back to the Songbird Estate?"

"Never. I don't even want to hear the name again."

"I can understand that. What about Stefan? Who does he think did it?"

"He's gone weird. I'd like to talk it over with him but he doesn't want to."

"Stefan has a solid alibi. He stayed in the same area the whole time between five and six-thirty."

"Is that the time it happened? I've seen three cops a total of five times and none of them gave out anything."

"They probably didn't know until the post-mortem examination results were issued and the time of death established. Probably forgot about it afterwards or maybe you were sharp with them."

"The girl was all right. Saw her twice at the beginning. Then some loser came in looking like he was bored. The last straw was this morning when Mr Frosty arrived."

"It's unfortunate. And now me. I hate to think what you're going to say after I've gone."

"I'll talk to you and answer your questions. You're okay... just okay."

"No. I want us to do better than that. I want you and me to get back at Greg Darrow. Only, I can't think of anything just yet."

"Well, think of something and I'll see what I can do to help!"

"Excellent! That's the spirit. First, let's talk real estate. Believe it or not, I am actually in the market to buy a house. Not in Belton, though; in Newhampton."

"Really? This isn't just a line?"

"Really and truly. I have my heart set on something very suburban."

"Give me some details." She took out a form to fill in. "We have an office in the city, as well. I go there twice a week."

"That helps. Let's see, three bedrooms will do. It can be run down but not dilapidated and it mustn't be ugly. I like things to have proper proportions or be double-fronted. The one thing it must have, and this is absolutely critical, it must have a large back garden with a southern exposure. If it's all lawn at the back, I'd be happy. A few small trees are okay. I don't want to be cutting down a forest, though. In fact, I wouldn't do that because I like trees. I want to take up gardening. It has been a long-cherished but as yet unfulfilled ambition of mine."

"I like gardening, too. It's a lot of work, though. I hire someone to do the lawns and beds. That way, I can work on the interesting things and cut the flowers for arrangements."

"How do you protect your nails? They look very well-cared for."

"They do get messed up now and again. Usually, I wear two thin pairs of gloves. Seems to do the trick. Do you have a preferred area?"

"Not really. A quiet area, I think. It can be anywhere but not out in the sticks. I don't want a long commute to downtown. Here's my card. The address is wrong on it but the phone number's still good. I'll print new ones with the new address."

"Thanks." Martha took the card and stapled it to the form. "Price range?"

"Hmm, I was thinking about six hundred thousand."

"That limits you a bit. Most of the properties in that bracket are further out. Closer to the centre, the price escalates quickly. 'Specially for a large lot. I'll show you some listings we have on our books."

Martha swivelled her monitor around so Brent could see it and typed details into the query form. After a few seconds, photographs of listings populated the screen.

"What's that one there?"

"What, this one? It's seven hundred and forty-five thousand and it's an easy distance to the city centre... see it on the map. Let's take a look at it."

Photographs came up of a late seventies, architect-designed house with a large, empty garden at the rear. The kitchen was very dated and the interior was bare.

"I like the house," said Brent. "Four bedrooms... It's larger than I wanted."

"Um, do you have a partner? Children?"

"No, to both questions."

"I'm surprised."

"So am I."

"I'm sorry, I didn't mean anything personal. It's just you're looking for three bedrooms. It's up to you what you do with them."

"I have yet to find a soul mate. When I do, I'll have a house and garden waiting for her."

"Be careful she doesn't marry you *for* your house and garden." Martha laughed knowingly.

"There is that to be considered. What do you think of the house?"

"It's good quality. You can see that in the attention to detail and its features. That design in the brickwork on the side. It added hours to the labour costs to put it in. Little things like that make me think that quality should be found throughout. Now, the kitchen is a disaster. The bathrooms look okay. You'd need an inspection for the mechanicals, foundation, roof, plumbing, and wiring. See the tall window over the front door? That would be expensive to replace if the seals are gone. It could be redesigned or replaced. It would cost either way."

"Is it worth the asking price?"

"Hmm, in that area in that condition I'd say it was a little overpriced. If you put a hundred thousand into it, I'm only guessing you know, then it would be worth over eight-fifty probably nine. If you could get it at a discount it would probably be worth doing."

"We're a long way from six hundred thousand. More like eight hundred."

"True. There are plenty of other houses. By the way, you should get yourself pre-approved for a mortgage unless you're selling another property."

"It's a cash deal. I have another property but I want to keep that."

"Oh, I see." Martha raised her eyebrows on hearing these details.

"Look, it's three-thirty now and I have a meeting at five. I'll sign something to make you my buying agent. You come up with a list of suitable properties for me to look at - as soon as possible, please, because that place is growing on me."

"Here's my fee schedule, then. You give me an exclusive for ninety days and I will find you your dream home."

"I'm sure you will. But first, you can give me a discount on your fees."

"Why should I?"

"Because they're too high. You sound like you know what you're talking about and that reassures me greatly. I'll pay half."

"Sixty per cent."

"Done. Now, if I got that place for six-fifty and all the costs are within what we were discussing, I'd give you a bonus of five thousand."

"I'll see what I can do."

"Okay. So, now we have a murder to discuss. I'll keep it brief."

"Sure. And, don't forget, we've got to do something for Darrow." Martha smiled as she said this.

Chapter Ten

Plain sailing

B rent cut it a little fine in getting to the five o'clock meeting. He parked his old, blue Jeep in the parking lot. As he impatiently waited for an elevator, he was thinking alternately about murder and real estate.

Once inside and ascending, he looked at his appearance in the mirror to smarten himself up. On the fourth floor, he passed the open door of Greg Darrow's office where the detective was straightening up some things on his desk, preparatory to leaving to go to the small conference room where the 5 p.m. meeting was to be held.

"Very nicely done," said Brent, keeping a straight face as he stood in the doorway.

"Oh, what are you referring to?" asked Greg with an air of innocence.

"Getting the information from Martha. She was very helpful."

"Was she?"

"Yes. Very helpful. I have the answers to your two questions. Firstly, no, she did not see Charles Babbington in any place outside of the restaurant or store. Secondly, Martha says, that, although she had seen Sheila Babbington in the past, she had not met her personally. Sheila had been a guest speaker at a Belton Business Improvement Association's luncheon where Sheila had been promoting her wine selection and talking about the hardships of women in business. Martha says that Sheila was not a *great* speaker but was good enough that she could empathize with what Sheila was saying. Personally speaking, I find the word empathy is overused these days but that is what Martha said."

"Ah, thank you."

"No problem. Happy to do that for you."

"And, uh, how did *your* questions work out?"

"Very well indeed. Could not have gone better. Charming woman."

"Is she?" Greg Darrow was visibly on the brink of saying something more but controlled himself.

"Going to the meeting?" asked Brent.

"Yes. I'll be there in a minute."

Brent nodded and turned to go. "Oh, I nearly forgot." He turned back and took his phone from his pocket. "Martha would like you to see these."

The investigator set his phone down on the desk in front of Greg. The photo, taken in the real estate office, was of Brent's and Martha's smiling faces with their cheeks touching. He swiped and the second photo was of Martha now kissing Brent on the cheek. There was a prominent red lipstick mark already on his face. The third and final photograph was of both Brent and Martha facing the camera with their tongues sticking out.

"See you at the meeting."

He picked up his phone and left. Greg had not moved a muscle and was left staring at the desktop.

When Brent entered the conference room, Jennifer was already seated.

"How is it going?" she asked.

"Difficult to say. The murder investigation is good, though. We can cross one name off the list, as far as I'm concerned."

Jennifer gave him a quizzical look. "Who is it?"

"That will come out in a minute. I'm looking for a slightly dramatic moment for the denouement. If it doesn't come off, I promise to tell you everything later on."

"I guess I'll accept that," said Jennifer.

"Sorry. I know I'm on probation and I must report to you. Let's just see what happens. Ah, who's this?" Brent stood up.

"Detective Damian Field, this is Brent Umber who is here to help us with the investigation," said Jennifer in a business-like manner.

"Brent," said Damian.

"Pleased to meet you," said Brent.

They both sat down and almost immediately Greg came into the room.

"Sorry I'm late," he said. "I was organizing a few things."

He looked around the room. "Now, I think we need to state where we are at in order to give Mr Umber an idea of how we are approaching the case."

"Oh, I agree," interjected Brent. "That would be very useful. But first I must explain the terms and conditions of my mandate. As you know, I am a private investigator by trade. I have been asked by your senior management to come in and review the work done so far in order that I may then conduct my own inquiries where necessary according to my own methods. Everything I discover I will share with all of you. I am not a competitor and I hope you will accept me as an auxiliary to your team. I've been instructed to report to Jennifer and I always use first names where possible because it sounds friendly. She is to oversee my activities and, if I get out of line, I suppose she will fire me. I'm quite content with this arrangement. If I have to clear any of my activities that are out of the ordinary, Jennifer will say yea or nay. That is how it has been set up." Brent had glanced from one person to the next during this speech but now he looked at Greg as he continued,

"I've said all this so that there is no misunderstanding as to my position here. I probably will not be with you for more than a few days and I apologize for taking up your valuable time."

"Okay," said Damian, nodding his approval.

"Very good," said Greg. "At least we all know where we stand. You have to remember that we're all police officers here and to have a civilian come in and work in the same area that we usually control, well, let me say, it is very unusual."

"I sympathize," said Brent. "I would be irritated if I were in your place. I hope to cause no further irritation. I may have interrupted you, Greg. I believe we were going to review the case as it currently stands."

"Yes. Who will go first? Anyone got anything new?"

Damian went first. His report was brief and to the point. Jennifer followed and her report encompassed the few things she had managed to get done since the last meeting, neatly summarizing in a way that Greg would approve. Greg came last. He added a few more items and now the stalled case had been laid out before the group.

"May I add something?" asked Brent.

Jennifer nodded. She had been waiting patiently for his update.

"I believe Martha Badowski can be crossed off the list of suspects. I realize you would prefer I present evidence and that she could be provided with an alibi but I interviewed her this afternoon and several things struck me. Firstly, her reactions to several situations that have arisen recently were entirely genuine. Even if she were the best of actresses, she would not make her reactions so overblown and melodramatic as to be extraordinary. In any event, they were not the reactions one would expect from a murderer. Secondly, she is extremely stressed because her husband, Stefan, refuses to speak about the murder at all. He is dismissive and gets annoyed if she tries to get him to talk about it. He is clearly upset and is doing the silent-manly thing. As a consequence of this situation, I became something of a sounding board for Martha's impressions, thoughts, and fears. I received a few too many Badowski marital insights. However, what this deluge revealed to me was that she is not a murderer, hasn't the mind of a criminal, and is quite trustworthy unless you are buying real estate from her when she can be extraordinarily sharp." Brent stopped speaking for a moment or two but, finding the silence rather nerve-racking, continued his spiel.

"Something of an aside, Martha can sound quite sickly in her sales patter when on the phone talking to a client. I heard her and it's truly awful. So, I asked her about it. Martha said that a lot of her clients expect her to sound like that. She went on to say that she doesn't do it with everyone but only those who seem to need leading to make a decision. Sorry, if I'm off track but I found it fascinating. Anyway, to conclude, I'm convinced she didn't do it. I believe Greg can back me up on this point."

Damian and Jennifer turned their attention to Greg to find him nodding slowly in agreement. Very great was their surprise when Greg went on to say,

"I think I owe you all an apology and an explanation. I want to clear the air. I don't much care for travelling away from home. I'm interested in the case but I don't like being away from my family. I stay in Belton some nights and have extra travelling others. I was sent here by my division commander so it was not my choice." Up to this point, Greg had seemed his usual self-assured self. When he continued that self-assurance was noticeably diminished and, for the first time in their presence, he appeared somewhat uncomfortable.

"The next thing is that I can't help but take charge in any situation. I normally *am* officially in charge in my regular work in the city. With my senior rank and work habits, I simply took over here without asking. I should have realized that I am a guest in Belton and that we should be working as a team. I think we are, despite myself, but then I didn't ask for your input... I just took over." His audience was mute, such was its surprise.

"When Brent appeared today, I can't tell you how annoyed I got. So, I set him up. I spoke to Martha Badowski this morning. She became very angry and threw me out of her office. So the set-up was this: I asked Brent to go and see her and made out that she was easy to get along with. I, also, by the way, was coming to the conclusion that she's innocent - no murderer in her right mind would act towards the police as Martha has. Anyway, I had really hoped that Brent would receive even worse treatment than I had - by rights, he should have because the witness was already at the end of her tether before she set eyes on him. Let me tell you, Martha Badowski can be pretty outrageously bad when she gets going. Brent, show them the photographs."

"Are you sure?" asked Brent.

"Yes, yes, I deserve it. You'll see for yourselves how our associate here... and he's only been with us a few hours... well, just you look how he turned the tables on me. I'm not sure how he did it but that woman was so angry with me and the police in general that you wouldn't believe it unless you were there. I'm impressed with Brent and he has behaved like a gentleman over the matter."

Brent showed the photographs.

"How'd you do that?" asked Damian.

Jennifer looked a little disgusted at first.

"I'm not putting anything about this in my report," she said. "They'll think we're crazy. You *are* crazy, Brent. This could get you fired. *She* is a *witness*."

"I honestly did think about clearing the photos with you first but I decided it would take too long to explain properly. Please don't fire me yet."

"You did get results, I suppose. Try and keep it decent, will you?" replied Jennifer.

"If you knew me I would be shocked by your request. You don't know me therefore you are forgiven. I do assure you I am thoroughly honourable and always morally well-intentioned."

"I think there's a catch in there somewhere. You're still on probation."

"Understood. Would you mind if I went out to the Songbird Estate? I know it's nearly six but I'd like to have a chat with Charles Babbington today."

"He's very upset," replied Jennifer. "Promise me you won't annoy him?"

"I absolutely will show respect to the grief he is going through. I will be tender with the children should I meet them. I can't quite imagine how he's coping. I hope to find out."

"All right," said Jennifer.

"Thanks. I'm gone. See you all, later." Brent left the room in a rush.

"He's quite a character," said Damian. "Is he unstable, do you think?"

"I don't know," said Jennifer. "I hope not."

"He has a theory about the murder already," said Greg. "Explained it to me earlier. He thinks the murder was targeted or the work of a serial killer. Gave some good reasons to support it. He might prove difficult to get along with on a number of levels but I'm getting a sense he'll do some good work."

"Should we look into it... the theory?" asked Damian.

"I asked someone in my own department to take a look through the databases. They'll let us know what they find."

"It crossed my mind... what do you think he did to get noticed by upstairs?" asked Jennifer.

"I don't know. Did you see him with Baker?"

"Yes. Wilson was there and he was acting like an uncle, wishing Brent all the best, patting him on the back."

"Then Wilson brought him," said Damian. "What was that about?"

"If you want to find out something about our guy," said Greg, "ask him."

"Yes, that's right," said Jennifer. "He's pretty open about everything even with a total stranger. In the test interview, he spoke to John Finch like a friend."

"So, Greg," said Damian, "where do *we* go from here?"

"Yes, well, that's for you to say."

"So how about you still supervise the case and divide up the duties like you've been doing only I don't get all the lousy stuff."

Greg looked at Jennifer. "Okay with you?"

"Sure. You're the one with the experience. We're beginners by comparison."

"What I'll do is identify what needs doing, we discuss it, and then you both can choose what you do off the list. Is that fair?"

"Fair," said Damian.

"Yes, that sounds about right. What about Brent?"

"I think we pretty much have to let him do his own thing. Whatever he does, we need to get evidence. Nothing's changed that."

"You're worried about what he'll do, aren't you?" asked Damian of Jennifer.

"I am. I hope this isn't a bad idea."

"Don't sweat it," said Greg. "I mean, how much trouble can he cause?"

Chapter Eleven

Red, red wine

The old, blue Jeep had left the busier roads and built-up areas behind and was only a few minutes away from the winery. The road in front of Brent was now forced to follow the winding of a river. Every so often, a small bridge appeared. Then, for the next mile, the road parted company with the water to avoid the flood plain created by a broad loop, effectively hidden from the road by a tall, forest border of uniformly recent growth. The next bridge, quite high because of its long span, was the one that led to Brent's destination. As he crossed, he caught glimpses, now through ancient willows, of the riverside vines of the Songbird Estate, laid out in sharp regularity on the opposite bank.

Once off the bridge, the Jeep climbed a gentle slope for several hundred yards; a sharp bend and the entrance to the winery appeared unexpectedly in the corner before the road sharply turned again to go up a steep hill. Brent slowed down but still a cloud arose from the dusty, thinly gravelled driveway as he drove onto the property and came to a stop. The store and restaurant were shut. Blinds were drawn over the restaurant windows. A now faded, dark green wreath with drooping white lilies hung on the door.

"Oh, no," said Brent. His face dropped. The case which had thus far been for him academic - an extremely interesting and novel adventure - and a just cause to rally behind, had now turned into that old track of simple, dreary, crushing grief as expressed in changed lives and faces that could not smile without first having forgotten, for a moment, the persistent aching loss. Brent knew these sad things lay behind the doors and windows of the large, well-kept house. The human loss of Sheila was before him.

The odd assortment of buildings grouped together blended into a cohesive whole of interest and charm. The buildings had been constructed during each decade of the last one hundred and twenty years with each housing a separate process relating to wine production or the upkeep of a large, agricultural property. There was so much to explore and it lay so inviting in the summer sunlight. A hundred interesting nooks and a hundred crannies into which to peer. 'But,' the wreath said, 'what is the point of charm, interest, and curiosity? Leave it at the door. Come inside and weep, for we all come to this in the end. We shall weep or be the one wept over.'

The sun shone in the clear sky, although the day was nearing its end, but even the pale orange skyline, warm-tinted wisps of cloud, and warm, mild evening air full of scents of earth and plants failed to counter the sadness that had settled upon the place. Before Brent got out, he saw a fox in the distance on the track next to some vines. The grief was not palpable, then. The fox did not notice it. The air of grief was not a physical force but only a mastering emotion and a strong clamp on one's thoughts. One's master can be changed and one's thoughts can be renewed. Eventually, the wreath will be thrown away. Brent got out with his pack over his shoulder and went to knock on the door. He saw tall weeds among the flowerbeds beneath the windows. Sheila was no longer able to attend to them and no one else had remembered the beds as being important.

Charles Babbington opened the door. Mindful that he was in mourning, Brent tried not to search the man's face for evidence of grief and distress but failed in his restraint. He saw those things there readily enough.

"Mr Babbington. My name is Brent Umber. I hope I'm not disturbing you."

"Hello. No. I'm not doing anything."

"I'm very sorry for your loss. I didn't know Sheila personally but I feel as though I did. You see, I'm working with the Belton Police Department. Here's my card and here is Detective Allen's card. I believe you've met her."

Babbington took the cards, glanced at them as though he did not know what he was supposed to do with them, then handed them back to Brent.

"Yes. Twice, I think."

"I'm a private investigator working on the case. If you feel like it, we could have a talk. I'd like to get a picture of Sheila in my mind."

"A picture?"

"Yes. I'd like to understand what she was like. What her interests were. It seems to me that she must have been very proud of the vineyard. I should imagine it takes a lot of dedication to run a place like this and do it well."

"Oh, it does. She worked very hard to get it where it is now."

"Was it more her project than yours?"

"It was. I'm an engineer and it was her dream to run a winery. Oh, excuse me. Please, come in."

"Thank you." Brent was now standing in a dim vestibule from which a long narrow passage, with stairs to the right, led past two reception rooms and a kitchen. At the end were open double doors into what was obviously a very large lounge or sunroom. It was brilliant with golden light from the sun going down over the river.

"Go through to the back."

In silence, they walked the hall and into the lounge.

"What a beautiful, beautiful room. And the view is stunning."

The room was the entire width of the house and was filled with comfortable, overstuffed chairs and a set of rattan furniture. Numerous potted plants, including a weeping fig and an impressively plaited Money Tree, stood on the diamond-patterned, glossy red, terra cotta tiled floor. Large picture windows rose up two stories on three sides while a second-floor gallery could be reached by an iron spiral staircase. Patio doors led out to a narrow stone terrace which had six steps descending to a small, ornamental garden. Beyond that, the ground fell away sharply into a flat, level plain covered in vines. Everything was touched golden in the light and the shadows were long. The land, striped by golden-green vines and golden grey shadows between them, presented as some fabulous cloth of immense proportions. The broad field ran downhill to the river where the lines diminished in thickness, compacted by distance and the lie of the land. Where it ran uphill, the vines seemed taller and more open as though the field were bent over a frame to reveal the tan-coloured warp and weft structure of the imaginary cloth.

Brent noticed where the uphill vines disappeared behind a line of trees and bushes and suddenly recalled why he was there in this house. He turned to his silent host who was also looking at the view.

"It is beautiful, isn't it? We never take it for granted," said Charles, as though his wife was only out of the room for the moment.

"Yes. A sight like this can't be possessed but only enjoyed. Mind you, the laying out of the vines is your contribution."

"Ah, it was a vineyard when we bought the place. We extended it and made improvements. This scene hasn't changed much in a hundred years."

Brent nodded. "Are the children in the house?" he asked.

"Uh, no. I thought it best they stay with Auntie for a while. She's taking very good care of them."

"I see. I'm sorry to be so direct but I don't think you're doing very well."

"No, I'm not. I've fallen in a heap, really."

"Let's sit down, then. Which is your favourite chair?"

"That one." Charles pointed to an armchair, hesitated, then went over to sit in it.

"Do you drink tea?"

"No. It's too late for coffee."

"Well, you must have some wine on hand."

"Oh, yes. Plenty. I'll get a bottle. Be back in a moment."

"Thanks. I'm very interested to sample some."

Charles went to the kitchen and was gone for some minutes. When he returned, he was carrying four bottles, each with a different label. He put the bottles down on the glass top of the rattan table. Three had similar labels in striking, single colours, incorporating a bird's silhouette and were easily identified as:- SongBird Lark - a white Chardonnay; SongBird Robin - Cabernet Sauvignon; SongBird Nightingale - a blended, red wine. The fourth bottle was black with a plain white label. A flowing gold script stated it was a three-year-old vintage Pinot Noir. Brent picked it up and found another simple white label on the back stating the bare minimum of details. However, there were two gold medal graphics at the bottom. The bottle had traces of light dust on it. Charles must have wiped it clean before bringing it in.

"Shall I get the glasses?"

"No, no. I had to get a bottle up from the cellar. I'll get them." When he came back, he said,

"We should have some food. Have you eaten?"

"I didn't mean to put you to any trouble."

"It's no trouble. I like to be busy. I can't focus on my engineering work at present but I can still cook. I have fresh trout. Do you like trout?"

"I do. You realize, I only came to ask some awkward questions?"

"I know. We'll save the Chardonnay for the meal. I'm not much for wine except a glass with dinner."

"I'm the same. And I'm no expert so I won't be able to give you an informed opinion."

"Just say if you like it - that's my test. Sheila was the expert."

"Did she write those convoluted taste descriptions about wood notes, blackberries, and cheesecake? I find those baffling."

"She didn't write them but she could rattle them off very quickly. She loved the production side and the marketing as well. We'll try the Nightingale first."

He proceeded to uncork the bottle.

"Did you have much involvement in the vineyard?"

"At first, I did... when we were starting out. Here, see what you think."

Charles gave Brent a half glass of the dark red wine. He sipped it.

"Oh, that's nice. Very drinkable. A stupid question but this is from there?" He pointed to the field outside.

"Yes. They all are. We don't buy anything in for blending. Sometimes, we sell a little bit wholesale. Sheila wanted to raise the profile of the Estate and was focused on brand awareness. Marketing terms - she learned those very quickly. She was good at it."

"What did you want?"

"Me? I liked the idea of a winery. We had to scrape the money together and get loans to buy it. I suppose I saw myself taking it easy in the middle of a pretty place and easing into an early retirement. Far from it... Brent, isn't it? I'm bad with names. Twenty-hour days sometimes. I wondered what I had gotten into. A couple of times I said we should sell up. She wouldn't hear of it. It was her passion. I wanted for her to be happy. Sheila was happy. She found happiness working hard and getting results."

"If this wine is anything to go by then she achieved a measurable result of success."

"This one is my favourite." Charles sipped from the glass. "The Chardonnay is good but I'm told it's only a table wine and nothing special. Same for the Cabernet Sauvignon." He sipped again.

"What about the other bottle, the Pinot Noir?"

"That is in a completely different class. We have to drink it last. It dominates everything."

"Hmm. All the wine I've ever had has been modestly priced."

"The wine business is a strange industry. It's full of prejudices, tradition, and pride. I'm told that our Pinot equals the best French Pinot Noir. I've never compared them so I couldn't say. What I do know is that whenever I have drunk that wine I feel uncomfortable. It's as though I'm on trial and some clever pronouncement is expected of me. It is a lovely wine but I don't quite see it's worth the price. Perhaps I have an untutored palette."

"It looks expensive. What does a bottle go for?"

"Three hundred. Sheila said it was under-priced because we do not have much of a reputation in the wine world. We're in an outlying region and our output is quite small. She said if it were French it would be three thousand. I thought she was joking. She wasn't. I heard it from others, as well."

"So, if you produced, what, a couple of thousand bottles? And could get three thousand a piece that's…"

"Six million. But that's retail. We have one hectare of Pinot Noir and the production is greater than your example. Emily or Sergio would have to explain it to you about controlling the yield for maximum quality. It is a very tricky process to get right. All I know is the vineyard is quite profitable and worth a lot more than when we bought it."

"And would be more valuable still if your reputation grew."

"That's what Sheila had been working on lately."

"I think I saw that you've been here eleven years?"

"That's right. Many of the vines have been replaced in that time. We tried to make a champagne at first. We put in the Pinot Noir and a Gamay. The sparkling wine wasn't very good and we had production issues so we gave up on that. But, by chance, where we planted the Pinot Noir were the very best conditions possible. The soil is perfect. And the trees around the vines act as a sort of a slight heat trap. You probably know that stresses on the vine make it produce better-quality juice. Would you like some more before we eat?"

"Just a little drop. I have to drive home."

"Of course. You don't mind me talking like this? I guess I've been feeling pretty lonely."

"Not at all. I came round to talk."

"Did you say you're a policeman?"

"Private Investigator, assigned to the case by the police."

"They keep coming round, asking questions. They don't seem any nearer to finding the murderer. Not that they say much. I have to find out most things from the media."

"That's their practice - speaking cautiously and being conservative."

"Doesn't help me." Charles paused before saying in a small voice, "Why was she murdered? I don't understand it."

"I don't, either. It is what I'm working towards. There doesn't seem to be anyone in sight with an obvious motive. Plenty of people had opportunity but there's no apparent reason for any of them to kill. This is what is causing the delay."

"Even if the police had a suspect they wouldn't say anything."

"You're right. Only when they are sure enough to make an arrest would you be told the reasons - along with everyone else."

"It doesn't bring her back."

"No, it sets the matter straight. Not understanding something like this slows the grieving process down to a snail's pace. People talk about closure. I don't think there ever is closure for some things but there can be distance from the pain of the event. It is a move from overwhelming, incapacitating grief to a place of occasionally recalling sad memories. My opinion is that time helps with a lot of that but to get started is the important thing."

"Finding the murderer and seeing him sentenced begins that?"

"Understanding what happened begins the journey. The two things you said are important way-markers."

"Seems about right. I just feel numb and stupid at the moment."

"I think you're doing better than I would be if I were in your place."

"You didn't see me last week. I'll get dinner going. It won't take long."

"I'll help you."

Charles prepared a good dinner. Brent said the white wine went well with the trout, although he did not say that he had not actually cared for it that much despite drinking two glasses. With the cheese came the Cabernet Sauvignon. Brent liked it. Talking all the time, they finished the bottle between them and then a second one was opened and consumed as they sat once more in the sunroom. Old-fashioned shaded lamps made the spacious room cozy, despite the high, glass ceiling. Outside was a wall of darkness with a few faint stars showing. A slight glow from distant Belton's street lights could be seen to the southeast. The light from the room fell on the terrace. Beyond that, the vineyard was featureless and completely hidden.

"Do you think you will sell up?" asked Brent.

"I don't know. Sometimes, I think I will. I received a letter of condolence from Magnum Inter-Wine last week." Charles got up and went over to a small desk. He took a letter from the drawer. "At the end they said, quite tactfully I thought, that they would be interested in the estate if a decision to sell was ever made. Then I got this today. Here, you read it."

Brent did so. The letterhead was from a company called Bartlett Beverage Group. The first two sentences expressed conventional deepest sympathy. The rest of the two-page letter was a hard-sell outline of an offer to purchase. No punches were pulled in the language and there was an urgent request to get the matter settled quickly for the included price, to buy everything, of 5.4 million. It was signed, Claude Gaudin.

"The way he writes, I'm surprised he waited as long as he did," said Brent.

"He didn't. He wrote to me twice before and he came to the funeral. The first letter was quite sympathetic. The second was more business-oriented, I forget what he said exactly."

"Do you have them still?"

"I do. You want them? Are they important?"

"They are very important until they are proved to be unimportant."

"I'll get them." He went to the desk again.

"Has there been anything else like this or anything unusual?"

"Not really. A lot of well-wishers from the industry sent letters, cards, and flowers. They all had better manners." He brought the letters back.

"I'll take these with me and I'll give you a receipt. Just hold them for a second."

Brent pulled out a pair of surgical gloves from his bag, put them on, and carefully took hold of the letters by their corners. He put them in an evidence bag. Then he wrote out a receipt and gave it to Charles. He then wrote on the bag a description of its contents with a few notes.

"This looks very serious," said Charles as he watched Brent.

"It might be."

"More wine?" asked Charles.

"Um, I'm feeling a bit light-headed as it is. I think I'm past driving. Will a taxi come out this far?"

"Oh, yes. But I've a better idea. Stay the night. There's a spare bedroom."

Brent thought for a moment. "Yes, I will. Thank you for your hospitality."

"I need company." Charles got up and left the room. When he returned, he was carrying two more bottles. "I don't understand, Brent. Why murder her?"

"I know. It's inexplicable. It is so hard to say why people do such things. Are we getting drunk?"

"Oh, I see. How much have we had?"

"There's a tiny bit left in the first bottle, still. Then there was the bottle of white. And two of the Sauvignon."

"One, wasn't it? No, you're right. I got a second."

"I think your wine is too drinkable."

"It is. I hadn't really noticed before. Just a glass with dinner is what I usually have."

"I'm the same." It was the third time they had established this notable fact.

"It doesn't seem to have much of an effect."

"Perhaps it's having more of an effect than we realize."

They both laughed at this.

The night wore on and the bottles were emptied. Another Sauvignon was opened and finally, the two men made an attempt on the Pinot Noir.

"Must be room temperature by now," said Charles.

"Must be. I think it is."

"Good. There. Now. New glasses. We must have new glass-es."

"Mein host, I shall get them 'mmediately." Brent stood up and stared at nothing. "Whoa! Don't get up quickly."

Brent was a long time in the kitchen before coming back with the glasses.

"Where'd you go?"

"Kitchen. Here you are." Brent put the glasses down and nearly fell into his chair.

"Oh, the kitchen. Now, then, pour carefully. Don't spill a drop. Don't shake the bottle. There. Perfect. Try that for size."

Brent picked up the glass and sniffed at it before taking a sip.

"Charley, that is the best wine I have ever tasted."

"You like it?"

"Yes. Why, my friend, have we been drinking all that other rubbish when we could have been drinking this?"

"It's not rubbish."

"By comparison it is. Go on, try some. You'll see I'm right."

Charles drank a little from his glass while Brent watched him intently - his head at a very curious angle. Charles drained the glass.

"You are right!" he said, noisily. "It is all rubbish!" He swept his arm in the direction of the other bottles.

"See, I told you so."

"This is ambrosia."

"Charlie. I have heard of ambrosia but I don't know what it is."

"It's what some old, silly gods drank."

"Yes, but what is it?"

"Fill your glass and we will gooooogul it because I do not know, either."

Chapter Twelve

Ouch

B rent arose before 6:00 a.m. with a splitting headache and an uncertainty as to where he was. He knew it was Wednesday.

He washed, dressed and went downstairs quietly. Charles Babbington was still asleep. By six-fifteen, Brent was on the terrace drinking coffee and taking aspirin. The fresh, mild air served to wake him up enough to realize that he should never drink anything alcoholic again no matter how good the reasons to do so might be. He was pleased with the evidence and information he had gathered: the value of the property; the offer from Gaudin's company. What troubled him was that Charles was believed to be the murderer by some of Sheila's family and his own family was not particularly supportive. Inoffensive, sad Charles Babbington was thought to be a murderer. How easy to condemn a person without evidence. It was what people did, though. A husband is the most obvious choice in the absence of a definite suspect.

Poor Charles. Brent knew he was innocent. He had heard the man, sober and drunk, over the course of seven hours, without once hearing anything to alarm him.

Brent got up to go through the small garden and down to the track alongside the vines. He followed it. Swifts flew overhead and birdsong was in the trees. Gathering clouds threatened rain later but, for now, the birds could sing. He passed the small restaurant. He could see it was not really a stand-alone establishment but an adjunct of the tours through the vineyard. He passed the shuttered buildings - some built of old limestone, some brick, steel sheds for machinery, and a large central building which possessed many additions housed the winery's operations. Beyond guessing that equipment was stored in large sheds, he had no real idea what they did in the rest of the buildings except obviously somewhere the fermenting of juice in vats. How they bottled - or did they use barrels? - he did not know.

The track became very steep and lay roughly parallel with the road outside. Brent stopped to look back. He could see almost all the buildings below him. Anyone on the patio at the back of the restaurant would see him easily. On the day, there had been at least six people on the patio the entire time between five and six-thirty. He continued walking and turning to look back until the track took a sharp right turn. Ten paces more and all but the edge of the patio and some roofs had disappeared from view. The track continued for another hundred yards and from here all was hidden. Even the road was effectively blocked off. A car passed and Brent could hear the sound it made but could barely see it through the trees and undergrowth.

He continued on and now began to scan along the rows, looking for the exact place where Sheila had died. He felt he knew her better now. Her husband had talked a lot about his wife. Charles was deeply wounded. A metaphorical knife had pierced his heart, too. After hours of talk Brent could sketch her but would need still more insight to finish Sheila's portrait.

It was important for him to have a complete picture for that is how he would ultimately determine the murderer's identity. He created a picture, a mental image, populating it with the cast of characters who featured in the murder. He wanted to see the victim clearly. He also wanted to see the murderer in whose hand was held a knife, raised in the act of destroying Sheila. He would switch face after suspect's face into the assailant's, at present, unformed visage until one of them fitted like a puzzle piece, to the exclusion of all other candidates. He was far away from that triumphal moment. This was the process he had used before when his friend had been murdered and he had tried to bring the killers to justice. In that case, his moment of triumph was soon dampened by a shower of legal technicalities which left only frustration in its wake.

It took a while but Brent found the place where Sheila had died. The police tape had been removed. He noticed that several vines in one area near the entrance of a row had not been pruned as rigorously as those surrounding them. That was really the only tell-tale sign. He accepted his observation as fact and went in between the rows to begin a close examination of the ground and plants.

He could not find anything of real interest. The ground in between the rows was hard-packed, as it had been on the day. The only loose, impressionable soil was around the plant stems. Caught around a stone was a fragment of clear plastic - part of some kind of wrapper. Brent picked it up with tweezers and put it into a bag but thought it likely to be contamination after the fact. He stood up and stepped back to take several photographs. Having completed his examination he looked about the field. Absent-mindedly, he plucked the top wire, bare between the laterals of two vines, and found it sounded a dull note.

"Why in this row?" he said aloud. Looking around, he began to think about Sheila's actions. *She parked her car to come through that gap in the corner of the field. She followed the track down. She could have walked about on the track, waiting for someone to arrive... maybe she did. While she waited, she checked the condition of these plants. These represent reputation, wealth. These vines are the means by which she can achieve all her goals. Yes. Then she saw someone. It had to be the person she expected. Did Sheila stand still or walk towards the newcomer? If she saw him early enough she would have walked towards him. If the person approached unnoticed then she would have stayed in this area. Within... what? Twenty feet? Yes. Within twenty feet she had to have noticed someone approaching. The person she expected. Then what?*

Brent could not get any further in his reconstruction. He was dissatisfied because something was wrong with his theories as they stood. Brent could not imagine an assassin would willingly confine him or herself to a tour group. He could not see why Sheila would be waiting to meet someone she did not know. There was a flaw in his reasoning and he could not put his finger on it. Besides, his head was muzzy.

He climbed the track to its end to examine the ground, the vegetation of the field's perimeter, and to look out over the whole sweeping field. The sun was rising above the tree line and would soon heat the ground and plants. The vines would lose moisture and intensify all their precious compounds and flavours into the immature fruit. The plants, forced into a life of stress, had no choice but to form fruit and survive by replication, rather than grow outward with leaf, stem, and branch, and so survive by becoming large and extensive. Left untended, each plant would compete for space, soil nutrients, and water as the more favoured outgrew the weaker vines. Fruit, then, if there were any, would be tasteless and small.

These heavily pruned, trained and trellised plants were engines. The output was pale yellow and blood red wines of exquisite richness. The fuel was sunlight. The field, then, was an organic production line that would not exist if vinis vinifera were not so greatly desired with its history so intricately intertwined with civilization and religion.

The plants might be ruthlessly ruled by humanity but the magic of a cluster-bearing shoot twined itself around the hearts of those who sought to possess the fruit. Wealth, lives, lands, businesses, and marriages had been both gained and lost because of grape juice - fermented and bottled.

In the morning light, Brent wondered if it was all worth it. He decided it wasn't. His head told him that this was so.

Chapter Thirteen

Staff troubles

H is search of the track yielded nothing to add to what was already known in the case. At least the investigator had a spatial sense of where everything and everyone had been. Now the question that bothered him was - where had the cyclist come from and gone to? The person and bike were witnessed facts but their connection with the vineyard was tenuous. *The cyclist could have shoved the bike into some bushes to hide it and walked in. Could have ridden in through the gap, coming fast, downhill, to a sudden stop because the quarry was sighted among the vines. Could then have leapt clear of the cycle left to fall on the ground... run up and stabbed Sheila before she could scream. Perhaps she screamed and nobody heard. No. There was no struggle. She had to have either known or expected the person who approached. This is endless.*

Coming back down the track, at just before seven, Brent noticed a young man entering a large steel shed. The work-day at the vineyard began early. He had hoped to talk to the employees sooner or later and his overnight stay permitted it to be sooner. A startled rabbit, persona non-grata in the vineyard, ran out of the vine rows and into the undergrowth ahead of him.

A tractor's engine was started inside the steel shed and the large door was slid open by the young man, who caught sight of Brent, fifty yards away. Then a large, new yellow tractor emerged and stopped. It hid the man from Brent's view while also bringing the quiet of the vineyard to an abrupt end. The tractor was towing a piece of machinery whose purpose Brent found quite inscrutable.

It was obvious that the man on the far side had spoken to the driver, who had turned sharply to look in Brent's direction. The driver switched the engine off and got out. She proved to be a slender young woman. She was carrying a large wrench and was walking quickly towards Brent, who stopped in his tracks. The man reappeared, hurrying to catch up with the woman. He was carrying a shovel. It occurred to Brent that he might well be in the wrong place at the wrong time.

"Keep your hands in sight and stay where you are," called out the woman in an angry shout. "What are you doing here? This is private property," she said a little more quietly but no less angrily, as she halted five or six yards in front of Brent. She appeared to be in her mid-twenties and had dark brown hair in a bun. She looked as angry as she sounded and Brent was left in no doubt that she could easily start swinging the wrench she was gripping tightly in her hand. The man standing next to her was muscular, about the same age, and also looked most unfriendly.

"I'm a private investigator. I'm working with the police."

"Prove it," said the woman in a sharp tone. "Put some ID on the ground and step back."

Brent rightly guessed their aggressively defensive attitude was the result of recent events in the vineyard. He complied with her request, laying out business cards and his driver's licence on the track, and taking a few steps back.

"Further," she said.

When she was satisfied that Brent was a safe enough distance away, she and the young man approached to pick up Brent's ID and scrutinize it together.

"Brent Umber... looks legit," said the man.

"Why are you snooping around so early? Should've asked someone," said the woman.

"It's true, I am snooping. Although, I hadn't thought of it quite like that. I came yesterday and stayed the night."

"What! With Mr Babbington?"

"Yes, Charles and I had a long discussion into the wee hours."

"I'll check that out," said the woman. She put the wrench down and took out her phone.

While they were waiting, Brent said,

"You must be Emily Harfield. And, I think you must Thomas Block."

"Right... er, hi," said Thomas.

"Hi. I completely forgot that you would all be coming in early to start work. I'm a city boy, that's my excuse."

"No problem."

The call connected.

"Good morning, Mr Babbington," said Emily.

"Good morning, Em."

"We've found a guy wandering around on the property. His name is Brent Umber. Do you know him?"

"Yes. He's fine, Em. Give Brent what help you can and don't be too hard on him."

"I already have been. I'll make it up. Thanks."

She put her phone away. Picking up the wrench, and holding it now in a relaxed way, she said,

"Sorry about the reception we gave you. Thought you might be a reporter - or even the murderer."

"You mean, returning to the scene of the crime? I can see how you might think that. But a reporter? You must have had trouble with them."

"I don't mind them," said Emily. "They've got a job to do. But I'm not letting them bother Mr Babbington."

"Then I am very glad I'm not a journalist. You looked so ferocious you quite frightened me."

Emily smiled. She looked like an elf with freckles when she did so.

"How did he sound?" asked Thomas.

"You know, he sounded better today," replied Emily.

"Charles was telling me how bad he's been feeling," said Brent.

"Yeah? Well, it's Sheila's family that's causing problems now. One of them came round and had an argument with him. She accused *him* of killing Sheila of all ridiculous things. That was four days after the funeral."

"Charles didn't mention that specifically. He did tell me of the bad feelings that have started up. Can I get something out of my pack now?"

Emily smiled again. Brent decided that it was worthwhile to get her to smile. He got out a notepad and pen.

"What was the lady's name?"

"Nora Butcher. Sheila's sister. She came looking for a job. But she's not the only one of them against him."

"Em, I gotta go set the crew on their rows," said Thomas.

Emily nodded.

"Can we chat later when you're not so busy?" Brent asked Thomas.

"Sure. But we're always busy, dude. Always something doing." He walked away.

"Anyone else?" resumed Brent to Emily.

"Mr Babbington doesn't say much. He kinda lets things drop in a conversation without going into details."

"In what way? Give me an example."

"I knew there was a fight because I heard them. Later, he said, 'Sheila's family think I did it'. He said it in a way that made me think it was more than just the Lindsay woman mouthing off."

"You like Mr Babbington?"

"Yeah. He's a nice guy. Never seen him angry. Always supported Sheila. It was his idea to do a really big harvest celebration dinner for all the field-hands. Every year we have it under a big tent and there's stuff for the kids. I don't know if we'll have one this year."

"Would Sheila want you to have a celebration this year?"

"Oh, yes. She would definitely want that."

"Then, have one - that is, if you have any say in the matter."

"He needs time to think about what he's going to do. He's really depressed."

"And you are his protector as well as the senior viticulturist."

"Yeah. I loved Sheila. She was a friend. I started here straight after university and the Babbingtons gave me a chance. I owe both of them."

"When was that?"

"Seven years ago. They had been struggling with... well, everything. One thing my predecessor did that was really good was to put the PNs at the top of the hill. But he wasn't getting the best juice from them. He was going for quantity and not quality. Kept watering and spraying everything. I keep spraying to a minimum. Getting a high yield makes sense for the ordinary vines everywhere else but not up there."

"More stress on the vines and they produce better quality juice?"

"That's it."

"This is all new to me. On the day of the murder, you were up near the top section. What were you doing?"

"I was looking over a few rows. I did some pruning and was thinking about taking out the CS and putting in more PN."

"That's Cabernet Sauvignon you were thinking of taking out?"

"Right. You see, about seventy per cent of the Pinot produces really well The highest elevation is where that comes from. Some vines around the edges and the bottom thirty per cent don't give the best results. Don't get me wrong. They make a good Pinot but not a great one. The good PN sells for a lot more than the CS we're producing. You following me?"

"Oh, yes. Please, continue."

"It's been on my mind to extend the PN down a few rows. It would mean more profit on the juice. I have to justify the switch to Sheila... oh, I keep doing that. Thinking she's still here."

"Must be difficult for you."

"It hasn't gotten easier yet. Anyway, there's a cost to switching out perfectly good CS for PN. The vines themselves. The labour. Then, we don't get any yield at all for the first three years and the three years after that will only yield average quality. It takes at least five years and more like seven for the vines to produce quality that notices."

"I see. So, it's a serious investment to make a change."

"Yeah. It's hard for me to decide. I can make a case either way so I'm leaving it as it stands. I don't like taking out good vines. I'd transplant them to fill in any gaps that occur elsewhere and *that* is a job and a half."

"Then on the day, you were thinking this problem over?"

"That's correct. See, Serg is a real master vintner. I want to give him the best I can from the vines."

"I can appreciate why you would want to do that. Did you see Sheila at all?"

"No. I didn't see anyone. I was busy pruning by hand so I might not have noticed. We do a mechanical dormant prune on all the rows and then a second mechanical prune later for most of them. After that, we prune by hand. The PN vines are entirely hand-pruned."

"I think I understand. What is that object on the back of the tractor?"

"It's a cultivator. It loosens hard-packed soil to keep weeds down and help soil aeration."

"I saw hard soil like that earlier." Brent pointed further up the track. "Are you going there now?"

"Yeah, well, I was going to do it weeks ago. Then she was murdered. I haven't liked to do too much in that section since."

"I can understand that. I noticed a few vines looking a bit hairier than the rest."

"That's where it happened. I can't touch them. I'll have to get someone else to do it."

"I was thinking about that. I can see how you might not want a memorial in a commercial vineyard. What do you think of training the vines into a shape?"

"How do you mean? Like a heart or something?"

"Exactly. That's a good and appropriate idea. Then, the place is not lost among all the thousands of vines."

"I can do that. I'll do it now."

"Shall I come with you?"

"No, because I'm going to ball my eyes out and I'd like to do that in private."

"Okay. I have to see Sergio Calabrese. Is he here and where can I find him if he is?"

"He should be about somewhere. Let's go back to the tractor."

Outside of the steel shed, Emily Harfield suddenly bellowed out,

"Serg!!!"

Brent was astonished that she had produced such a sound. There was a delay of several seconds before a faint shout returned.

"What?!!"

"Visitor!!!"

"What?"

"Vis-ee-tor!!!!"

"Okay!"

"You could have warned me you were going to do that," said a wide-eyed Brent. "If I were a cat I would have just lost a life."

Emily smiled. "He's in the fermentation room. It's the second door round the corner."

"Seriously, is that how you communicate?"

"Saves walking. You any closer to catching someone?"

"Not yet. We're working hard on it, though."

"Get it done."

She quickly climbed into the tractor's cab and started the engine. She waved goodbye and set off up the track, leaving Brent to find Sergio Calabrese.

Chapter Fourteen

Wine industry

"Ah, and who might you be?" Sergio Calabrese smiled and held out his hand. He was a short, stocky man in his fifties with thick black and slightly greying hair. His clothes were incongruous. He was wearing standard dark blue work trousers and a denim shirt. Over the top, he wore a smart, expensive tan sports jacket and was shod with a pair of brown Italian loafers. A red silk handkerchief was in his breast pocket. The smell of recently applied scent hung in the air about him.

Brent imagined that, had he been five minutes longer, the transformation would have been complete with trousers matching the jacket, an expensive shirt, and a silk tie. There were then, he surmised, two Sergios - the one who worked and the other who met the visitors and was concerned with appearances - with a complete outfit for each persona.

"My name is Brent Umber." They shook hands. "Here's my card. I'm working with the Belton police on the investigation into Mrs Babbington's murder."

"Oh, I see. It is a very sad business. I have been much distressed. Mr Babbington, he is like a shell of a man. I will assist you in every way."

"Thank you. I only wish to ask a few questions."

"Of course. Please, we will go into the little office and be more comfortable."

Once inside the office and as Sergio shut the door after them, Brent saw a pair of carefully pressed trousers, a match for Sergio's jacket, on a hanger behind the door. From a hook on a coat-stand hung a grey lab coat and, from another hook, a hanger preserved the newly laundered look of a white shirt. Brent could not see a tie but he was sure there was one secreted somewhere in the room.

"Please, Mr Umber." Sergio seated himself and waited.

"Thank you. I want to tell you how sad I find it to meet under these circumstances when you're all still reeling from the loss of Mrs Babbington. I wish I had met her. What was she like?"

"A lovely woman. Warm, generous... very nice. She dressed well - always very smart - and she loved this business. Completely dedicated with a serious mind. Personally, it is a great loss to me. In the wine industry, she leaves a big gap. Many wine growers came to the funeral. I hope you find the murderer. It is a vile thing he has done."

"I've heard nothing but good things about her. I would like to have known her."

"Now you cannot."

"No. What makes you think the murderer is a man?"

"I don't know. I assume. Why, you have a woman suspect?"

"Unfortunately, we have no suspect at present."

Sergio shook his head and compressed his lips.

"I hope to find the murderer," continued Brent. "Can you tell me what you were doing on the day of her death?"

"Yes. I was in here and in the storage room. Some pipes were being replaced that afternoon and I was not satisfied with the mechanic's work. I gave him clear instructions and he make a serious mistake when I am out of the room. Just as he is clearing away his tools and he has the big, stupid smile on his face, I look over his work. He put in the wrong gauge pipe! He uses a step-down fitting. He and I, we have words. I tell him he is not being paid unless he fix it properly. He says that it is according to specifications. That the pipe was too large before. I tell him that is how I want it. He says he does not have the same size pipe so he replace according to specification. I get so angry… I have to leave. The Doctor says I must watch my blood pressure. It is best I go. I go outside and walk about. When I return, the mechanic has gone. He remove all the pipes he put in and take them away. I am so furious. I call his office and tell them what I think. We do no more business with them. Last week, an older gentleman come in and he do everything perfectly. We have a coffee together. He is my mechanic now."

"I'm glad that worked out for you. When you were outside, regulating your blood pressure, where did you go?"

"I walk down to the river and back again. Then I sit. Then I go round the front and that is when I see the cyclist. I take no notice but I see him. He looked to me like he was from the city."

"He was riding a mountain bike."

"Yes. Not a proper racing bike with the thin tires and the outfit of a racer. No, he looks like a teenager on a bike. I did not see his face.

After that, I sit, I walk and I go into the restaurant for a coffee. That is when the mechanic, whhheep, he takes off and I don't see him."

Brent made some notes as Sergio was talking.

"Earlier, when the mechanic was working, where did you go?"

"I take inventory of supplies. See what we need for the season. We have to order more bottles. Sheila was thinking of re-designing the labels. I tell her she must be quick to make sure we can have them delivered in time. But, she had not finished with the design. I call the label company. They say we should give minimum one month lead time. I think, ah, I think many things. Me? I like the labels we have. Designs should be done in the wintertime."

"Why are you involved with the labels? Sorry, if that sounds stupid."

"No. It's okay. You see, Mr Umber, everything - good corks, the labels, and the clean bottles have to be on hand. When the wine is ready to be bottled we cannot wait. We call in a mobile bottling company at the exact moment. If everything is not ready - poof! Nothing but headaches."

"So, you don't do your own bottling?"

"Nope. A bottling line is expensive. Minimum, half a million. Then you need experienced bottlers. Where do you find them in this area? No, it is all about the wine and preserving its quality. If it has no quality, what is it? Grape juice or vinegar. That's all. Timing is so important. Utmost importance. That is why the labels must be ready so we do not, I do not, worry about it."

"What was holding Sheila back, then?"

"I don't know. She's very busy. She was so good at the marketing. She was going to a convention and I think she wanted to see what the competition was coming out with and, I don't know, perhaps she was going to do something different and didn't want them to see what she would do."

"Do you think it strange that Claude Gaudin was on the tour?"

"Him? No. It was not. Personally, he is not so bad. Lot of talk - big shot - but he knows his job. No, I am not surprised. We talked a little of my work here, good wines. He was talking about his family a lot. His mother has Parkinson's. As always, he is looking for the deal and a way of building the Bartlett company. He was telling me about a deal he wanted to do in France. You know, he offered me a job at Bartlett's. Not now, before."

"Oh, when was this?"

"Eh, January. End of January this year. It was a big offer."

"Why did you not accept?"

"The top guy at Bartlett's is no good. They offer me fifty per cent more than I make now, a signing bonus, and relocation expenses. But I said, no. I'll tell you why I said no. See, Bartlett's, it has no soul. It's all about money. They want to get everything cheap. People, they work hard and build something. That company just want to take the best and add it to their portfolio.

Now with me, they want that this vineyard not do so well. Take me out of it and the wine will not be so good. Take Em out of it and the juice will not be so good. Then, when the vineyard is not doing as well, they buy it cheap.

Maybe they fire me afterwards. It won't stop them from making a flagship Pinot and adding it to their lines. But it would not be as good as it is now. They promote the name and take out the quality. The rest of this place, they won't care what happens as long as they get quantity and market share. Always, the market share. You understand this?"

"I do. Did they offer Emily a job?"

"I don't think so. She wouldn't go. Em's loyal. It's all like family here. And we were happy until our poor Sheila, she gets murdered."

"Okay. Who is the head of Bartlett's?"

"Oscar Flint. His heart is like his name. And, I tell you something else. He's done some dirty things in the past. Legal but dirty."

"How do you know?"

"It's what a lot of people say. But, I know a man in Italy, he's retired now, who was a manager at a small vineyard that produced very beautiful wines. Bartlett's Italian operation bought it and this is what they did. They tore up sixty-year-old vines like they were nothing." He snapped his fingers. "Sixty years old. Low yield? Yes, they were. But the wine from them was aromatic and sumptuous. They increase the yield four-fold with the new vines but the quality was nothing." He sneered on the last word. "That, also, is a murder." He paused for a moment. "No, I should not have said that. In memory of my dear Sheila, I should not have spoken such words and she, taken from us in such a tragic way. But, Mr Umber, to remove the superior and put in the inferior is against everything I stand for. I could never work for a company like that."

"I want to thank you for telling me all these things. It helps me to understand Sheila and the situation around her much better. I was thinking, what will this year's harvest be like?"

"God willing, it will be a good one. But the grapes are not in the basket yet."

"What do you think Charles Babbington will do?"

"I don't know. Really, I do not. I hope he continues on but it will never be the same. I think he needs someone to do the marketing. Sheila has a part-time assistant. Maybe she could be full-time. I don't know nothing about those things."

"I hope he does, too. Thank you for your time. I know you're busy so I'll let you get back to work. I apologize for the interruption."

They stood up and shook hands.

"No, no. It has been a pleasure to talk with you. You are sympathetic. It would be very nice if you could catch this filthy killer."

"Yes, it would be a good thing to find out who it was and have the police make an arrest. We're making progress but it's slow going. Goodbye."

"Ciao," said Sergio.

Brent went out of the building. As he passed by the window of the little office, he caught a glimpse of Sergio, sitting down once more, but looking miserable.

Chapter Fifteen

The old days

It was now just after 8:00 a.m. and Brent had finished talking with Thomas Block who was working near the vineyard's river end. The young man had not added much of any significance. His statements agreed with other things Brent had heard or seen written in statements. The one item that did seem significant was that he confirmed the work that Emily had been doing in the top section after 5:00 p.m. the day of the murder. They had all finished at six which, with the return to the buildings and the cleanup, allowed Emily about twenty minutes in the area.

Brent had thought the working day in the vineyard was very long and said as much. It proved to be that the workers did extra hours some days to get a half-day or a full day off at another time. The people on the tour expected to see a working vineyard. Thomas, or Tom as he preferred to be called, said he and Em liked it that way. The crews appreciated it, too. The young man went on to say that the Babbingtons were liberal with bonuses and the rates of pay were the best in the region. Tom, also, did not wish to work anywhere else.

Brent returned to the house. Charles Babbington gave him a cheerful greeting as he crossed the terrace.

"Did you sleep well?"

"I did, thanks. The quality I found to be good but the quantity was not sufficient. Sergio has been instructing me in such things."

"I saw that you got up early. How are you feeling?"

"Better than I did at six, thanks. Aspirin and coffee helped. How about you?"

"It's very strange, Brent. I feel more alive than I have for weeks. I think I could have a crying fit at any time but it's as though I've got past something. Like a barrier has been broken."

"That's encouraging to hear."

"Yes, thanks. I believe I can get on with a few things now - such as my engineering work. Also, I have to come to a decision about the vineyard."

"Oh...? Perhaps it is none of my business but I've spoken to your key employees this morning and, as sad as they are under the circumstances, I get the impression that they all want to continue on at the Songbird Estate. You have some very loyal people here."

"I have no intention of selling. It is more that I'm not sure how to proceed going forward."

"I'm so relieved to hear that. Someone mentioned that Sheila has an assistant."

"Patti! That is a good idea. I know she works at another couple of places and only comes in here when needed. Do you think she would come on board full-time?"

"Ask her. Then you'll know."

"I'll do that today. Have you had breakfast?"

"Now you're talking, Charlie. I think I could manage it now. No wine with it, though."

"Ha. I'm good for the foreseeable future, as well. Let's get at it."

"You lead and I'll follow. By the way, do you mind me calling you Charlie?"

"Not at all. The last time anyone called me Charlie, I was a teenager."

As they entered the house, Brent said,

"Charlie, I think I would like to put my name down for a case of this season's Pinot Noir. Is that how it's done?"

"That costs quite a bit, you know?"

"I understand. You see, I can then tell everyone that I have a dozen bottles of the world's greatest wine. They won't believe me but I can say it."

They were in the kitchen now.

"I can do something about the price."

"No. Absolutely not. I will be offended if you give me a discount. Whatever the going rate is that's what I'll pay."

"I can be stubborn as well, sometimes."

"Oh, a challenge. I love it. What's for breakfast?"

Brent and Charles had said goodbye and the front door closed. The two other employees, Janet Jones and Rita Inglis, would not be arriving for another hour but Brent needed to get to Belton as soon as he could. He made a call and told Jennifer some of his findings.

Before he left, Brent found a trowel and bucket. Working as quickly as he could, he got the flower beds at the front of the house to look halfway respectable. Afterwards, he climbed into his Jeep and was in a better frame of mind leaving than he had been when he arrived. If only Charlie would take up the fallen reins and, in deeds as well as words, make a real go of it.

"You think there's something solid in this?" asked Jennifer.

"I don't know," said Brent. "I can't see that Bartlett's would want Sheila dead - assuming she was obstructing their plans.

Why have her murdered when she brought considerable value into the operation?"

They were sitting in Jennifer's office at headquarters.

"Damian's looking into the company. Flint has no priors. Where does that put Gaudin?"

"The theory is that Flint wants the Songbird Estate. Sheila won't sell - though we have no proof she was ever contacted directly. The company hires a killer to get her out of the way. With her dead, Charles Babbington can be coerced into selling. It fits but it doesn't seem plausible. If Bartlett's was doing this routinely there would be a trail of bodies. It's a big line to step over and the flaw is that Charles might not sell to them, either. Now Gaudin would have to have knowledge of it. He writes the letters. He contacts Sergio Calabrese. He was present on the tour. He badly wants to acquire the vineyard or he wants the best parts of it. Is it worth the risk?"

"I would say no," replied Jennifer. "But, hey, it is possible. It means that Flint could be behind it and Gaudin is in on it with him or Gaudin is acting independently."

"Yes. Gaudin. Where is he now?"

"Greg's tried to get him in here but Gaudin says he's busy and can't come in today. He's putting it off until next week."

"I think I know a way to get him here tomorrow."

"Do you?"

"Yes. My good friend, Charles, should tell him he's considering the offer. I should think that would cause Gaudin to drop everything and come running."

"It might. So... you'd be there?"

"Oh, yes. It would have to be just me, though. Could I wear a wire?"

"We couldn't use it as evidence. I'm not sure."

"Right. But at least you would hear everything he had to say. Please, I've always wanted to wear a wire. Ask upstairs and see what Baker says."

"We can try it. But one of us has to see Babbington. He'd need to be coached."

"That presents a problem. I don't want him stressed because he might give the game away, among other reasons."

"You want to run the whole thing with Babbington unaware of what is going on? I don't think I can allow it."

"Ah. It was a nice idea."

"What? You're not going to see Gaudin?" Jennifer was becoming a little exasperated.

"I wouldn't say that. I don't think it would be good for Charles to be troubled at present, that's all."

"I have to draw the line somewhere," said Jennifer. "It would be you getting one suspect talking to another suspect. You could blow everything to pieces. Any lawyer could easily destroy the credibility of the case."

"That is a fair observation. You're right, of course. However, I don't think Charles is a suspect. He is my new best friend."

"I don't trust you. You've got something else in mind."

"Have I? How can you tell?"

"You look far too pleased with yourself. Your plan B better not be worse than your plan A."

"When I marry, I hope my future wife keeps me in line like you do. Think how exciting it will be."

"That poor woman. She'll have nothing but headaches."

"Just a heads up," said Greg Darrow. "Erica Stevens will be here in about ten minutes. The Richards are coming at eleven and the Forbes guy said he'd come in at one. Do you want to see any of them?"

"All of them, thanks," answered Brent who was sitting at his desk, writing up a report.

"Okay. What did you make of Babbington?"

"His grief is real and his mind troubled. I got no sense that he is anything other than someone who has been hit hard and doesn't know why."

"Speak to anyone else?"

Yes. Emily and Thomas are out as far as I'm concerned. Do you know, she thought I was an intruder and came at me waving a wrench. I have no doubts she would have used it if she had thought I was the murderer. Thomas had a spade. It was looking like she was going to bludgeon me and he would bury me. I ask you if those two were behaving like that towards a perceived intruder, what chances are there that either of them is the murderer?"

"Yeah, sure. Did you see Brown, the tour guide?"

"They've suspended the tours so we'll have to find her or bring her in. I didn't see Janet Jones and Rita Inglis, either."

"Calabrese?"

"Spoke to him. He's innocent."

"How do you reckon that?"

"For the simple reason that Sheila had not finished the redesign of the labels. The labels were worrying Sergio and, ridiculous as it may seem, there is no way he would consider murdering Sheila until the label question had been dealt with."

"Are you serious?"

"Sometimes. Sergio is all about the quality of the wine he makes. It's a passion with him. Delay in getting the labels could mean a delay in bottling. Then, as he says, 'Poof! - nothing but problems.'"

"Whatever. I take it he came across as an unlikely suspect. I've spoken to all the employees and I can't see a candidate among them. Calabrese seemed okay to me, too. I'll tell you who I have a problem with and that's Janet Jones. She's holding something back."

"Related to the case?"

"Maybe. She's got a guilty conscience about something."

"I'll make a note of that." Brent did so in a ring binder.

"I want Gaudin," said Greg. "I've yet to meet him and he needs to answer some questions. The fingerprint results came in. Two sets on the first two letters. Same sets on the offer plus a different set."

"Can't really make anything of that, I suppose," said Brent. "Did you not even get to speak to him?"

"Got his voice mail at the office. Then his assistant called me back with a busy schedule excuse. I think he's avoiding me."

"That's not very friendly of him."

"I heard you wanted to have a meeting with him and Babbington."

"Right, but it's off now."

"Go easy on Jennifer. She's a good detective. If you mess up it could reflect on her. It might harm her career."

"There is no way I would have her suffer for my antics. I'll make sure she is fully insulated from anything I might do."

"I'm not exactly reassured but I believe you'll try. Here comes Ms Stevens."

Detective Darrow interviewed the witness first. When he had finished, Brent was allowed a few minutes of conversation in the interview room. He explained to Erica Stevens how he was involved in the case.

"You're not going over the same questions, are you?" asked Erica.

"I hope not. That would be very boring. I had a thought, though. Do you want to sit in here in front of the two-way mirror or shall we go in there and sit behind it?"

"Why would we do that?"

"I thought it would be more interesting."

"Interesting? I don't really have time for this. Besides, aren't you supposed to have a female police officer present?"

"She is... on the other side of the glass. I thought we could join her there and it would be a lot friendlier for all of us."

"No, I'm fine where I am. I think it would be better if she was in here, as well, rather than being hidden behind a mirror."

Brent waved at the glass.

"The name of your salon is Hairicity. How did you come up with the name?"

Jennifer came into the room and sat down.

"It was at a party. Years ago, before the salon opened. I couldn't think of a good name that hadn't been taken already. We were all a little drunk and running out of stupid ideas when someone shouted out, 'Hairicity'. I thought, 'That's it!' Everyone loved it. It seems to work even though it looks like Hairy City when it's written. It's all about branding, anyway. The name doesn't really matter that much."

"I suppose not. What sort of clientele do you get?"

"Mainly women. Many are regulars. We used to get a lot of occasional traffic but a salon opened up across the street two years ago and we took a hit."

"That must be hard for you. Do you have a partner in the business?"

"No. I have two stylists who come in regularly and three part-timers who help when it's busy."

"Did you know that you keep looking at my hair?"

"Sorry," Erica smiled. "That's a bad habit of mine. A few people have noticed I do that. It's because I do it all day at work."

"What do you think? Do I need a trim?"

"Your hair's not bad. Needs a little tidying. You don't use gel?"

"No. I have an aversion to putting things on my hair. Why do you ask?"

"Because you have a little tuft sticking up on the back of your head."

"You're kidding me. Where?" Brent looked in the two-way mirror but could not see what she was talking about. "You'll have to show me."

Erica got up and came over to stand behind Brent.

"Move your chair so it faces straight to the mirror."

They were both looking at each other in the reflection.

"Okay. Did you bring scissors?"

"No," Erica smiled. "Do you always kid around?"

"As often as I can. There are plenty of things in the world to get one down if one allows it. I fight the good fight by acting the fool."

"You're not a fool."

"I think I'm a bit conceited, though. I don't like being that way."

"Why are you telling me this?" She pulled a wry face.

"You are my hairstylist. I thought I was supposed to confide in you."

"Very funny. I'll pull the tuft. There."

"Right at the back where I had no chance of seeing it. Well, I'll be."

"Whoever did your last cut must have seen it. It's just the natural lie of your hair. If it was longer it would lie flat. What they should have done is let it grow out a little instead of layering it."

"What's the prognosis?"

"I'd say, just a suggestion you know, that you grow your hair longer. That will take care of the back. Then, we can sweep it behind your ears like this. It will look all of a piece then. You'll need it trimmed so that it doesn't look messy until you get to the look you want."

"My mane is a mop at the moment, now I come to study it. When shall I come in for an appointment?"

"Oh.... Is next week okay?"

"I want to see you and at a time when it's not busy."

"Wednesday afternoons are quiet, say two o'clock next Wednesday?"

"Wednesday afternoon... yes, I can do that. Thank you."

With the hair consultation concluded they both resumed their previous seating arrangements. Jennifer was still sitting quietly in the corner, trying not to raise her eyes to heaven visibly.

"Now, down to business," said Brent. "I know you must hate this intrusion when your friend has died. But, if you feel like it, would you tell me what Sheila was like, please?"

"I don't know where to start, really."

"What was she like at school?"

"She was a swot. Worked hard and got good grades but she liked her downtime, too."

"Was she good at sports?"

"Okay. She liked swimming and tennis. We spent a lot of time playing tennis."

"Who is the 'we'?"

"Margot, Sheila, and me. There were a few others, boys and girls."

"So, early teens and Margot was the organizer?"

"That's right. How did you know?"

"The way you phrased it. Must have been nice. A big group of you, all playing against each other on sunny days."

"Yeah. We'd take our bikes out, too. Went for miles sometimes. Farther than we were supposed to."

"Of course. Sounds like a beautiful snapshot. Anything change after that?"

"How do you mean?"

"Like boys, for example."

"Yes. Well, we all got interested. But Margot had to play up to Kevin... he was Sheila's first love."

"That spoiled things, I suppose."

"For a while. They didn't speak. Then Kevin seemed to disappear out of the group and everything was fine again."

"Good. Perhaps it was all a misunderstanding."

"Yes... only... it doesn't matter. It was a long time ago."

"I wonder. Did history repeat itself?"

"Not exactly, although when we were all about seventeen and Sheila had another boyfriend... I can't remember his name... anyway, Margot kept flirting with him, knowing that he was Sheila's boyfriend."

"Do you think Margot was jealous?"

"I think so. I mean, why else would she do that? They were really good friends but as soon as a boy came into Sheila's life Margot went weird."

"It looks that way. How did they move past that?"

"Oh, then Margot found the love of *her* life. I can't remember what happened afterwards... we all started to move away from each other. You know how it goes. Sheila went to university and made a new set of friends. Well, when she came back to Belton for good, after she got her degree, we all started meeting up again. Not often, just once in a while. Sheila and Margot seemed friendly towards each other from then on."

"That's good. I like happy endings."

"But that isn't the end. Sheila met Charles Babbington when she was... twenty-three, I think. You could tell that he was *the* one for her. It seemed to me that it was only a question of time before they married. Sheila was big on getting married. Anyway, Margot, who had been as sweet as anything, started in again. It was ridiculous. She kept saying bad things to Sheila about Charles behind his back."

"Do you like him?"

"Yeah. He's a decent guy. I can't imagine what he's going through right now."

"I can tell you. Sheila's family... let me rephrase that, a few members of Sheila's family think he is the murderer."

"No. I don't believe it. Not Charles."

"You were saying that Margot changed tactics."

"Yes, she did. Sheila told me about what she was saying and I'd heard a few things separately. Then, suddenly, Margot drops it all and tells everyone what a wonderful husband Charles will be to Sheila."

"That's odd. How was her own love life at the time?"

"Didn't I say? She had a partner and then a baby."

"What do you think? Did the arrival of the baby have anything to do with Margot's change in attitude?"

"That's what I thought! It's obvious. Margot must have some kind of strong maternal instinct and she was projecting it onto Sheila."

"Then, she was acting like an over-protective mother at this time and had been acting like a domineering sister before that?"

"I suppose so. She was always bossy."

"Ah, an organizer of other people's affairs. Some people are just naturally like that. They mean well but they can be very annoying. Then they get annoyed when people don't do as they say."

"That's how I look at it. She just didn't know when to stop."

"Did you have other close friends?"

"Yes, quite a few."

"How was Margot with you?"

"Oh, fine. I didn't like it when she was mean to Sheila. I told her so. We didn't speak for a few weeks the first time it happened, though she was always friendly to me after that."

"But this past history troubles you, I think?"

"It does. I had decided not to say anything. But I had a really, really bad nightmare. I saw Margot killing Sheila. Makes me feel sick thinking about it."

"I imagine it would."

"Do you think my dream might be true? That this is what really might have happened?"

"No, I don't think so. My view is that troubling dreams are a way for the mind to deal with a deep-seated problem. Sheila has died. Somebody has killed her. You are trying to deal with that. The stress of coping with such knowledge has insinuated itself into your dream. The mind can only use what it knows to manufacture a dream. I think, in dealing with Sheila's death, your dream life fixed on a trigger point from the past. You saw Margot because of Sheila's past issues with Margot."

"Maybe. I hope you're right. I wouldn't have said anything normally. Margot's a good friend but if she did... I can't bring myself to say it." Tears began to well up in Erica's eyes until they overflowed.

"I doubt that she did. Margot will be coming in for an interview soon and I'll get to speak to her. I won't mention anything of what you've said. Hopefully, she will be forthcoming just as you have been. But let's broaden it a little. Is there anyone you know that had a grudge against Sheila?"

"Not that I can think of and I've been thinking about it a lot. I really liked Sheila. Loved her. We've always been good friends but I'd say we were never best friends. It hurts... what happened to her. I can't stop thinking about it. I nicked somebody's ear with the scissors I was so distracted."

"Oh. Should I defer my appointment? I like my ears the way they are."

"You're so silly." Erica smiled while she was crying. "I'm okay, now. It was the day after the funeral. I should have taken some time off but I thought working was the best way to forget for a while."

"Trying to ease the pain. It's an awful business. Hopefully, some of it will be resolved soon. You will have played a part in that resolution. Thank you for coming in."

"I don't mind. Like you said, anything I can do to help find the killer, I'll do it."

"That's it. So, until next Wednesday, then. In the meantime, I must go and slap gel on the back of my head."

Once Brent had seen Erica out of the room, he turned to Jennifer, who was now standing up.

"What do you make of it?" he asked.

"I don't see it. Too long ago and no real damage was done. I can't see Margot Vaughan holding some kind of grudge that long. Unless she's a psychopath."

"I agree with you. The interesting part is that it would have to be Erica and Margot murdering Sheila together. Their statements are in agreement. That makes them, as a murdering duo, such a remote possibility. I could get no sense that Erica had a grudge against Sheila. They were not even best friends. The only way Sheila would have made an enemy out of Erica was if she had deliberately harmed her. Nothing like that has been mentioned. What struck me was that Erica was looking at the dynamic between Sheila and Margot as an outsider."

"I suppose she was. The main friendship *was* between Sheila and Margot. Erica had enough standing to take sides and get involved but not enough commitment to remain unfriendly with Margot. This all takes me back to some drama during my time at school. It's toxic while it's going on and stupid in hindsight."

"Boys take to punching and kicking over similar stupidities. The only way that there could have been collusion was if Margot worked on Erica to convince her that Sheila had done something very bad... so bad that she should die. There is not a hint of this anywhere. I doubt if anything like that can be found. Still, it's all about crossing the possibles off the list until a single name remains."

"Brent?"

"What have I done now?"

"A haircut? I am so trained in not interacting with witnesses and here you are, all friends with them, making appointments, getting children's drawings, and I hate to think what you were doing all night at the Songbird estate. More stuff I can't tell Baker."

"When you can put up with me no longer I will tell you everything. No, that can't be. I promise to tell you almost everything."

"What with you *and* Damian I can hardly get my own job done."

"Who causes the most trouble?"

"Oh, definitely you and you know it. By a huge margin. You do realize that this is only your second day?"

"Is that all it is? You're such a nice person I feel that I've known you for much longer. Do you want to go to a restaurant? It's on me."

"I've brought my lunch."

"Well, how about this, then? The whole team goes for a magnificent dinner in a great restaurant, significant others included, and it's my treat. We go as soon as we've cracked the case. You can't refuse an offer like that. "

"That sounds nice but you're not paying for it. We'll split it. Except, that won't be for a while."

"I think we'll be finished by next Thursday. Anytime after that would be good for our slap-up feast and I'll have my new haircut."

"Next Thursday? You wish! I've got a lot of work to do. You'll have to see the Richards on your own."

"That's right." Brent looked at his watch. "They should be in with Greg about now. What did you make of them?"

"In one word - creepy. See you later. Remember she's a witness and he's a suspect."

"Got it. I will uphold the honour of the department and bear in mind your nervous disposition."

Chapter Sixteen

Things get weird

"Mother wishes to know why we have to see yet another policeman?" Stuart Richards was standing behind his mother's chair and was a tall, heavy-set fifty-year-old. The skin of his face and hands was pale - as though he spent too much time indoors - and his hair was dark, long, and appeared infrequently brushed. He looked as though he had shaved two days ago and, instead of achieving the rugged, fashionable appearance for which some men strive, it merely made Stuart look lazy. His clothes were of expensive brands but they were old - looking crumpled and unwashed - and were more suitable for a man in his twenties. Stuart's voice was educated but had a very slight whine in it.

"What did he say?" asked the bird-like, elderly woman, sitting in a chair. Arlene Richards' dark eyes were fixed on Brent as she spoke to her son. She was dressed very expensively, immaculately, in warm pastel colours that suited her. Arlene's hair was a fine cloud of short, silver-grey curls. Both hands rested on the handle of a black walking cane with silver mounts and ferrule.

"He hasn't said anything, mo'm." The whine became more pronounced when he said 'mom'.

"My name is Brent Umber and I'm a private investigator assisting the police in this case. I know you have just seen Detective Darrow. All I need are some answers to a couple of questions that will differ from those the police have asked you and I won't take up too much of your time."

"Tell him to get on with it," said Arlene.

"Mother tires easily. Seeing one detective and answering the same questions as she did before is exhausting for her and it is best if you can keep it short."

"I shall do so. Please, sit down, Mr Richards."

"Because the interview will be short, I prefer to stand." He seemed to be staring.

"As you wish." Brent sat down across the desk from Arlene. He imagined that the Richards had declined to meet in an interview room, with all its connotations of arrest and inter-rogation, and had insisted on an office. He wondered how Greg had handled them. Brent opened a file and, glancing up, looked at Arlene. He noticed she did not seem to blink very often because, when she did, it was as though it were a deliberate action, requiring thought and effort. It was not a tic. He found the habit disconcerting. He was also aware of a compound smell in the room of part stale, unwashed person and part expensive perfume.

"I hope your family is well, Mrs Richards?"

"What do they have to do with the case? Ask him that." She spoke to Stuart.

"If you could be brief and to the point, Mr Umber."

"I shall. It is about your will, Mrs Richards. How is your estate divided between your children?"

Brent began to write some notes in his ring binder.

"I think," said Stuart, "that you are way out of line."

"No, I'm not. I ask because it is possible that someone in the family is trying to frame you for murder, Mr Richards. I wish to explore that possibility."

136

"Who's framing you? Is it Clive?" For the first time, Arlene became engaged by the conversation.

"It wouldn't surprise me, mo'm. He has always been after your money."

"He's not getting a penny of it. Nor Bertram and Lucinda. You're my only child."

She reached for Stuart's hand which he took hold of and then patted with his free hand in a gesture of reassurance.

"Ours is not a harmonious family. My brothers and sister see Mother only as a source of income to maintain their lifestyles. They do not care for her."

"But my youngest is true," said Arlene, smiling up at Stuart.

"I see," said Brent. "It's sad to hear of such a fracture within your family."

"As to your question," said Stuart, "it is not my place to answer you and Mother prefers to keep such matters private. What I wish to know is what I have done that makes me appear suspicious in your eyes?"

"After the tour, you left Mrs Richards on the patio for nearly twenty minutes at about five-forty."

"You had to," said Arlene. Brent looked up from his note-taking to find Arlene, once more, staring at him, blinking, while addressing Stuart.

"Unfortunately, I have a number of medical conditions. I require treatment and I prefer to self-medicate as it is the most expedient method to deal with my many issues."

"That would be cannabis, then?" asked Brent.

"I ingest certain natural, organic compounds as they are the most beneficial for me."

"You have to, dear, don't you?"

"I do, mo'm."

"Does it take twenty minutes for this ingestion to take place?"

"Five or six minutes. I found a quiet place and sat there, contemplating my condition and how I was coping with being outside. It is difficult... very difficult for me to leave home but I did so want Mother to be happy. She had expressed an interest in visiting the winery and I could not disappoint her."

"In this secluded spot that you found for your contemplations, did you see anyone or notice anything?"

"I was among some trees near the river. I believe I passed some workers on the way there. While sitting, I saw another worker coming towards me but he abruptly turned around and walked back. He seemed agitated."

"I think I know who that was," said Brent.

"Who was it?" Arlene's question was sharp, direct.

"An employee of the winery who had been having difficulties with a repair."

"Oh. Not Clive, then. It wasn't Clive, dear, so don't worry."

Brent looked up from writing his most recent note to find Stuart, leaning forward, attempting to read what was written upside down. They locked eyes.

"No," said Stuart, unabashed at being caught out. "Mr Umber, I cannot see how I could be framed in any of this. I never went near the place where the woman was murdered. It was nothing to do with me and it is not right that I be associated with this criminal investigation."

"Nothing to do with us at all," said Arlene, suddenly blinking rapidly.

"It does seem far-fetched, doesn't it? But there you are; we have to explore every possibility no matter how ridiculous it seems on the surface. From what you have told me I can see that you do not have the inclination to be a murderer, and, if any family member had an idea to frame you, I doubt they would be able to get past your mother's careful vigilance."

"That is so true," said Arlene. "Come along, Stuart. We must go now. Help me up."

"Yes, mo'm. You must be careful as you stand. You have been sitting for a very long time. Take it slowly until the circulation has returned properly."

Brent watched as Stuart attended to his mother. It was apparent that she did not need her son's help but she expected it nonetheless. He observed their habits and could see what they were doing was an often-repeated performance. The mother needed the son; the son needed the mother; and the rest of the family was not required. That was the appearance they gave.

"Goodbye and thank you for coming in," said Brent.

"Goodbye, Mr Umber. I hope that is the end of the questions." Having said this, Stuart Richards carefully supported his mother all the way to the elevators.

Left alone in the office, Brent looked at his notes. There was no condemnation or undue suspicion written into the text. He was bothered, though, by Stuart reading what was written. He would have to do something about keeping his thoughts from prying eyes. An idea came to him. He began to draw some symbols on the page. He only need develop a key - a list of symbols and letter combinations to represent persons and situations within the case. *That should do it*, he thought.

At one-twenty, Greg had finished interviewing Stanley Forbes and it was now Brent's turn to see him.

"I fail to see why I must be questioned again. You police do not appear to be very well organized. It's no wonder you haven't caught anyone yet."

This refrain was beginning to annoy Brent. He supposed the detectives handled it in their various ways - were professional and patient in the face of opposition and rudeness. He looked at Mr Stan Forbes. Here was a wealthy man. His clothes, demeanour, voice - everything about him bore witness to the descriptor 'supercilious' - that was what forcibly struck Brent. A snap decision? Yes, it was. Brent found himself unable to maintain politeness and patience. He realized that he was not so much annoyed with how nearly every witness expressed tedium over the repetitious questions and interviews, but that he was annoyed specifically with this particular man sitting across the desk from him. A woman had been murdered, her life brought to an untimely end and snuffed out. Some witnesses acted as though this were no more than an inconvenience to their own private lives, and Forbes typified and concentrated this indifference. Brent had taken an unwonted aversion to the man. Seconds had elapsed with Brent staring at Stan Forbes in silence.

"Well, I'm not here to waste time. Get on with it."

"I am getting on with it." Brent relapsed into silence and stared at Forbes.

"This is ridiculous. I'm leaving."

"If you do, I'll swear out a warrant for your arrest." Brent knew he would have a hard time convincing Jennifer and Greg of this necessity because, as yet, he had nothing on the man.

"You'll do what?" Forbes was now visibly annoyed. It pleased Brent.

"You heard me. I think you're the murderer of Sheila Babbington. Unless you can convince me otherwise and prove your innocence this will be a bad day for you."

Brent waited again. He knew what the next few moves would be. Forbes would want a lawyer. Brent knew how he, himself, would respond. Then the man would talk. He watched as Forbes considered his options.

"I think I should have a lawyer present."

"You haven't been arrested but here you go." Brent turned and slid the telephone across the desk to Forbes. "You can dial straight out. Before you do, please understand that you will be formally charged when your lawyer arrives because we wish to hold you. Then your lawyer will apply for bail to shorten your time in the cells. Although all that could be avoided if you and I can establish your innocence. We'll chat and see where we get. What do you want to do?"

Forbes had declined the offer of the telephone and had begun to scroll through the numbers on his own phone, looking for his divorce attorney. He hoped that she could suggest an experienced criminal lawyer. He stopped what he was doing when Brent asked the question and looked up. He was clearly in two minds.

"You have been holding something back. I know that. This is a murder case, Mr Forbes. We have not found the murderer. Naturally, I assume the information you are holding back is connected with Sheila Babbington's death."

If Forbes had been worried he had not been showing it. Yet now he became noticeably more relaxed. Brent could not tell if it was studied or genuine.

"I suppose we all have little secrets," he said, his super-cilious confidence returning. "There are in fact two things I have neglected to put in my statement because I did not think them important or relevant."

"What would they be?" asked Brent.

"I believe I had said I had been acquainted with Sheila for some months, but I neglected to say how we met."

"Go on."

"It was in December of last year and I was in a traffic accident. It was not my fault. The roads were icy. A car came round a bend, quite slowly, skidded, crossed the median and crashed into me. My SUV was scraped along the side and a headlight was broken. A door needed replacing. There was very little damage to the other car. The driver was Sheila." Forbes stopped speaking and waited.

"Were either of you hurt?" asked Brent.

"No, no. But my vehicle looked a mess. It was quite irritating."

"I should imagine it was." Brent tried to sound sympathetic.

"I am something of a perfectionist and, to tell the truth, the vehicle was spoiled for me."

"Oh. I can see how that might be aggravating. However, the repairs they do these days are very good. One can't tell that a vehicle has been in an accident once they're done."

"Except, I would know it."

"Hmm... so how was this matter settled?"

"I got rid of the car and bought a new one."

"Did you have the old one repaired?"

"No."

"What about Sheila's insurance? That would have covered it, surely?"

"I suppose it would. I was not concerned about the money."

"You didn't put through a claim, then?"

"I did not."

Brent paused. He had examined Forbes' file and read of his personal wealth which was immense.

"Sheila bumped into you and then you became friends?"

"That was the other matter. It is personal but I can see you are leaving me no choice. At the time of the accident, she was so apologetic and so concerned for my well-being that I was touched. She was clearly so upset by what she had done that it struck a chord with me. We exchanged all our details and parted. As I mentioned, I was very annoyed about my vehicle but that subsided. I found myself thinking about her quite often. I was attracted to her." Brent could not stop himself from reacting to this as though he were in his new friend Charlie's shoes and thought *You swine!*

"You have probably seen," continued Forbes, "that I am a wealthy man by inheritance. At present, I am divorced. It can be lonely sometimes. Sheila showed an interest in me that I am unused to. I started to pursue her. Not in an overt way. She was very pleasant to talk to."

"How did you communicate?"

"I met her a couple of times but usually it was by telephone. I think I had begun to love her although I have not for one minute deceived myself into thinking that she felt anything but a warm friendship towards me."

"So, things were progressing on your side but not on Sheila's."

"Yes. I chose not to pester her. It would spoil the relationship we did have. I kept a respectful distance."

"She was married with a family."

"I know. She seemed content but I wasn't. I know she was under stress because of business and I was thinking that I might do something to relieve her of that burden. I don't understand why people put themselves through such agony to achieve success in business. I thought I would offer her a way of escape."

"Would your presence on the tour be connected with that plan?"

"Yes. I thought I would see the place and buy it. She could then stay on as a manager and do the things she liked."

"Then, through this, she might open her heart to you?"

"Something like that."

"What did you think of the Songbird Estate?"

"It is very well run. They have an excellent wine that I was already familiar with."

"The Pinot Noir?"

"Yes. It is a very mature and pleasing wine. To my palette, when the vines are another ten years older, the wine will have few equals."

"Ah, yes. It is a very good wine. I am partial to it myself. I consider that it already rivals the best French Pinot Noir."

"Really? That is surprising."

"On the day of the tour, you were not observed by any other person for a period of some thirty minutes from five to five-thirty. According to your statement, at five o'clock, you went to your car to sit and listen to music."

"That is what I did. Afterwards, I went into the restaurant for a refreshment before leaving."

"Then, you went for a long drive. I think you were upset."

The answer from Forbes came slowly. "I was."

"You had spoken to Sheila, I know. What about?"

"She joined in for a little of the tour... long enough to greet people and wish them a pleasant stay. It was impossible for me to say what I had intended at that moment so I hoped to talk to her privately about my ideas when the tour was over. She told me that she was departing very soon for a wine-growers' conference. I thought that it would be an opportune moment to say I would buy the vineyard. It was something she could think about while she was travelling. I knew she would need time to grow acclimatized to the idea. For the entire tour, I was content, thinking my plan was un-folding well." Forbes was doing his best to appear animatedly boyish at this point but failed in his attempt to gain Brent's sympathy.

"Imagine my disgust when I found that she had already left the vineyard without so much as a word to me!"

"Yes, very trying, I should think. Were you very angry?"

"I hate to admit it but I was."

"When someone is slighted like that, it could recall past offences."

"I tried to think rationally about it... But my damaged car did come to mind. And the fact that I had been waiting... patiently waiting for her for all those months...."

"Very disturbing. You must have had a very bad half an hour. Then you go into the restaurant."

"I snapped out of my bad mood. I came to the conclusion that I simply needed only to call her, although I had really wanted to see her face when we spoke about my idea."

"Now, while you were in your car, you did not see the cyclist pass by?"

"Correct. I could only see the road through the rear-view mirror - my car was facing a wall. I wasn't looking in the mirror."

"Please think carefully - did you hear anything?"

"I don't believe I did. Nothing out of the ordinary. I heard the usual things. A loud truck passed on the road. Several people were talking together nearby. I remember that because I wished to be alone but they soon left. I know someone went to their car to get something but they made little noise about it so it didn't bother me."

"Is that everything you can remember?"

"A crow made a noise... that really is everything."

"Then your music must have been playing quietly."

"I put on Dukas' Sorcerer's Apprentice until I realized I did not want dramatic and loud. I changed to a Chopin nocturne. I needed to be soothed and it did the trick. I switched off the music after that."

"Music hath charms to soothe a savage breast," said Brent.

"You do surprise me, Mr Umber. I find Congreve is usually and so often misquoted. He made a valid point, though, because it worked for me."

"Would I be right in thinking that, in the half-hour you were sitting in your car, you came to the conclusion that Sheila Babbington was no longer a necessity to you?"

"You could say that," replied Forbes.

"I think that is all for now, Mr Forbes. Thank you for coming in. I have to warn you, there may be some follow-up questions at another time but, for now, my suspicions have been allayed."

"I suppose I should have mentioned these things earlier. I can see how you might be wondering what I was doing when there appeared to be a gap in my statement. I will be happy to answer any further questions you have - without a lawyer, of course." Stan Forbes' assured condescending manner had reasserted itself.

Chapter Seventeen

Beginning to gel

S hortly after Forbes had left, Greg Darrow found Brent at his desk, feverishly scanning through copies of witness statements.

"What did you make of them?" asked Greg.

"You can only be referring to the Richards. The greater the distance between them and me the better I like it. Jennifer said they were creepy. I agree, they are the essence of creepiness. The word may first have been coined with them in mind. I honestly cannot say which is the worse of the two."

"Yep, pretty bad. Did you know that Stuart was making eyes at Jennifer when she spoke to them?"

"Making eyes? As in fabricating eyeballs in front of her or was he only leering at our brave Jennifer?"

"Leering. She said he was repulsive."

"I can imagine that must have been awful. I felt like I needed a shower as soon as they left and no one leered at *me*, though Arlene was blinking dramatically."

"I don't see him as a suspect," said Greg.

"No. It appears he was at the wrong end of the vineyard, smoking a spliff. He may have ingested by a different method but that is how I envision him self-medicating, as he puts it.

Anyway, he said enough that rang true to convince me he is not a murderer and probably was the farthest from the crime scene which is why no one could see him."

"What about Forbes?"

"Grade A suspect. Could have done the murder, having motives that fit perfectly. Could answer the possible clandestine meeting aspect of Sheila hiding her car. Forbes and Gaudin are neck and neck, in my opinion. Did you know that Forbes and Sheila were in a traffic accident?"

"No." Greg sat down. "Tell me about it."

Brent summarized the traffic incident and continued on to describe Forbes' romantic feelings.

"So, you see, Greg, Forbes may have killed Sheila because she smashed into his car. He may have killed her because she was not returning his affections. He may have killed her because she didn't make herself available when he wanted to speak to her. With the first two possibilities, he may have planned her death in advance and then hired an assassin to do it if he didn't do it himself."

"That's all a bit too extreme for me... the reasons, I mean."

"Normally, yes, I would agree. But Forbes is definitely one of those people who cannot stand to be thwarted. Furthermore, he expressed no regret at Sheila's passing which was strange, considering his professed attraction to her. Mind you, the Richards didn't express regret, either, but Forbes as good as confessed to me that he was in love. He fell out of love with her in thirty minutes, sitting in his car while playing his favourite moody tunes. He is so self-absorbed that he could apply for membership and become a card-carrying member of the Richards family."

"Sure. He's selfish. That doesn't make him a killer."

"Greg, I'm surprised at you. She bumped his car. Captured his heart. Stood him up. We're looking for motives and here we have a selfish, vain man who doesn't think like you or me and believes himself better than everyone else. He condescends to be attracted by Sheila - a married woman with children. The fact that she is happily married does not seem to bother him in the slightest. He will pursue her anyway. The sheer arrogance of the creature suggests to me that, if thwarted, whatever complex emotion he is calling love would turn to hatred in... in half an hour."

"The knife was prepared in advance," said Greg.

"True. Perhaps he's lying. He would know that we would look at the knife carefully and he can assume we would dismiss him as a suspect because the murder weapon points at pre-meditation. He gets away by looking guilty but not guilty enough. Anyway, he has sufficient money to hire a thousand assassins."

"He might mess that up... the part where we give him a pass for seeming guilty."

"His defence lawyer wouldn't. Forbes might even enjoy the notoriety of a trial."

"It's not a bad theory," said Greg. "It doesn't set me on fire, though. I like evidence."

"Then you're in luck. Though you don't deserve to be told it for speaking against my beautiful theory. Forbes provided something."

"What?"

"He said that while he was sitting in his car, he heard someone go to their vehicle. He didn't see them. He intimated they were unobtrusive, saying they made 'little noise'."

"And?"

"It was what I've just been searching for. Nowhere in these statements does anyone admit to going to their vehicle or that they saw anyone else go to theirs. There were no arrivals to or departures from the area at the front during the half-hour Forbes was present in his car."

"Now that is interesting," said Greg.

"You are truly pedestrian. In future, I will only confide in Jennifer."

"Andy. How are you?" Brent had called Deadpan just before 3:00 p.m.

"Can't complain, Brent. Can't complain. And yourself?"

"I'm doing very well. Listen, I need information on two people. Number one is Stanley Forbes. He's..."

"I know him very well - if you mean the wealthy man, recently divorced, who lives in Ferndale. I've done work for him in the past."

"Really? That is... I mean, does that make it awkward for you?"

"Not at all. He had my associates and me investigate his former wife for his divorce. Then I worked for him again, investigating that lady in Belton who was murdered."

"No. That's not possible!"

"Why would that be, Brent?"

"I'm working on her murder case with the police."

"How exactly do you mean that? Are you working with them or are you a suspect?"

"Working with... Are you at liberty to answer some questions or do you have a code of silence about your cases?"

"Essentially, I buy and sell information. As you can appreciate, I provide this information and what the recipient does with it is no concern of mine. I had this happen once before, where both parties in a divorce matter hired my services."

"What did you do?"

"I earned two fees. What would you have done?"

"I think I'm less objective than you are, Andy. I think I would have chosen one side over the other."

"I could have done that but I didn't like either of them so I didn't mind."

"I think I've learned more about you in the last three minutes than I have in the last three years."

"Very likely."

"What would you do if you were offered a fee to investigate me?"

"*That* is a very awkward question because we've known each other for so long. I'd say, I'd give you a warning. Then we could work something out... if you take my meaning."

"Good man. Thanks for the, uh, hypothetical sporting chance."

"No problem, Brent."

"So, what can you give me on Forbes?"

"You'll want some current stuff and I'll give you the back history on both jobs at the same time."

"Anything spring to mind that I might find useful?"

"He was obsessed with the Babbington woman. Wanted to know her weekly routine, her friends, business associates, and background. The funny thing was, he asked for the exact same type of information about his former wife. I'd say he was planning to marry Babbington or something close to it. What we observed was that she had very little contact with him directly and he would call her about once a week. It was all on his side."

"That sounds about right. I questioned Forbes today and the way he spoke and what he said lines up with what you're saying. Anything else?"

"He wanted to get hold of her vineyard."

"He mentioned this. When did he tell you?"

"It was all during March. Do you know how cold it was in March? One of my associates nearly caught pneumonia keeping the place under surveillance. Though Forbes was decent enough to pay extra for the hardship."

"Why did he want the vineyard?"

"No idea. Not really part of my job to know what motivates my clients."

"Anything else that struck you?"

"Only, when she was murdered, I immediately thought of Forbes. I assumed he did it."

"I can see how you would. Any evidence?"

"None. Just an association of ideas, I expect. What do you want on him at present?"

"Surveillance round the clock. A list of contacts. I'm particularly interested if he has any criminal links or, at least, links with anything suspicious. I'd want those followed up immediately. And, if you are able, find anything that might link him to this murder and do everything with the assumption that he murdered Sheila Babbington."

"Certainly, Brent. What was the other matter?"

"Same angle for two people at the Bartlett Beverage Group but they're out of town."

"I don't know that company. Send me some information. I'll have to farm that work out unless you can wait."

"No, I need that soon, as well. The two names I'm sending you are those of men who are both suspects, also. Sending it now."

"What's happened to the police? They asleep?"

"Far from it. Evidence in the case is very hard to come by."

"So they hired you? That is very interesting and, um, if I may say, bold, on your part. The information's come in."

"I know. You're being diplomatic. I think you mean I'm idiotic."

"You have your reasons, I'm sure. Do they know anything? Oh, they wouldn't, would they? They'd be from Belton."

"Thank God, not a single thing. Although there's a city homicide detective on the case named Greg Darrow."

"Does he know Bennett? He's the one to watch out for. He's got a long memory, that man has."

"I haven't asked and I don't intend to."

"Darrow, eh? I've heard of him... Yes, I remember it. He was the lead investigator on the Tony Falcao case, that crime boss who was killed at the airport. He had it pinned on Robbie Samson but it was a mistrial and then it was dropped."

"Samson. That thug had to have done it. But I thought he was dead. What happened?"

"Judge threw the case out on a technicality. Someone explained everything to me, although I wasn't involved professionally. My informant said that, afterwards, Samson was bragging about the murder and how he'd got away with it. Then he got his and he stopped bragging. It's nice talking, Brent, but I'd better be going. There's a lot to do here. I'll let you know as soon as I have anything."

"Yes, sure. Goodbye, Andy. Oh, before you go. There's a cyclist wearing a hood on a warm day. He might be a hired killer."

"Doesn't ring any bells right now. Let you know if it does. Goodbye."

Brent held his phone in his hand and lightly tapped his chin with it. He sat staring, thinking. This was how Jennifer found him.

"What's up?"

"Oh... too many thoughts and not enough certainty. I'm seeing Margot Vaughan next."

"She's coming in?"

"No. I'm going out to see her. Are you having any luck?"

"I've knocked a few things off my to-do list but found nothing new that leads anywhere. What happened with Forbes?"

"Don't know yet. For me, he's a prime suspect. I explained why to Greg but he didn't seem very impressed."

"Oh." Jennifer's face became a mask.

"I told Greg that I would speak only to you in future. You are my handler and he is your guest and if I didn't observe the proper protocols this time, I apologize."

"It's okay... we're a team. What did Forbes say?"

"I've got it written up in a brief summary. I'll send you a copy. What I do know is that Forbes had an obsession with

Sheila and the Songbird Estate. He wanted them both... or, he wanted one to obtain the other and I do not know which was the most important to him."

"How sure are you of this?"

"I'm after more information. As it stands, he leads the suspect race."

"And Greg didn't find that interesting?"

"When I told him I knew less than I do now. To be fair, he said he wants solid evidence and I have none so far. But... I hope to get something soon."

"This is good. Damian has a lot on Bartlett's. Oscar Flint has the reputation of being ruthless in his business dealings. What I saw makes him look like a candidate, too. At least I can now give something to Baker."

"Am I earning my keep?"

"Looks like it."

"I'll have to miss the meeting at five. Can we chat later? There are a couple of things on my mind that I should discuss with you."

"Sure. I'm staying late tonight... probably until around ten or so."

"Good. I'll see you before then."

Brent got up and left.

Batna Insurance was a large, regional insurance provider. The fifteen-story office building Brent entered was no more than five years old and Batna's local office occupied two floors - the second and most of the third.

Margot Vaughan, Office Manager, was the third highest-ranking executive on site. She did not have the ear of the head office executives to any great extent, as did the District Sales Manager. Neither did she have much direct contact with the commissioned agents, as the Development Manager had. However, everyone else belonged to her - from janitors to the IT department - all one hundred and seventy-five of them.

Brent waited at reception, the office manager having been made aware that her appointment had arrived. The office was busy at just after 4:00 with a few employees leaving and couriers arriving for pick-ups and deliveries. While he waited, he tried to interest himself, without success, in the latest edition of 'The Insurance Journal' he had found on the glass table before him. All the articles and news items were too deeply focused within the industry for an outsider to find a compelling read.

At 4:10, a young woman approached Brent.

"Hi, I'm Ms Vaughan's assistant. Sorry to have kept you waiting but she is free now. If you would follow me, I'll show you to her office."

"Thank you," replied Brent who dutifully arose and followed, chatting pleasantly the length of the office with the young woman.

When they arrived at the appropriate oak door, the assistant asked Brent to wait. She knocked, partially opened the door, and put her head in to say,

"Mr Umber is here to see you."

"Send him in," came the reply from Margot Vaughan. Her voice was somewhat high - high and youthful enough to remind Brent of a schoolgirl's voice.

Brent was ushered into the room by the smiling assistant who, once he was safely inside, closed the door quietly behind him. Ms Vaughan stood up, proving to be about five-ten in height with shoulder-length black hair parted in the middle and wearing a mid-grey business suit with a pearl-coloured silk blouse. Her manner was business-like.

"Please, take a seat."

"Thank you for seeing me on such short notice. I should imagine that you are kept very busy - running an office as large as this."

"Yes, it can be challenging. You said you wanted to ask me a few questions."

"I'll come straight to the point. I think your friendship with Sheila has been quite complicated with some misunderstandings in the past. Why was that?"

"I'm sorry,... what does this have to do with the case?"

"Nothing at all, I hope."

"I don't approve of this."

"I'm sure you don't. I wouldn't, either. Here am I, a complete stranger to you, asking about something that superficially has nothing to do with the case and has every appearance of prying into your personal life. If I were you, I would throw me out."

Margot looked puzzled. She hesitated before answering.

"I've seen the police four times and answered all their questions. I don't think I can add anything to my existing statements."

"You haven't heard the rest of *my* questions, yet. I mentioned to your assistant, Clara, that I am a private investigator. There is a distinction between how the police operate and how I am conducting myself on this case. They are looking for evidence. I look for motives. That is the most obvious distinction. Going deeper, the police accumulate evidence to produce a conviction. On the other hand, I look for something in the person I'm interviewing that says to me, 'No, she could not have killed Sheila.' It is not psychology so much as my looking for the condition of innocence in a person. When I cannot find the innocence I'm looking for, it is likely I will find the murderer."

"Then, you are looking to prove me to be innocent?"

"That's it. I must satisfy my mind on that score. Once I have done that, I promise I will no longer be an aggravating nuisance to you."

Margot glanced at him. She was clearly coming to a decision.

"I can always leave," said Brent.

"If you do, then you'll be thinking I might have murdered Sheila." She said this coolly and evenly.

"That is the starting position for everyone who had opportunity."

"But I was with Erica the whole time."

"That makes no difference. It is an alibi that only you and Erica substantiate. No one else can corroborate what you two told the police."

"You're insinuating that she and I killed Sheila? This is…"

"'Outrageous' is my suggestion. 'Horrible' is another or you could use 'despicable', too. I want to find the murderer, to see that person's face in my mind's eye, and know that they will answer for the crime. This is what I do to arrive at that point."

"If I throw you out, as you suggest, then you'll put it in some lousy report that I wouldn't answer your questions?"

"No. I've only asked a single question so far. Whatever your answers will be I will not put them in my report unless they prove to have a direct bearing on the case. If they don't, I'll give you my word that what you say will not go beyond these four walls. Just so you know, I have already spoken to Erica."

"What did she say?" Margot briefly looked annoyed.

"According to my code of conduct, I will not tell you. I promised you confidentiality and I must do the same for her. Remember, I am working hard to clear both of you."

"Very well. I don't seem to have a choice."

She was quiet, leaning back in her chair which she swivelled to look through the wall of glass window and thereby avoid eye contact with Brent. It crossed his mind that this easy action of hers, signalling acceptance of the situation, was one that Margot would do if Brent were her therapist.

"Sheila is my best friend. Was my best friend. You want me to come to the point... I will. I found her annoying sometimes. She was very talkative and open about things. Got on well with people. I'm different. I'm always a bit fearful of meeting new people and it hasn't improved over the years. If it's not work-related I don't know how to read them and I become awkward. I put up barriers. So I was always a little jealous of her... for the way she connected and I didn't. Not all the time... a few times. I suppose I became possessive of her affections. I don't want to bore you... I wasn't very nice to her. She was a good friend and we got past it. Then, she did something that I could never forgive her for."

Margot stopped.

"What would that have been?"

"Um, I had better tell you. She asked two people to be bridesmaids at her wedding before she asked me. It's obvious she thought very little of me."

"I see. Could it have been a mistake?"

"How could it? She simply ranked me lower than the others."

"You said she was talkative... perhaps she was so excited about her wedding that she just blurted it out when she had the opportunity with the others?"

"No, she should have asked me first."

"Were you a bridesmaid?"

"Yes."

"Did you discuss this with Sheila?"

"No... Now, I can't."

"If you *could* discuss it with her now what would she say?"

"I hope she would say she was sorry."

"Sheila says she is sorry," said Brent.

Margot sat up in her chair and looked round at Brent.

"You can't apologize on her behalf." Her tone showed slight incredulity.

"I just did and there's no taking it back. Sheila would want you to move past all of this. I think she must wonder why you didn't bring it up before. Speaking personally, I don't see that you really have cause for this grievance. Not a significant one, anyway. You only *believe* yourself to be a victim in this. You manage this important office and that is a testament to your abilities. That you are haunted by the past, about things that could easily have been remedied at the time, demonstrates that you must like to nurture a grievance against someone because, in some respects, it gives you control over the relationship."

"What are you saying? That I wanted this?"

"You don't need to answer to me for anything. You could easily have cleared up this matter with Sheila. What do you do when two employees don't get along and it starts to get ugly. What would you do?"

"Hear both sides and try to reconcile the differences. If that doesn't work, then an arbiter might be brought in. If work is affected then a more serious view is taken of the situation. But I don't see how that's relevant."

"Think about it. No quick fix but a steady working through of issues to resolve them. Did you do that with Sheila over the bridesmaid issue?"

Margot said nothing and turned back to look out of the window again.

"I'll go now," said Brent.

"What? Oh, yes, okay. Goodbye."

Brent left her sitting in her swivel chair, still staring through the glass at the vista of buildings, roads, and trees beyond.

Chapter Eighteen

Artistic discussion

"If you sit in that chair, I can continue working while we talk," said Patricia Epstein.

Her studio was small and gave the impression that an explosion of colour had recently occurred and very little in the way of cleaning up had been done afterwards. Paint was on everything - dabs, smears, lumps - only Patricia's clothing seemed to have escaped the blast. One of her pale cheeks had a violet smear across it - as though she had a scar. It contrasted with her abundantly thick and long, red-brown, curly hair which was barely restrained by colourful ties. Brent wanted to rest his arm on the old wooden table next to him but he dared not for fear of damaging his clothes. Looking around, he saw two finished paintings that he liked out of the many he saw scattered everywhere. These two were very restful, stylized landscapes with a carefully chosen and unusual palette of colours - quite different to the others in their various stages of progress. The majority of the completed ones were large canvases - mostly soft, geometric impasto shapes in a limited range of sombre colours.

"I don't believe I have ever been in an artist's studio while the artist was actually at work."

Brent watched as Patricia finished applying broad strokes of brown before standing back to look at her work.

"Not very exciting, I'm afraid," said Patricia.

"I don't know. I find it interesting to see how it's done."

"You'll find it's a mundane business." She began to dab small, thickly applied amounts of grey in a line.

"I imagine lots of things are, behind the scenes. Theatre and movies must be terribly disjointed and tedious until the finished product is produced."

"Is that how you see art? As a product?"

"Yes. As a carpenter produces a chair or a chef produces a tempting dish so an artist produces an artefact for others to use and enjoy."

"Sounds like you have your head screwed on the right way. You wouldn't believe some of the gibberish I have to listen to sometimes. Do you like what I'm doing now?"

"I have no idea what it is. What is it?"

"It's called Spasmodic #4. I have to knock out some metaphorical theme pieces for a show. It's a charity fund-raiser. Ticket-holders are automatically entered into a lottery. First prize is one of my paintings. Second prize is two of my paintings." She turned round sharply when she said this.

"Why do you do it?" asked Brent, as he smiled back at her.

"It's expected of me. I'm supposed to churn out stuff that nobody can make sense of. I get paid for it. If it was your chef producing an equivalent dish it would be crème brûlée topped with baked beans. In other words, all the right ingredients but just plain hideous or revolting."

"Are you playing with me?" asked Brent.

"Yes. A habit of mine. I self-deprecate to gain attention."

"If you drop the pretence I might buy one of your paintings."

"Ooh, a paying customer with some backbone. That's a rarity. When I've finished this line of highly significant and symbolic dots I'll drop the pretence."

"Symbolic of what?"

"The number of days until the rent is due on this studio."

"That's hilarious... It will drive the cognoscenti insane... do another one... it's seventeen days until the first."

"Are you sure? Idiot! I was only counting until the last day of the month. I've gained another whole day. That is an immeasurable gift you have given me. But don't expect a discount on the price. My landlord is an old villain... wears a long moustache and a top hat. He has no heart."

"I should imagine your landlord is patience itself and goes by the name of Fred."

"Bob, actually. You seem to be quite human for a police officer."

"That's because I'm not. I'm a private investigator."

"Brent Umber?" Patricia picked a large tube of oil paint and came over to show it to Brent. "Burnt Umber. Is this a relation of yours?"

"It could be my nom de guerre. At least my mother thought the name Brent was a better choice than Burnt."

"So, are you a mystery man or are you serious about your mother? I like this. I would have chosen Alizarin Crimson - far more dramatic and dare-devilish. Do I have to marry you to find out your real name?" Patricia pulled up a high stool and sat opposite Brent.

"Is that a proposal? What happened to Michael McGinnis?"

"His train has just left the station. Mine has reached the end of the line. We haven't got around to discussing schedules yet."

"Oh, I see."

"You don't approve?"

"No. When I marry it will be for life."

"That sounds boring and you were doing so well. I'm the complete opposite. We would never get along."

"At least that's settled."

"Does that mean you're going to ask tedious questions now?"

"I'm afraid so. Did you have any reason to murder Sheila Babbington?"

"Is that your question? That's laughable. If I'm the murderer I would simply lie to you."

"There are lies. There are mistakes. Then there are motives to murder. If I thought you were the murderer I would catch you out. At present, I just want to prove you're innocent. So, tell me something you know. By the way, personal confidences are kept out of my reports unless you are the guilty party. I say this to everyone and, as yet, I've had no complaints. Mind you, this is my first murder case working with the police."

"Are you clever or naïve?"

"Both. How would you describe yourself?"

"Truthfully? Yes, I can see that's what you want. Angry... a little. Careless more than carefree. I love life but it so often spirals away from me. My painting is not an outlet for emotion or any deep-seated beliefs. I wish I were a better painter but I think I've reached my limits. I'd do something different if I could think of anything. I'd like to do cat portraits but I have allergies." Patricia folded her arms in front of her as she continued,

"Artistically, a cat portrait is a very frivolous thing but what I see in it is the devotion of the owner, the gentle peace of the project, and the representation of a safe world separated from news headlines of violence and political scandal. There lies a sanctity and separateness that I wish I could enter into. Much better than standing on a cliff's edge amid the raging storm."

"Those two paintings over there..." Brent pointed to the two he liked. "Did you paint those in happier times?"

"Yes. If you're interested in one of those, they are not for sale."

"That's a pity. If you painted something similar what would the price be?"

"If I could paint one of them again, it would cost you millions or nothing."

"I don't have that much on me and I haven't the bad manners to ask for a free painting. I understand what you're saying, though. Patricia, seriously now, could you paint me a painting like the beach scene and how much would it be?"

She turned to look at the canvas and smiled.

"You're on. Twenty-five hundred... might take me a few weeks, though - it will be a challenge."

"It's a deal. Here's five hundred as a deposit... balance on delivery."

"Wonderful! I can eat again. Do you want a beer?"

"Yes, but on the understanding you do not ask if I want a second one. I met a man last night who swore to me he only ever drank a glass of wine with his meal. He then proceeded to open seven or eight bottles which obliged me to keep up with him. I'm still suffering the ill effects of my indiscretion."

"Hair of the dog, they say. Beer's not wine but you should survive."

Patricia went out of the room and into a small annexe to bring back two bottles from a small fridge. Brent stood up and looked at a few things about the room while waiting for her to return.

"There you go," said Patricia as she handed a bottle to him.

"Thanks. I don't understand something," said Brent. "You've changed your painting style completely. Why is that?"

"It's what I can sell. I tried art for art's sake. Tried putting my soul into it. Neither of those worked. Then I gave what people wanted... wanted from me, anyway. Formless masses of colour. It's decorative in a way. Others read things into it. Who am I to say they're wrong? I scrape a living out of it. Some months are better than others."

"You know, when you were talking about cat portraits, I found that it rang true for me, also. You were very candid... unusually so. I'm not so different from you. I have a past history, the burden of which I carry around with me. It doesn't bear scrutiny in the light of day. To offset that, I keep myself busy on things that I feel make a difference. That, and weave a world of words around me to keep the past in check."

"Do you? Well, we have to do something or we'll drown."

"That's it exactly. You and I have a similar view. It's a relief to meet you because you seem to understand. What should we do, do you think?"

"Live on. There's no other choice."

"That's the conclusion I've come to. I'd want to frame the painting so I'd need a shallow stretcher."

"No problem. Doing something similar to that beach scene will be difficult. I was in love when I painted it."

"Perhaps that's what shines through. I think you can do it again. Your shop interior scene over there was only painted last year and it has a similar style."

"We'll see. So, how's the case going?"

"Getting closer."

"Why did the police have you assist them?"

"I solved a problem for a senior officer. He thought I might be of use in what was essentially a stalled case."

"And have you been useful?"

"I like to think so. My strong suit is I'm not a police officer so I don't have to follow official guidelines."

"Is that what you're doing now? You're investigating me through this chit-chat?"

"Yes. You're quite a challenging person in some ways. I find you to be truthful."

"I feel like I should be angry with you but I'm not. You're like a child in some ways and like a friend in others."

"I'm a chameleon. I change colours but I do it unconsciously. If you open up I'll open up. If you are afraid I will comfort you. If you are sad I will be sad with you. I can't seem to stop myself."

"This is too much. I'll tell you what, Brent. Let's get the questions done. I'll get on with your painting. If I ever think about marrying, I'll look you up."

"Deal," said Brent. "I have to see Michael. Today, if I can. Where will I find him?"

"He's on the road. He won't be back until late. You're wasting your time there, though. He is such a gentle creature it brings out the mother in me. There is no way he could murder anyone. It's not in him and he hasn't the courage to do it."

"I'll take your word for it. However, I still have to see him and I'll bear in mind what you've said. Could you have him call me as soon as he returns?"

"I'll do that. Can I continue painting while you talk?"

"Sure. Why did you go to the Songbird Estate?"

"I saw photos of vineyards on the internet." Patricia took up her palette and brushes again. "I liked the idea of a world within in a world. A vineyard has a dramatic and isolated appearance. I was going to do a painting. I made some sketches and took photographs on the tour. I went off the idea when the woman was found dead."

Patricia began to paint something very different on the canvas in front of her - thick red swirls.

"What did you think of Sheila Babbington?"

"Nice enough. I liked her. We only spoke briefly at the beginning of the tour. I asked if she would mind if I came back to set up an easel and see what I could do. She said 'No problem'. As I said, I haven't wanted to go back since. Why was she murdered?"

"I don't know. Everything I've found out about her makes her such an unlikely victim."

"I hope you catch whoever did it." As she spoke, Patricia changed the colour she was using and started making quick accurate strokes in a very dark blue and Brent watched as a face in profile began to appear in the centre of the canvas. The mouth was open, screaming.

"Is that Sheila?" asked Brent.

"It is the fear and pain she went through. I'm not sending this to the fund-raiser. I'll do a proper job on it and work it up into something that makes sense. Keep talking."

"That part troubles me... what she went through. I've only been on the case two days but I keep her in focus all the time. I want justice for her."

"Good. I like that. Go on."

"What appals me the most, apart from the crime itself, was that she lay alone out in the vineyard all night. She wasn't found until the staff came in the next morning. Although it was a temporary condition and not really the case, it was as though she had been overlooked."

"Hmm. Forgotten and alone. Yes?"

"Then there's the hole she's left in the lives of those who surrounded her. Her husband took it hard. Sheila's family thinks he is the murderer."

"Oh no. That's awful. Poor guy. You'll sort that out, though."

"I hope so. Was there anyone you saw on the tour, or anywhere else that afternoon for that matter, that struck you as odd?"

"I think many people are odd. I guess you mean potential murderer odd. I've thought about it. Hey, I've even wondered how I must look to the police. I can't say anyone comes to mind. There were a couple of people who I didn't care for much. One was a wine guy who wouldn't shut up."

"I know about him. Who was the other?"

"It was the family guy. Kept talking down to his boy - only he did it in a kind, irritating way. He was just a little boy but the dad kept telling him to do something or not to do something all the time in a patient, ineffectual tone."

"How does that equate to his being a potential murderer?"

"Doesn't really. He wants a perfect child and I don't think one has been born yet. Just annoyed me. But he was doing it to an extent that made me think he could murder someone if he didn't get his way... sort of snap."

"I've spoken to him and actually he seemed quite pleasant, although his child wasn't present at the time."

"Different dynamic. Wine guy didn't seem to like the children being there. Some people don't. I could see he was getting on the tour guide's nerves with his running commentary. That's it really."

"Did anyone seem anxious or ill at ease?"

"Yes. Michael McGinnis. He thought the vineyard should be a hundred per cent organic. You should have heard him when he spotted a pile of spraying equipment."

"Thanks. You've been very helpful."

"Don't tell me you're going now? I like having you around."

"I would love to stay but I have a lot of work to do and you seem to be producing an effective piece."

"I hadn't realized it but I needed to do this more than I thought. Perhaps I do have to work out my emotions through art after all. This will need a lot more work. The background needs changing."

She stood back and Brent joined her to view what she had done. The swiftly executed profile was unmistakably one of Sheila. He began to wonder how Patricia had remembered Sheila so well. It was then he noticed a small print-out of Sheila's photograph clipped to the edge of the easel. There were paint marks on it in several different colours so it had been there for some time. Brent pointed to it.

"All my talk is only a façade, you know. My defence. I've been wanting to do something for her and it's coming out now. I'm very cut up about her death."

"You have captured her perfectly," said Brent. "Goodbye."

"See you," said Patricia who went back to her painting.

The private investigator was at a loose end. He sat in a restaurant, eating an unsatisfactory dinner. The fish did not seem as fresh as it should have been but he was too tired to complain in a place to which he would never return. He picked at his meal. At least the salad was not bad. Seven-thirty and Brent had run out of time to go and see Luke Valinho, the courier, because he lived in Newhampton. Janet Jones and Rita Inglis, Songbird staff, had been questioned by Greg as recently as yesterday, prior to Brent's own visit to the vineyard. He would interview them himself soon when he went to check up on his new pal, Charles. As he finished his salad, the names of all the other suspects came one by one into his mind.

Gaudin. Brent was anxious to see him. He wanted to corner and force something definitive from the man. What was he like, though? How best to do it?

Forbes. He could not help but see him as the murderer but it was a cloudy picture - unsatisfying, like the fish in front of him. *Do I want him to be the killer?... I think I do.*

Valerie Brown. He would have to meet her before deciding anything but, superficially, he could not place her anywhere in the big picture as there was no hint of suspicion.

John Finch. *Where's my drawing, John? Tell Master Kevin to get on with it.*

Stefan Badowski. *He has the perfect alibi... on the patio the whole time. I have to see him.*

The Richards. *What were they doing there? Did they lie?*

The Cyclist. *Did you kill her or are you a distraction?*

Oscar Flint.

Brent took out his phone to call Damian. It was 7:45.

"Hello, it's Brent."

"Hey, Brent. What can I do for you?" Damian sounded more upbeat than usual.

"Got anything on Flint?"

"Yeah, like a load of stuff. Nothing attaches to him directly but he has friends of friends who are pretty shady. Gambling interests mainly. These are the type of guys with a legit front who you know are doing something illegal behind it. One or two have records but nothing major and mostly old."

"Did you see a connection between Flint and say, racketeering, money laundering, fraud?"

"No. He looks clean. The wine business is not his only interest, though. He's the kind of guy who's in luck all the time. He buys a property for a million and then a new development is announced and he sells it for eight. That kind of luck. Only, it's not luck. He'll grease palms to get the information before the announcement and then he buys in."

"That gives me an idea. Any sense he'd employ violence to achieve his objectives?"

"I thought about that." Damian sounded relaxed, confident. "I'd say, he would have a person killed *if* he felt threatened. As a way of operating? No, I don't see it."

"That's good to know. Anything else?"

"The company is financially solid. Doesn't owe anything and has big cash reserves according to their bank. Now, Gaudin is another matter. A big spender and lots of debt."

"Enough to make him desperate?"

"Maybe. He'll need a big deal to get out of the hole he's in. He isn't bankrupt but he's not going anywhere either, you know what I mean?"

"I do. Do you see one or both of them as a murderer?" asked Brent.

"Yes, it's possible." Damian sounded as though he was enjoying himself. "I see Gaudin as a facilitator with Flint directing him remotely. It's worth investigating, anyhow. I'll get the go-ahead in the morning to do just that."

171

"Good on you. Thanks for the information."

"No problems. See you tomorrow."

"Sure."

Chapter Nineteen

A different way

B rent thought about dozing in his old Jeep for a few minutes because he felt so tired. He really wanted to go home, clean himself up, and go to bed. Instead, he started the engine and headed for the Finch household.

Delia and John were focused on their children. The small, neat house could have had a neat garden to match but it had been surrendered to the dictates of two small humans. A bright red, rounded, plastic sit-in car straddled the path. A pair of orange plastic boots were on the top front stair while a pink stroller was parked at the bottom. Under a bush, a plastic bucket with a yellow dinosaur motif and a matching spade drew attention to the place where Kevin had been digging ineffectually.

Brent knocked, hoping he was not too late. He could hear childish voices beyond the closed door, followed by muffled adult responses. He guessed there was a bedtime rebellion in progress.

Eventually, a short, dark-haired woman opened the door. She smiled a welcoming smile which was strongly tempered, and made uncertain, by the immediate desire to deal with the situation farther inside the house and a hair-trigger readiness to be rid of a door-to-door salesperson.

Before she spoke, Brent said,

"I'm sorry to disturb you. My name is Brent Umber. I'm a private investigator working with the Belton police."

"Oh, yes." Her face brightened and her smile became real. "John mentioned he spoke to you. Please come in. We're just trying to get the kids to bed."

"Is that a difficult process?" asked Brent as he stepped inside.

"Very often it is. Zoe's no problem but Kevin refuses to go even when he's so tired his eyes are closing."

"Ah," said Brent. Children and the way parents were supposed to deal with them... the subject was a complete mystery to him.

They had not left the hall before a small boy, wearing cartoon-decorated pyjamas, padded in barefooted.

"Who are you?" asked the boy.

"I'm a policeman."

"A policeman... where's your uniform?"

"They haven't given me one yet. I'm a very new policeman."

"Kevin, this is Mr Brent Umber," said Delia.

"Hi, Brent," said Kevin.

"Hello, Kevin. Are you going to bed now?" asked Brent cheerfully.

"No, Daddy said I can stay up."

"I don't think he did, Kevin," said Delia. "Let's go and ask him."

She took hold of the boy's hand and led him along the hall. Brent followed.

John Finch was in the living room putting an armful of discarded toys back into the box where they were usually stored.

"Hello, Brent," said John. He looked slightly puzzled until he added, "Have you come about the drawing? I'm so sorry, I completely forgot all about it."

"What's this?" asked Delia, looking from one man to the other for an answer while still holding Kevin's hand.

"If John could just hang onto Kevin for a moment, then I can explain in private."

"Oh, sure," said Delia.

Quietly, in the kitchen, Brent asked Delia to allow her son to draw a picture before he went to bed. He told her of the necessity to have the drawing come out as naturally as possible, without prompting, and, when it was finished, to ask questions to see if it was anything like the description of the cyclist.

After twenty minutes, the sometimes difficult, sometimes willing Kevin produced a finished work. It was something only a mother could like but there was a bike of yellow and purple in it. Kevin had said goodnight and retired to bed, gently hauled along by patient Delia who was going to read to him.

Brent held the paper in his hands. He studied thick purple tires, a yellow frame, and an awkward, disproportionately small, red figure. Kevin said it was himself on the bike. Asked if he would wear a hood while cycling, Kevin replied, 'Sometimes. If it's raining. Not when the sun's out. That's silly.' Asked if he had seen someone on a bike wearing a hood he shook his head. Asked if he had seen a bicycle on the day he went to the vineyard, Kevin said he had and 'it went really slow and then it went really, really fast.' That was all Brent and Delia could extract from the witness.

A little before ten, Brent's Jeep rolled into the near-empty parking lot at the back of the police building. Inside, the policewoman on duty eyed his visitor's pass suspiciously. She was not satisfied with his explanation as to his presence there until she had got confirmation from Jennifer. She grudgingly let him through to the elevators.

"Still at it?" asked Brent.

"Just about done. Everything is now caught up."

"Too many forms and reports?"

"I can't understand why we don't have a single form to fill in and it populate everything in the database. We have two databases and I have to copy and paste from one system to another. It's okay once it's all set up - then they're synchronized." Jennifer had been frowning at her computer screen but now she turned to Brent and smiled.

"So, what do you want to talk about?" Jennifer gave Brent her full attention.

"This is by way of being a verbal status report. Written reports are to follow. I haven't seen everyone yet so consider this an interim assessment.

"Without going into details, in my opinion, the prime candidates for the position of murderer are these: Forbes directly or by employing an assassin. Gaudin, Flint, and an assassin. Gaudin may have acted alone in the matter. The cyclist is the most obvious person to be the hired killer. Could have been someone else but I doubt it. Do you like children's pictures? Master Kevin has contributed his witness statement. Here, you could pin it on your wall."

Brent handed her a clear plastic bag containing the drawing. Jennifer took it out.

"Is this what he saw?"

"Hard to say. I tried not to lead him. His statements were not very definite. It's possible to read what one wants into what he said. My take on it is this. Kevin saw a bike going slowly uphill and then, almost immediately, saw it quickly coming down again. There is a small chance that he saw the cyclist wearing a hoody but, if he did, I think he's forgotten the fact. The parents both say Kevin's observation had to have occurred just after four o'clock. This is not good courtroom material, I know. However, it leads me to believe that the killer cyclist was in the area for some time."

"Who hired the killer?" said Jennifer, more to herself than to Brent.

"This is why I wanted to see you quietly," said Brent.

"Oh, why the secrecy?"

"If we look at this case from a different perspective, there's a firming up of a few things."

"Such as?"

"Look at the people on the tour by category rather than as individuals. We have the Richards - very wealthy. Then we have Forbes - very wealthy. There's Gaudin - the representative of a wealthy company. Next, we have the Badowskis, real estate agents. Where do they all meet on the same day? The Songbird Estate. Bartlett's has already put in an offer on the place. Forbes spoke of buying it from Sheila for what sounded like a very flimsy reason. Since I spoke to you, Damian told me that Flint occasionally uses illegal means to buy up parcels of land before a city project goes in. My question is, what is going on out there?"

"No idea. I haven't heard anything. When I started on the case it was one of the first things I looked at."

"Could there be something, a big project, say, that hasn't been announced and is only in the planning stages at present?"

"Possible, I guess. I'll have to ask around."

"No. I wouldn't do that. Remember, we do not know who we're dealing with and Sheila Babbington may have died because of it."

"So, like, someone in the planning department who would know where a project's going in and might be in the habit of reporting to... whoever it is behind the murder, would also report if we investigate?"

"That's what I'm thinking. If I'm right, we have at least three or four factions as candidates. Until we know who it is we should tread carefully."

"Yes, I think so, too. If there's a ring operating a scheme we'll want to get them all. Baker needs to be brought in." She thought for a moment before adding, "The Richards? I don't see them in it."

"Why? Because they're weird and introspective?"

"She's eighty."

"The son isn't. She thinks it up and he carries it out. Why not? It's possible. And, consider this, Stuart forced himself to go to the vineyard even though he hinted at agoraphobia or something similar. Had to smoke cannabis to get through it, according to his story. That's a good alibi they have between them and one that is easily fabricated. The employees Stuart saw were also seen by Arlene. She only had to keep a count of them and of what time they appeared on the track and he rattles it off like he was there when he said he was. That would leave him free to be elsewhere, like meeting the cyclist or committing the murder."

"It's *possible* they worked it together. It's *possible* there's more to them than meets the eye. What was that about the cyclist?"

"Maybe innocent. I don't think so. For the three main factions, there could easily be a reason why one of them *had* to be present to oversee the hit, only we don't know what it is.

I put the Badowskis into a separate class. They could be connected to one of the other groups as their real estate agents or they are in it for themselves. Of all of these factions, they seem to be the most likely to be present by coincidence. I feel the wealth aspect is the greatest indicator we have."

"Mind you, the Badowskis could probably borrow money to get the estate."

"Yes, you're right, of course. I just hope that it isn't so."

"Why's that?"

"Didn't I tell you? Martha Badowski is looking into some real estate for me."

"Oh, Brent! How *could* you do that?"

The phone did not ring. All the way home, Brent wanted to hear from Andy Fowler. Feeling tired, he wanted to go to bed but knew he would not sleep unless he heard something.

When he was in his apartment, he had cleaned himself up, eaten something, had reviewed his investments, and checked his building's security system. He was still waiting for the call he hoped would come. Brent was reluctant to bother Andy and be an unprofessional nuisance.

By 1:00 a.m. he decided he would be a nuisance anyway.

"Hello, Andy. Got anything?"

"Brent. I was just about to call you. Nothing new on Forbes. I'm, uh, having difficulties with that Bartlett company. Neither of the two local contacts I have want to get involved. I'm very sorry about this." The familiar monotone contained no hint of apology.

"Oh. Why won't they touch it?"

"In different ways, they both said the same thing. Flint has a clean and solid reputation but there is the idea that he is connected to some nasty and very private people. If anyone starts looking into his affairs accidents follow. Gaudin gambles but I don't know if he owes anyone."

"Flint's a frontman. For whom?"

"They couldn't say specifically, although one of them mentioned the name, Clive Richards. He said there were others and those ones he didn't want to talk about at all. He wanted paying for that nugget of information. You'll see it itemized on my invoice."

"Hold on a moment. Clive Richards... yes. Any details about him?"

"You seem excited. I'd never heard of him before. My contact said he's some kind of behind the scenes political expert. Professional man. Advises people in all levels of government and different parties about finances. Record's clean. Must be good money in it because he lives well, so I'm told."

"This is excellent, Andy. Can you check his birth certificate in the morning? I need it asap."

"Certainly. You want me to find someone else to follow Flint and Gaudin?"

"Gaudin only, if you can find him. You leave Flint for the moment but get someone local to trail him. There's another matter that needs looking into."

"You're keeping very busy. What is it?"

"It's highly likely that Sheila Babbington was murdered by some gangster type. We have a young man on a bike at the time of the murder. No one has given a description other than he was riding in the area on a mountain bike at the right time. He was wearing a grey hooded sweatshirt with the hood up. It was a hot day. Remember Jerry Miller? He was up to no good when I saw him walking with his hood up on a warm night. These guys don't want to be seen and, by habit, they use the hood thinking they won't be noticed. Amateurish, but it makes me see the cyclist as an urban gangster out in the country, waiting around to knife Sheila. He simply sticks out as not belonging. Could be a woman but all witnesses thought it was a young man about five feet nine.

"Then there's the way he used the murder weapon - an old knife. Cleaned and sharpened it scrupulously but left it behind as though it was his trademark. Do you think it possible to find someone like that?"

"Interesting. Could be anyone and finding him or her would take time even if it's possible. Also, I have a bit of a technical difficulty in this matter. It would delay an investigation."

"What's that?"

"I only have so many contacts in the urban gang world. Because of your last job I'm reluctant to overwork some of them. Draws attention, you see - attention which can be injurious to my health and that of my associates."

"I suppose it would. Well, do what you can and stay safe."

"Um, Brent, there's another matter. I hate to bring it up."

"My account! It must be getting up there. How much do you need?"

"Twenty-five will do until we settle up."

"Right. I'll drop off a package first thing in the morning. Where do you want it delivered?"

"Thank you very kindly. I think the dry cleaners this time."

"They're open early... It will be there about seven-thirty. Thanks for your superb work."

"It's nothing at all. Goodnight."

Brent went to bed as soon as the call was finished. The room was welcoming, and the design on the grey and black comforter stated it was a man's room. The Handel lamp on the bedside table cast a warm light through the tropical sunset coloured glass shade with its aquamarine border. He lay back and looked at the indistinct shadow on the white wall of the lamp's palm tree pattern. As he switched off the light, he thought he would never be able to get to sleep. Within five minutes he was dead to the world.

Chapter Twenty

Undercurrents

The next morning, Thursday, the detectives' daily 5 p.m. meeting took place at 8:05 a.m. The flow of information to get everyone up to speed resulted in Greg immediately asking, and obtaining, his superior's approval for an extension of tenure on the case.

At 9:35, Brent heard from Andy Fowler. Clive Richards proved indeed to be Arlene Richards' eldest son.

When the meeting was finished at 9:50, Jennifer brought Commander Baker into the loop. He approved all the plans the detectives laid out before him.

Greg was to return to the city and begin two investigations. The first was the search for a gangster-killer answering the familiar description. The second was of an entirely different nature. It was the beginning of a multi-jurisdictional investigation into the affairs of Bartlett's Beverage Company, including its executives and network of associates and interested parties. Greg Darrow, being a homicide detective, would not be the lead in that case but had to familiarize the detectives who were assigned the Bartlett's file with its contents and with the fact that an ongoing murder case had to be considered in how they were to proceed.

Damian was going to look into the extended and local Richards family to find any possible connections to the murder or to Bartlett's.

Jennifer would be researching government projects that might influence the value of the Songbird Estate. If she found something useful she would pursue it. If not, then she would switch to investigating Forbes. Brent realized he must warn Andy as soon as he could. He was determined that Andy and Jennifer should not meet under any circumstances and, in particular, that they should not trip over one another when observing Forbes.

Technically, Brent now had nothing to do. The police were in their element and had clear objectives. He could never rival their abilities or capacities. In the heated rush of revelation and excitement that arose during the meeting, he had largely been forgotten and had no clear tasks assigned to him. So, functioning under his original mandate, he remained focused on Sheila Babbington. Nothing had changed that for him. It was his sole focus and the other things, the shady dealings of the moneyed, he saw as distractions which might or might not eventually lead to a murderer. His unaltered task was to find the killer - if he could. Brent decided to seek out Gaudin and get him to talk. He neglected to tell anyone of his plan as they all seemed very busy. He had to leave Belton and return to Newhampton.

The noisy, blue Jeep came to a stop near the entrance of a nineteen-seventies, two-story office building that appeared to have been architecturally slapped onto the front of a very large, brown metal-sided warehouse. Gaudin had been found, followed, and run to ground at a Bartlett distribution centre by one of Andy Fowler's associates. Claude Gaudin was usually stationed in Bartlett's head office at its expensive address near the airport which was convenient for his frequent travelling.

Brent parked in a reserved spot next to a year-old, bright yellow Corvette. The car was entirely out of keeping with the thirty or so vehicles that occupied the other parking spaces. If Brent had not already known the fact, he would have guessed that the yellow car belonged to Bartlett's super-salesman. Brent got out of his fourteen-year-old vehicle that was definitely showing its age and mileage. The driver's door no longer shut properly without it being first lifted and then shoved home.

He looked through the Corvette's smoke-grey tinted passenger window at a scrupulously clean, black leather interior. The sports car was in showroom condition - unlike his own receipt-littered Jeep with its worn, scratched, and faded innards.

Going through the glass doors of the entrance, Brent found himself in the rubber matted reception area of an open-plan office. The pale blue carpet, which extended as far as the eye could see, looked so old and tattered that it did not seem worth the protection of a mat. The lighting was old fluorescent, the paint was old white, and the few prints on the wall - a half-hearted attempt at tying the office into the reason for its existence - were enlarged, poor resolution, faded photographs of wine barrels, bottles, and bunches of grapes.

There was no one at the reception desk, which was really a large L-shaped workstation with a frosted glass baffle topped by a shelf. The pale wood-grain patterned Formica trim was damaged with small pieces missing. Someone had been sitting there recently - the computer monitor showed a half-filled invoice on its screen. Brent looked along the office. Four desks were occupied but if the people had seen him enter they did not care enough to walk the ten or twenty yards to speak to him. Brent saw a Bartlett's Beverage promotional pen of the cheapest kind. He picked it up.

"Can I help you?" bellowed a formidable-looking woman from the back of the office. Her face and voice gave the impression that she hated Brent. Behind her were two shelving units. One, stuffed with ring binders, visibly sagged. The other was an ancient, grey-green metal unit piled high with computer print-outs and stacks of loose paper. A single mauve vase with a plastic flower in it stood on the top shelf. The other three office workers looked up.

Before he could answer, a young Indian woman came through the door that connected to the warehouse.

"Sorry, I was out the back." She was smiling and pleasant. "How can I help you?"

"Hello," said Brent. He glanced back along the office and the formidable woman, without the expression of distaste leaving her face, sat down and attended to her work. "I'm here to see Claude Gaudin."

"Oh. Um," she said awkwardly, and then looked along the office for guidance. Everyone had their heads down. She turned back to Brent. "He's not seeing anyone because he's working on a project. Do you have an appointment?"

"I don't. Here's my card. I'll write a note on the back. If you could take it to him perhaps he might see me."

"Okay." She smiled again.

Brent picked up the pen but it didn't work. He took out his own pen.

"I'm very sorry," she said. She removed the defunct pen and put it in the waste-paper basket.

"Don't apologize," replied Brent as he wrote a brief sentence on the back of his business card. "You seem to be the only cheerful person in here."

She made a sound with her lips that implied she did not care for the place.

"Next week is my last. I've got another job."

"That's good. A step up?" Brent handed her his card.

"Yes. Oh... private investigator?" She looked up at him with a keen, enquiring gaze.

"You're probably wondering why I'm here."

"No. It is not my business."

"But you're curious, right?"

She smiled and, with a slight move of her head, said, "Of course I am. Nothing happens here... it is so boring."

"Will you be glad to leave?" asked Brent.

"I cannot *wait* to go."

"Why's that?"

She stared at him before saying, "They are so cheap here. Wages are okay but everything is like that pen. Doesn't work. I was away from my desk when you came in because I had to go and count the inventory. I can't ship an order unless I count first. Inventory in the system is always wrong. No one's stealing but some people do not know what they are doing." She glanced along the office at the formidable woman.

"I see," said Brent. "So, when you go, you won't miss any of the staff?"

"Not in the front office. Out the back they're okay."

"Hmm, then I'll tell you why I am here. It's about the murder case."

"Really?" Her dark eyes widened.

"Yes. What's your name, by the way?"

"Sashi. How can you be here about the murder case when you are not police?"

"I'm working with them as an assistant."

"Oh. Okay." Sashi accepted what he said but did not seem convinced.

"What I'm interested in is why Claude Gaudin was at the Songbird Estate that day."

"I don't know. One of the drivers said the police had been to Head Office. That's all I heard. I have been working here three months and I have only seen Mr Gaudin twice before this week."

"When would that have been?"

"First week I started I saw him for a few minutes. Then… like six weeks ago he was here all day."

"Was anyone with him?"

"No, I don't think so. A package came for him."

"You received a package… six weeks ago?"

"Yes. He was waiting for it to arrive."

"How big was the package?"

"You are being an investigator? How much does it pay?"

"The pay is pretty good but getting enough work regularly is difficult."

"Oh. Okay. It was about eighteen inches long and twelve by twelve."

"You're very observant and have a precise memory. Do you recall who sent it?"

"Head Office. Immediate Delivery."

"What was inside, do you think?"

"It was not very heavy… a few pounds. How is this connected with the murder?"

"I don't know that it is. It could all be entirely innocent but I have to pursue things that look unusual. I think that it's odd that Mr Gaudin should come to this office."

"That is what I think," said Sashi.

The formidable woman came up close to them.

"What's going on here?" she asked.

"I have a meeting with Mr Gaudin about a real estate contract. Sashi, could you take my card up, please?"

"Certainly, Mr Umber." Sashi nimbly moved away from her desk and headed upstairs.

"Hi, are you the office manager?"

"No. I'm the Inventory Control Manager."

"I see. That must keep you busy."

"It does. There are three other distribution centres and I'm responsible for all of them."

"Must be quite challenging."

"Yeah, it is. Well, I can't be chatting all day."

Having effectively closed down the conversation, she returned to her desk. Brent watched her go. Sashi returned shortly afterwards.

"He will see you right away," she said with intense glee and flashing eyes.

"You read the back of the card?"

Sashi hesitated before answering, "Of course, I did."

"I would have, too. What did you think?"

"I'd like to sit in on the meeting. I want to hear what you're going to say."

"I wonder if that's possible?"

"No, no, I can't. I'd love to but I have a job to do."

"Only one more week."

"Yes. And just when it is getting exciting, I'm leaving. But, anyway, it would not look proper. He would not speak in front of me."

"Don't tell anyone else, will you?"

"No, no, no. My lips... they are sealed."

Brent smiled at her and then went to ascend the open tread staircase with its cracked and discoloured, grey vinyl tiles.

"What's this trash?"

Gaudin was angry. Standing by his chair, he flung Brent's card across the desk towards him as soon as Brent entered the office. He was tall, framed perfectly by the picture window behind him. Claude Gaudin was a well-dressed, tanned, and handsome man who had once been an athlete but was now a lover of good things, to excess. His sun-bleached hair was thinning but well-groomed. His obviously expensive pale blue shirt was new and crisp. The heavy, expensive watch was qualitatively matched by a thick gold link bracelet and two rings with gemstones. Brent saw they were a black onyx and a large tiger's eye.

"It's trash if you can disprove it. It's true if you cannot or will not."

"Funny guy. You're not even a cop."

"People frequently remind me of that fact. Make no mistake, I do have the power of citizen's arrest *and* I can call in the police any time I choose."

Gaudin began swearing loudly at Brent. The occupants of the other offices on the floor could not fail to hear what was being shouted.

"You are such a small-minded and obvious man," replied Brent. "Do you really think you can bluster your way out of this?"

"What do you mean!? I'm not *in* anything."

"Like the card said, 'You're the murderer and I can prove it.'"

"How?"

"Simple. Motive, opportunity, means - you have them all."

Gaudin took to swearing his denials and telling Brent what he thought of him.

"Call your lawyer." Brent spoke quietly and evenly so that no one could overhear. "Let's get him or her in here. Or, if you like, don't say anything. But if you continue like this, I'm going to swear out a warrant for your arrest and have the police deal with you. Make no mistake about that."

Claude Gaudin began pacing up and down behind the desk. He ran his hand through his hair and then shook his head. His actions demonstrated extreme irritation. Brent had yet to see the man composed so he could not gauge his present condition against something he knew to be normal behaviour. He guessed Gaudin was usually a smooth and persistent talker when it came to convincing someone about a deal. Oddly, Brent pictured Gaudin as a French Baron of medieval times. He imagined the angry knight, frustrated at his inability, because of modern restraints, to kick him, Brent, down the stairs, before using a whip, or an axe, to express his true feelings of displeasure.

"Are you French?" asked Brent.

"What? No. My grandfather was French and Claude was an uncle's name on my mother's side."

"Can you speak French?"

"A bit."

"Enough to buy wine in Europe?"

"Yes. What's this got to do with anything?"

"Not much. I'm interested, that's all."

"Why are you here?"

"To find Sheila Babbington's murderer. If it is not you, I need to know it now. However, you have been up to something... that I do know. You're going to tell me what it is or you will be arrested before the end of the day."

"Look, Umber, I didn't murder her."

"You have debts."

"So what?"

"You need money. Setting up Sheila's murder either got you some cash or you discharged an obligation."

"What *are* you talking about?" He poured amazement into his words as though an unseen arbiter was listening and needed persuading of his honesty.

"You owe some very dubious people a lot of money because they are better at cards than you are. I think we should discuss this outside. It's nice weather. As they say, 'the walls have ears.'"

Claude Gaudin looked ill at ease but, before Brent's eyes, he started to transform himself into a man who was a little more certain of the situation; who stood on firmer ground. "Sure, why not?" he said at last. He almost smiled.

Chapter Twenty-one

Stand-off

B rent followed Gaudin down the stairs - he thought it the wiser position to take under the circumstances. As they passed the reception desk, he noticed Sashi furtively glancing up several times - first at Gaudin, who was preoccupied, and then at himself. He winked at her and she had to stifle a convulsive laugh.

Once outside in the late morning sunshine, Gaudin stretched himself as though he were just waking up. The two men gravitated to where their cars were parked. Brent leaned against his Jeep, waiting for Gaudin to begin.

"I spoke out of turn in there," said Gaudin. "I should've kept it together. But you came in accusing me and what was I supposed to do?" He paced about and used his hands expressively. He was not nervous but neither was he ever still.

"I was a little rude," said Brent.

"Too right. If you had just asked to see me we'd have had no problems."

"Like the way Detective Darrow asked to see you yesterday and now you're hiding out here?"

Gaudin looked up sharply, then smiled. "You've got me there. See, Brent, I'm a busy guy and all these questions throw me off my game. The cops ask the same things over and over. Like I told them and I'm telling you now, I didn't see anything."

"Maybe," said Brent. "Let's go over it from my perspective. The means - a kitchen knife. You could have brought it with you...

"Aw, c'mon. There's no way you can believe that. Anyway, that goes for everyone who was there."

"Let me finish and we'll get done here a lot faster. Interrupt and we'll be making a day of it."

"You've got the floor."

Brent heard the disdain in his voice and saw how he acted it out in the way he stood and by how he used his hands. It was no wonder that Gaudin had gambling debts because he telegraphed too many things.

"You had the knife with you. It was fairly easy to conceal it. You spoke to Sheila privately... for some minutes. Others saw you and said that it was an ordinary conversation... some laughing... some serious moments. Now, how would you have worked it? You asked Sheila to meet you privately because you wanted to discuss an important, private matter. Important for both of you. But you could not do that with so many people nearby. Also, you would like her isolated from her husband so that you could make your pitch without a contrary opinion being voiced. You knew that she would make the final decision and, if you could get that decision before her husband interfered, you had a good chance of settling the matter."

Brent stopped leaning against his Jeep and began to pace in slow steps as he continued.

"You're a deal-maker. You believe in your abilities to sweet-talk people around to your way of thinking. That's your job. Knowing that Sheila would be leaving on her trip, you had to act fast. You convinced her to meet you secretly to hear you out. She agreed. You met in a remote section of the vineyard. There's a chink in your alibi, a time when you

194

were out of sight of any other witness and which gives you opportunity to have met with her." He stopped pacing to face Gaudin.

"Had she agreed to the deal you proposed, she would be alive today. She refused. You then killed her. You left the weapon because you could not dispose of it any other way... someone might see you with a bloody knife and you could have been splattered with blood. Your luck held going to and from the meeting and no one saw you. I think you did have some blood on you. You went first to your car to clean up... perhaps with water and a rag or perhaps with other things you'd brought with you because you expected some mess. You were heard going to your car, not this Corvette, a company car. When you looked presentable again, you returned to the group. How am I doing?"

Brent had watched Gaudin as he spoke. First, he had relaxed, then he smiled. After that, he shook his head.

"All wrong. Just wrong. Why was I doing all this crazy stuff? I mean, for what reason would I kill someone I'd known for years and do it in broad daylight?"

"You wanted the Songbird Estate or, at least, some kind of big pay-off from it to get rid of your debts."

"I'll give you that. You obviously know we've been after the property. The rest of it is all wrong. And, I don't think you have evidence for any of it."

"That's right. It's all conjecture," replied Brent. "That's not how it happened."

The two men stared at each other.

"Why'd you go through all that, then?" When Brent did not answer, Gaudin continued, "You said you can prove that I'm the murderer."

"So I did. That was not strictly true but then there isn't much space on the back of a business card. You're one of several conspirators. If you give up the others the police will very likely cut you a deal. My suggestion is this, go and see

Greg Darrow today and tell him everything you know. He's back in the city's homicide department. That's the only way you can get out of this because, as surely as we are standing here, you are going down. The people you're connected with will happily make you the fall guy. You have to move first before they do. Once they give you up, you'll be in prison a long time."

Now it was the turn of Gaudin to pace up and down between the two cars, running his fingers through his hair again as he did so.

"The police will find you," said Brent. "You won't get far in that." Brent pointed to the Corvette. "Is yellow your favourite colour?"

Gaudin did not answer.

"How's Oscar these days?" asked Brent.

"You know him?" asked Gaudin.

"I know of him. Are you good friends?"

"Ah, I wouldn't say that. He's my employer... Look, Oscar is... he kinda plays a mean game. Takes no prisoners. He asks me to do things. Sometimes they make sense, sometimes they don't. I do them because I make good money and he's been fair to me but I'm in a hole at the moment. You got that part right."

"What did he ask you to do?"

"He asked me to go and see Sheila and just see if she was interested in selling. Nothing more. Not push her or anything. Just find out where she stood on selling."

"So you went. No surprises, she wasn't interested. Something else happened, though, didn't it?"

"Yeah. He sent me out here the morning of the tour. A package had come. I was to put the contents in the trunk of my car which I was to leave unlocked when I parked at the vineyard. That's all. I thought it was a pay-off."

"What did the contents look like?"

"It was heavily wrapped in plastic film over one of those plastic envelopes the couriers have. I was pretty sure it was cash."

"How much do you think?"

"Don't know. Maybe fifty or a hundred thousand."

"Yes... It would depend on the denominations. Who was getting paid?"

"Honestly, I have no idea. I don't want to know, either."

"I can see that. What are you going to do?"

"If I go to Darrow, I could wind up dead."

"That's true. That is a matter you're going to have to work out on your own. I came to give you a warning."

"Why?"

"Because you are so obviously placed as a fall guy. One last question. Why the interest in the Songbird Estate?"

"I don't know. I thought Oscar just wanted to add a flagship brand to the existing lines. It's a good fit for the company because we don't have a top-notch Pinot Noir."

"I see. Do you picture Oscar Flint as a murderer?"

"I've heard some stories... I don't know if they're all true... but I wouldn't say he was a murderer. How could he have done it, anyway?"

"I don't know. That's what I have to find out. I think that's all for now. Any ideas what you will do?"

"I need to think about this."

"Don't take too long. Your opportunity is fast disappearing."

"You'll tell Darrow?"

"I should be seeing him some time today. I can't not tell him. At least you have a few hours in which to decide. If you do speak to him before I have to, there's no need to mention my visit. It will look better for you."

"I suppose I should be thankful. Why did I get involved!?" Claude Gaudin slapped his forehead angrily with the palm of his hand.

Brent got into his Jeep and started the engine. Through the open window, he said over the noise,

"I think you need to do the right thing. Whoever is behind this might kill you anyway."

"I know. That's been on my mind all along."

"Take care of yourself," said Brent.

He backed out his vehicle, turned, and then began to move forward. Claude Gaudin watched the ancient Jeep shoot away onto the road, gathering speed, and until it was obscured from view.

Returning to Belton, Brent had called ahead to the Rising Star Realty office to find out if Stefan Badowski was in his office. He was and said he would see Brent.

"How does having two offices work out for you?" asked Brent, once he was installed.

Stefan looked older than his forty-nine years. He seemed tired, as though it were an effort to hold a conversation.

"It's okay. Most of my business is in Belton. It's difficult to work the city market without being there all the time. It pays for itself and some of my local real estate investors like the service we can provide."

"I should think that's important. Do you ever get involved in vineyards and wineries?"

"Sold one years ago."

"The Songbird Estate?"

"No, it was a forty-acre vineyard. The client wanted to retire. It was bought by Dumont Wines... a near neighbour who was looking to expand."

"Convenient for everyone."

"Yeah, you could say that." Stefan smiled and then immediately winced.

"Are you all right?" asked Brent.

"Peptic ulcer. Plays up from time to time. Please excuse me."

"I'm sorry to be bothering you. I'd put off this meeting except there are a couple of important questions I need answered. When you went to the Songbird Estate, was it just for the tour or was there another reason?"

"Another reason, such as?"

"Like a potential real estate deal, for example."

"No."

"Were you interested in the estate?"

"No."

Brent hesitated for a moment before saying,

"Are there any new developments starting in that area?"

"New developments? What have you heard?"

"Do you know, Stefan, that Martha is acting as my agent in a transaction?"

"Oh, is that you? She mentioned something. I hadn't connected the dots."

"Stefan, does a stomach ulcer shut down a person's brain?"

"It's a peptic ulcer and, no, it doesn't. Why are you being smart?"

"Why are you prevaricating?"

"I'm not. I think you'd better leave. Martha won't be handling your deal from now on."

"A lot of people will be going to prison very soon. You'll be one of them. Just think, you haven't earned a commission or divided up the spoils and yet you'll be behind bars. Being there will give you plenty of time to nurse your ulcer and reflect that, had you spoken earlier, you could have escaped a lengthy sentence."

"Are you threatening me?"

"Yes. You're the second person I've threatened today. It's tedious work but obstinate people always persuade themselves that they're right and nothing can happen to them.

But you're wrong this time, you know. The legal fees for your defence will swallow up your company. Besides, who would want to do business with you when your reputation is shot?"

"What charges are we talking about?"

"You tell me. You don't answer my questions yet you expect me to answer yours."

"I think you're fishing. You haven't got anything."

"I will have and very soon at that. Everything is shaping up nicely. I've given you a chance and you're refusing to take it. You're on your own now. Should you change your mind, contact Detective Jennifer Allen."

Brent got up and left quickly. Stefan Badowski did not call him back.

Over a late lunch at a Chinese buffet, Brent reviewed his notes. He found a loose end going by the name of Janet Jones, the store manager at the vineyard. He called the number he had on file but it was no longer in service. He called Greg Darrow instead.

"Hi, Greg. Are you busy?"

"I was until you called. What is it?"

"You're such a friendly soul. I'll visit you in your lair some time today. Janet Jones... what makes you suspicious about her?"

"Too consistently nervous. She took the murder hard but instead of giving way, like many do, she seemed frightened to show her feelings."

"You can read something into that?"

"Yes. She wasn't natural. I don't see how she could be involved directly in any of this stuff we now know about so I think she must have some private matter she wants kept secret."

"Did you know her number has been disconnected?"

"That's news to me," said Greg.

"I'm going to follow up on her. Something else crossed my mind. You know the cell phone tower data dump that was requested, was anything interesting found in that?"

"There were three burner phones in the area. No calls made between them. A few people made or received calls but no one we're interested in."

"A dead end, then?"

"I wouldn't say that. Sheila Babbington made a very short call to an unidentified subscriber at around 2:30. It was traced to the Belton city hall area."

"And this wasn't put in the reports?"

"We didn't know what to make of it. Could be a wrong number. I've got it as a note and it will stay that way unless I can fit it in somewhere."

"I suppose it could have been a wrong number. Where's the region's land titles office?"

"Next to Belton city hall."

"Do you think Sheila knew something?"

"How do I know? It's wasted effort as far as I can see. The person she dialled might just have been walking past the building. It was probably a friend who wants to be anonymous on the phone networks. A lot of people don't like big brother and they're not all crooks." Greg's voice was becoming quite clipped and Brent guessed the call was about to be brought to an end. Sure enough, Greg continued,

"I've got to go to a meeting and I need to put a few things together first. Is that everything?"

"Yes, everything. Thanks, Greg."

Brent made another call.

"Hello, Charles. It's Brent. How are you?"

"Nice to hear from you. I'm doing well... today... so far."

"I'll be brief, I'm looking for Janet Jones. Do you know where I can find her?"

"Um, Janet... she's in the store now. Would you like me to have her call you?"

"No, that's fine. I'll come out right away. If you could mention that I'm on my way... I should be there about two forty-five."

"I'll do that immediately. She doesn't finish until six today."

Chapter Twenty-two

A pleasant time

Driving along the road coming up from the bridge and approaching the vineyard, two things forcibly struck Brent at the same time. The first was the undeniable beauty of the countryside, the road, the sky, the clear, perfect light upon a blessed land. The second was the perceptible cachet, that indescribable certainty of the right placement of everything, including the buildings. The wooden sign that read, 'Songbird Estate', was nothing remarkable by itself but today, it was *the* perfect sign in its proper place with sufficient wear and tear to make it authentic, alluring, and right. The whole vineyard, from panoramic view to intricate detail, appeared to be the product of a mind of immense genius who designed effortlessly and arranged to perfection.

Ordinarily, upon seeing these sights, Brent would have smiled, perhaps hummed or sung, but the other matter was too strongly and intrusively present. A violent death had turned beauty into mockery and dimmed the very light of the sun. The shade under the trees did not coolly beckon but posed a threat as a hiding place for evil. There, it was easy to surmise, the murderer had stood. Behind those bushes, the killer may have watched. Perhaps that man was still there but, if he had really gone, he had impressed some haunting fragment of his violent self upon that pretty part of the world for as long as people would remember it.

Janet Jones was sitting on an iron-framed bench with wooden slats which stood on the veranda next to the shop's entrance. She watched Brent drive up and get out.

The investigator saw a smart but casually dressed woman - a few years younger than himself. When she stood up he estimated she was about five foot six. He was struck by how pale and sad she looked - lacking any animation over his arrival.

"Hello, I'm Brent Umber. Are you Janet?"

"Hi. Yes, I am." She began to move towards the door.

"Why don't we sit outside? It's so nice out here and you looked comfortable."

"Sure."

She turned away from the door and sat down again at one end of the bench. Brent joined her and sat at the other end. They both sat facing an eighty-yard section of road, some of which was overhung with mature maples. Part of the far side of the road was a riotous wall of green growth at the front of which were the floating white blooms of Queen Anne's Lace, mixed with the subtle blue of cornflowers, and a short, buttery-yellow flower to which Brent could not put a name. All of these flowers were weeds but they looked beautiful, flanking the pale tan road. A car went past.

"I'm sorry to be bothering you like this."

"It's your job," replied Janet. She twisted her hands nervously.

"True. There are some aspects of my job that I really like and others that I wish I didn't have to do. It wouldn't surprise me if most people saw me as a nuisance."

Brent waited, in case Janet answered. She did not so he continued, saying,

"Do you like working here?"

"Uh, yes... I mean, I did, but... I don't know now."

"The light has gone out," said Brent. "Do you know why I'm here?"

"Something about the, uh, case?" Her tone was flat.

"Yes. That's a given but there is a more specific reason for my visit. You've spoken to Detective Darrow. He tells me you're hiding something. There's a matter you wish to keep secret. I'm here to find out what it is."

He was staring at the road and the scene before him but he noticed Janet's sudden movement when she looked at him.

"Is that what you don't like - prying into people's lives?"

"No, the opposite. I like talking to people and hearing what they say and, if that's prying, I'm guilty as charged. Aren't you curious about people, at least, some people, some of the time?"

"I guess so... It has nothing to do with Sheila's murder."

"I'm sure it hasn't. Are you coping with the way things are now?"

"Barely. I can't face coming in here anymore."

"That is a shame. I suppose it's harder now with the restaurant closed and no tours around the vineyard. You're left alone with your thoughts."

"It's like everything's changed. Sheila's gone, then Charles has completely withdrawn into himself, and the rest are hurting."

"Yes...Will you stay?"

"Until Charles makes up his mind what he's doing. Once he's decided, either way, I'm going to leave."

"This place is so beautiful. It's difficult to believe that anything bad happened... could ever happen here... What will you do?"

"Move to the city. A friend says there's an opening for me any time I ask for it."

"You'll do the same type of work?"

"No. It's a publishing company specializing in school text-books and children's illustrated stories."

"That is different."

"Yeah... I'll finally put my English degree to full use. I do a few jobs already in that line from time to time, like editing and proofreading."

"What stopped you taking the full-time job before?"

"Sheila was the reason. We are friends... or we were friends. I wanted her to make a success of it here. She used to talk to me all the time. We'd discuss the wine industry. She'd come up with new marketing ideas and we'd go over them. She listened to what I had to say and I appreciated that she valued my input. I enjoyed that part of the job. I knew I wasn't going anywhere if I stayed here... career-wise, I mean. I didn't really mind."

"Sounds like you had a special relationship and she depended upon you. Were you friends outside of work hours?"

Several starlings swooped in and landed. They began their quick, ungainly walk - pecking at things on the ground close to the veranda.

"Not exactly. I think we would have kept in touch if I had left before... before she died. Our relationship was all centred around this place and improving the business."

Brent nodded as he listened. "What was she working on recently?"

"She wanted to organize a winegrowers' association. There are two already but they focus on industry news and latest trends. Sheila was going to set up a co-operative. Her big thing was to try and get price stability and better prices in the wholesale market. You see, some large companies don't pay much for bulk sales of juice. That makes it hard for smaller vineyards to operate successfully on much smaller margins."

"Was the co-op for this region?"

"Yes, but she wanted to take it further. Build alliances with growers in other regions - that type of thing."

A large, blue and black butterfly landed on a bush a few feet away. They both watched as it slowly fanned its wings in the sunshine.

"Did that disturb anyone? Maybe the larger producers didn't take kindly to the idea."

They were now facing each other as they sat on the bench.

"Don't know. It was only in the fledgling stage. A few local vineyards were completely on board. Sheila wanted to talk to others at the conference she was going to and see what they thought."

"Very enterprising of her."

"I suppose so."

"You don't seem enthusiastic about it. Not that it matters now."

"It was my idea."

"Oh. Then it was very enterprising of *you*."

"Yes... I suppose I might as well tell you. We had an argument over it. A bad one. She had said, oh, about three weeks before the conference, that I would be going to it with her. Promised me I could go. Then she changed her mind. She only booked one flight ticket and didn't tell me until a few days before. Said she needed me to run the store. Said she would make it up later."

"Is this what has been upsetting you?"

Janet nodded. "I got really angry and lost it. I have a short fuse sometimes and I had been so looking forward to going. I said to her that I was so furious I could kill her. No, I didn't say it, I shouted it. Ever since I've been thinking I brought a curse down on her."

"It would be easy to think that. It isn't true, though. I've an idea there was a reason why she didn't want you to go."

"What's that?"

"I don't have the picture quite right yet but it seems several people were interested in buying the estate. It's likely she wanted to hear what would be said without you present... because she thought the subject might upset you."

"Could be. Were you meaning Claude Gaudin?"

"That is interesting. How do you know that?"

"He tried to recruit me as an ally. Offered me a commission if I could persuade Sheila to sell up. Also, he started flirting with me."

"I can understand the last part. I've half a mind to flirt with you myself but a few obvious things are hindering me."

"What?" Janet laughed. "You're not serious. Guys are never serious. It appeals to my vanity but it's kinda shallow."

"Perhaps it's a way of overcoming shyness."

"You're not really shy?"

"I am, actually. Despite the façade I put up, I worry about how people I deem important think of me."

"I'm seeing someone."

"Well, that settles that. No flirting allowed."

Janet laughed again.

"How did it go with Gaudin?" asked Brent.

"He is one smooth operator. Too smooth and too sure of himself. I heard him out and said I'd think about what he'd said and talk to Sheila if it seemed appropriate."

"Was this the day of the tour?"

"Yes, in the early afternoon. Later on, Serg told me that Claude had tried to hire *him*. It seemed to me that Claude was employing every trick he could think of to break up the business or get hold of the property."

"That's an interesting way of phrasing it. Did you tell Sheila about this meeting with Gaudin?"

"No. We were barely on speaking terms at the time. I know he'd spoken to her in the past. She never did say what they spoke about. I guess it was about selling."

"Do you remember when he first approached Sheila?"

"Sometime last year was the first time. October, I think. Then he dropped in unannounced at the beginning of May.

Then he was here again late May to go on the tour. It was odd, him doing that. All in all, he's visited here about six or seven times as far as I know. I can't see why he would suddenly want to go on the tour when he's seen everything already."

"Do you think he could have murdered Sheila?"

"Murdered her!? Are you serious?"

"Very serious. Some of his actions have been somewhat suspicious. I have to clear up the matter one way or another. I take it the idea has never occurred to you?"

"No, it has, actually. It is often quiet in the store... like now, for instance. Sometimes, I sit here and try to think who could be the murderer. I don't see him as a suspect."

"Then, who did you see in the role?"

"I shouldn't be saying anything about that. I'd hate to point the finger at an innocent person."

"Quite right, too. The way I like to work, myself, is to prove everyone's innocence. I test alibis and find out as much as I can but in the end, it is evidence that is really needed."

"I suppose you do suspect someone. Is it Claude, then?"

"I don't know, yet. There are a couple of others who are strong candidates."

"Like Stan Forbes?"

"He would be one of them. How did he seem to you?"

"He asked some strange questions when he was in the store. Asked if I liked my job." Janet became more animated as she recalled the event. "The weird thing was that he seemed to expect me to understand all about the wine-making process. I mean, I know some of it, but he was talking about soils and fermentation temperatures... things like that. I don't know if he was showing off or what."

"Did he buy anything?"

"He asked about the Pinot but we've been sold out for months. I told him he could put his name down for this year's harvest but he wasn't interested. Oh yes, that reminds me. You're buying a case, aren't you? I saw it in the register."

"Well spotted. Charles gave me a sample of it and I couldn't resist."

She gazed at him before saying, "You're a strange guy. You drive an old Jeep, work as a private eye, and yet you're buying a case of very expensive wine. You've made me curious."

"You're seeing someone, remember?"

"Very funny but I'm not letting you off the hook. Come on, tell me." Janet gently pushed his arm.

"Okay. I'm financially sound. I don't need to work but I'd go crazy if I didn't. There are a number of reasons why I do this particular kind of work but it would take too long to tell you right now. What I will say is that the work is challenging and rewarding on several levels."

"Oh, mystery man. Why a PI and not the police? How does that work anyway?"

"The police would be too restrictive for me. They brought me in because I happened to solve a difficult problem for someone quite high up in the force and then they thought I might be able to help with the case."

"Have you helped them?"

"I'm supposed to be questioning *you*. I think I've helped a little bit."

A car slowed and turned in at the vineyard's entrance.

"A customer," said Janet. She sounded disappointed.

"I'd better be going," said Brent. "I'll check in with Charles before I leave." They both stood up. "Thanks for talking with me. A question. If you were single and I asked you out to have dinner with me, would you go?"

Janet smiled. "I think I would."

"Then let me know if you are ever free."

"You've cheered me up so much I might just do that."

Chapter Twenty-three

A surprising turn of events

"What you got, Brent? Anything new?" Damian was leaning over the wall of Brent's cubicle at about five-thirty.

"Lots of small things that might add up to something. But I think you have news. You look like the cat that got the cream."

"Oh, ye-ah. Seeing as uncle Greg ain't holding court at five anymore, I'll tell you. Stuart Richards has a serious drug problem. Snort, shoot, smoke - he does it all - only in binges. What I heard is that people are surprised to hear he's still alive."

"He certainly looked very unhealthy when I saw him," said Brent. "Are you sure about this because he's intelligent, albeit in a peculiar way? If the conversation pertains to him then he knows exactly what's going on. I didn't see him as someone destroying his mind."

"You didn't let me finish. I was gonna say, he takes drugs but he ain't addicted. He's like one of those guys who likes experimenting to increase their awareness. He takes different drugs to enhance his mood or to give himself what he would consider profound insight. That's what he does."

"He has it under control, then? You said serious."

"Richards takes big hits of whatever it is he's doing. It's like he's conditioned himself to drug abuse."

"Where does he get the money for this?"

"You would think it was mama but it's not. He gets it for free."

"Free? You've got me there. I can't see how that can happen."

Damian had a slow smile spreading across his face. He was clearly enjoying the situation.

"It was really hard to get this information... I had to call in a favour. Stuart Richards is invested in drug distribution. He supplies a number of wealthy individuals with what they need to make them happy. Richards doesn't handle the stuff but he takes the orders and the goods are delivered and are paid for directly. He takes his percentage in product instead of cash."

"Talk about different," Brent shook his head. "Who's the supplier or is there more than one?"

"One from Newhampton. Supposed to be an outfit run by a guy called Toussaint."

"Well, well. What a small world it is."

"You know him?"

"Yes. We're not on friendly terms and, should we ever meet, something will have gone seriously wrong."

"Whatever. That's the scoop on Stuart Richards. Besides that, he has some money of his own and doesn't need to work. Lives in his mother's mansion which is close to city hall."

"Hmm, that could tie in with something." Brent made a note in his ring binder. "What about Arlene?"

"Not much yet. She goes swimming twice a week and sees a lot of seniors her own age. Has a badminton net set up in her back garden and a few friends come over for a game."

"So she's not incapacitated in any sense?" asked Brent.

"No, not at all. She's very active. I got this from her gardener. He said she has a treadmill and a rowing machine in the house that she uses daily."

"Why the pretence of an invalid? When I saw them they were trying for, 'doting son attends to ailing mother'. What is it with these people?"

"They're weird *and* they look suspicious. I don't know about a connection to the case. I'll keep working at it to see if I can get more."

Ten minutes after Damian had gone, Jennifer arrived at Brent's workstation. She wheeled a swivel chair over to sit on. She looked very relaxed.

"So, Brent. What have you been up to today?"

"You've got something, haven't you? Jen, you must never play poker. Today, I saw Janet Jones. Greg was fussing about her hiding something. Turns out she had argued with Sheila just days before she was killed. Sheila was supposed to have taken Janet to a conference with her and then reneged on it. I don't know why she did but I suspect some private matter was to be discussed at the conference and she didn't want Janet present. That's only a guess on my part. When the argument hits fever pitch, Janet says to Sheila, 'I could kill you.' They barely talk to each other for a couple of days. Then Sheila is murdered. Janet's conscience is stricken and she feels like she called down Sheila's death upon her in some way."

"That sounds only natural. You say these kinds of words in an argument," said Jennifer, "but you don't mean them. She really got caught out on that one. What else?"

"I saw Stefan Badowski, he of the solid gold alibi. Turns out he's not telling us everything. I'm convinced he was at the vineyard with an ulterior motive but I couldn't get him to open up despite my dire warnings of what could happen to him. I'm certain Martha Badowski is not involved and that stubborn Stefan is flying solo on this one. I think he knows more about the Songbird Estate than we do... You blinked. You've found out what it's all about."

Jennifer was smiling. "This is so weird and yet it makes so much sense. There's follow-up work to be done but it's a big move forward." Jennifer settled herself in her chair. "Okay. So, everyone is interested in the winery and we haven't known why. There's a hydro-electric project to be built in a gorge on the Sand River."

"I think I've heard of that. Go on."

"Well, it's been through all kinds of environmental assessments and, while it was still being considered, the project developers requested an amendment to raise the maximum water level behind the dam by three feet. They all went back at it. There were meetings, a delay, and then the approval came through in..."

"In May! Sorry for interrupting."

"Yes, in May. The river that flows past the Songbird is a tributary of the Sand. It's the only major area that will be affected by the rise in the water level. A few other properties will be adversely affected but, basically, a large loop in the river gets submerged and..."

"Oh, go on, say it," said Brent. "Don't play with me."

"The lower part of the Songbird Estate will disappear. Compensation for all the other properties is minimal because the affected land isn't used for anything but the payout for the Songbird is huge because of the loss of future earnings. There's a complicated compensation formula but, if I got it right, the owner of the estate gets fourteen million for loss of just over forty acres and gets to keep the buildings and the valuable upper section."

"You are fantastic. This explains so much. Now, was it Clive Richards who worked out the formula for the compensation?"

"How did you know that, Brent?"

"A lucky guess but it makes perfect sense. You have done brilliant things today."

Momentarily, Jennifer had a broad grin on her face. It was followed by a serious expression.

"Have you told me *everything* you've done today?"

"Not exactly," admitted Brent. "I was writing it up when you dropped by. That will be the clean version for Commander Baker to read at his leisure. The dirty version is, I went to see Claude Gaudin."

"Oh, did you?" Jennifer looked annoyed.

"You left me on my own, without guidance, so I thought it would be a good idea if I had a chat with him. I found him in a Bartlett's warehouse in Newhampton. Our meeting started with angry words but it ended up with me urging him to go to Greg Darrow with his story and we parted on relatively good terms."

"What did you say to him?"

"I suggested that he was being set up as the fall guy for the murder and he agreed it might be the case. He also thinks he will be killed if he squeals."

"Fall guy? I don't understand."

"Somebody is playing a game. I'm not sure who it is exactly. Could be Bartlett's, the Richards, or even Stan Forbes. And, as always, it seems there might be another player in the game. Along with this star-studded cast, Stefan Badowski also plays a part as well as Gaudin. At present, I don't see how they're all interconnected.

"Oscar Flint of Bartlett's sent a sealed package to Gaudin, instructing him to leave it in his unlocked car at the vineyard. Someone was to pick it up and, presumably, that someone was the cyclist.

"My guess is that the cyclist arrived in the area in his own vehicle, took out the bike, and rode around for a while. When the coast was clear, he retrieved the package from Gaudin's car. That was the payment for his services. The cyclist, now a commissioned assassin, went into hiding somewhere until

Sheila arrived at the prearranged spot. When she was there, the cyclist came out from cover, killed her, and then took off.

"The big question is: who got Sheila to go to the quiet part of the vineyard? Was it Oscar Flint through his proxy, Claude Gaudin? Or Stan Forbes, who probably needs psychiatric help? Then there are our dear friends the Richards, who appear to have stepped out of a psychological horror movie. There had to be an inducement or a compelling reason for Sheila to go. If we knew *why* she went to the rendezvous we would almost certainly know who conspired against her.

"The irritating part of this is that another party could easily be involved. Someone with understanding that the Songbird Estate would lose half its acreage but would retain the most valuable part with the Pinot Noir because it would remain above water. Buy it at five million, lose approximately two million in value and gain fourteen million in compensation. That amounts to a net profit of twelve million."

Jennifer whistled.

"The party best placed for the subterfuge," continued Brent, "is the Richards combine with Clive as the point man. The best placed from the wine industry perspective is Bartlett's. The best placed because of incipient insanity is Stan Forbes. All are wealthy, all stand to make easy money from the deal, and all present themselves with enough motivation and lack of ordinary humanity to fit into the role of the employer of an assassin.

"Now here is the part that remains obscure to me. What if they were all present for the same reason and were in it together? Some of them are strange enough to go on a vineyard and murder tour for the fun of it. What do you make of all that, O Jennifer, my leader?"

"This is the most interesting case I have ever worked. And, you know, I don't think we would have broken it unless you had been here. Certainly not as quickly without you. To answer, we need to find when everybody could have known about the change to the water level. It looks to me as though either Clive Richards or he and another person in the know, has been selling information."

"Good point. We'll probably find it was an employee in a clerical position who sold the information about the approvals to Forbes and Bartlett's. The Richards appear to have their own conduit of information."

"We can look into that. What are you doing now?"

"Finishing off reports. That, and waiting for Greg Darrow to call about Gaudin. I started two hares today and both seem to have got away from me."

Chapter Twenty-four

A new friend, an old enemy

J ust before eight, Brent was in Belton receiving a call from Greg Darrow in the Homicide Department in Newhampton.

"I thought you were coming into the office," said Greg.

"I had meant to but I got busy with a few matters. What's up?"

"Gaudin walked into my office looking for me. He then proceeded to tell me a long story about a package in his car and a payoff to an unknown person. Gave all the background information that led up to it. We took down a nice statement from him which he signed."

"That's excellent!"

"I note your enthusiasm. The funny thing is this, and correct me if I'm wrong, the entire time he was speaking, right from the moment he arrived, I got the distinct impression that someone had urged him to come in."

"That would have been me."

"Right, right, that's what I thought. Aside from the serious issue I have with you messing with a potential murder suspect, why did you send him to me?"

"I thought you might be lonely. Also, you're more conveniently placed if Gaudin felt he needed to explain matters. It was a shorter distance for him to travel. Just so you know, I tried sending Stefan Badowski to Jennifer. That was to equal things up. I don't like playing favourites."

"Badowski, eh? Look, I have to warn you, Brent, your actions could be considered as interference. I know you're helping but you should have told me first."

"My humble apologies. I should have but I thought it better not to. If he had been a no-show I'd have told you what he said."

"I know you would. Don't get me wrong. I'm not doubting your motives. It's your execution. Just say it went wrong with Gaudin and his testimony can't be used in court because something you had done messed it up. You'd be exposed to a charge for your own actions. Doesn't matter that you've been hired and are working on the case. You see where I'm going with this?"

"I do. I understand the setup. If anything goes wrong I'll be held responsible for anything I do."

"As long as we're clear. You coming over? There are some interesting things you should look at."

"I'm on my way. Can I bring anything in for you?"

"Ah, yes, that would be good. A large black coffee no sugar. It's going to be a long night for me."

Before Brent left the Belton office, Andy Fowler called. Stan Forbes had been followed to the Rising Star Realty offices. It was not known who he had met there but he had stayed for about an hour before leaving with a large envelope. Next, he had gone to the law offices of Agnew, Persaud, and Bishop, carrying the envelope with him. He was there for twenty minutes and left without the first envelope but with a different one under his arm.

Forbes had then gone to the main Belton branch of Fidelity Domestic Bank with the second envelope. From there he returned home. At seven, he had gone to a Japanese restaurant, meeting there a group of five people consisting of three women and two men of a similar age to Forbes. They were still there, reported Andy, making a convivial night of it.

Greg met Brent in the vestibule of the Newhampton police headquarters. It was an older building, in service from the nineteen-sixties, with some modernization and refurbishment from the nineties. The cramped, angular modernity of the earlier era seemed anxious to throw off the now dated and worn overlay of the later one. Stone, steel, and glass waited for grey carpets, dull wallpaper, and awkwardly sized offices to be replaced by fitting renovations that resulted in something more useful and dignified.

The brass plate surround of the elevator buttons had a soft glow from daily polishing. Greg pressed the button. Both elevators were in use. Brent held a small tray with coffees and some food - sandwiches, snacks, and a couple of doughnuts. As he stood, thinking how to phrase a policeman and doughnut joke for Greg's enjoyment, a third man joined them.

"Hello, Greg," said the big, burly man.

"Ian. They've got you working late, too?"

"Yeah. Two perps held up a loan office around six. Professional and they got away clean with about fifty thousand. What are you up to?"

"Sheila Babbington case. There've been developments and we've gotta chase down all the leads."

"Oh," said Ian Bennett who glanced at Brent. He looked at him again.

"Yes, you know me, Mr Bennett. How's the family."

"Brent Umber. Well, well, well. Have you been nailed at last?"

"Ah, not yet."

"What's *he* doing here?" Bennett addressed this question to Greg while jerking his thumb towards Brent. The elevator arrived.

"He's helping with the investigation." The three men stood aside to allow the occupant to leave the elevator before they boarded it.

Once they were inside, Greg pressed buttons for two floors, and Bennett asked,

"Witness or suspect?" He was staring hard at Brent, who was cringing inwardly.

"I don't know what's between you two," said Greg, "but Mr Umber is on the investigation team."

"On the team?" asked Bennett with an incredulous lilt in his voice. "Like, he's investigating a murder?"

"That's right. Takes some getting used to."

Bennett was silent, scowling. The elevator came to the third floor. He made no move, neither did Greg. Brent deduced it was Bennett's floor. He pressed the 'open door' button and held it.

"What is it you wish to say?" asked Brent.

"That's enough from you," said Bennett. He then spoke to Greg while pointing at Brent. "Don't trust this guy. I'd have put him away a dozen times but he's too slippery. Whoever brought him in must be some kind of stupid."

"Ian," said Greg, "thanks for the warning. I've got a lot of work to do tonight."

"Yeah, sure. Don't we all."

Bennett left the elevator, his bulk filling the opening. Brent allowed the doors to shut. The two men travelled on in silence.

Chapter Twenty-five

Two heads are better than one

Greg Darrow's desk was ancient and heavy. Its old and immovable appearance had probably prevented it from ever being shifted by renovators and re-organizers to another part of the office. Situated by a window, which let in the morning light but not the heat and glare of the afternoon sun, Greg's chair was against an interior wall. Its position would give him a panoramic inside view of all other desks and an exterior view over a small park with mature trees and a cityscape of good proportions with no real obstruction by any single building. At that moment, the sun had set and the lights from adjacent office buildings and the street in front of the park dominated the scene outside.

Spread across Greg's desk were numerous open file folders and printouts with details and photographs of persons who had come into close contact with the police over the years.

As they approached, Brent asked,

"Where shall I put these?" He held out the coffees.

"Oh, yes. Thanks. Over there will do. Which one's mine?"

"On your left."

"Just what I need."

"Don't you have coffee in your department?"

"Ha. We do. There was supposed to be a coffee fund but some people forgot to contribute on a regular basis so we were always running out. At the moment, we're trying a bring-your-own-pods deal and I used my last one earlier. Going to Belton has thrown my routine for a loop."

"Free coffee in Belton," said Brent. "Though it tastes odd. I thought it might be the water. There's a lot of chlorine in it."

"I noticed that. Could affect the flavour. Anyhow, let's get down to business."

"Um, before we do I'd like to clear the air," said Brent.

"You mean Bennett?"

"Yes. You must be wondering what went on there. And I'm wondering how you'll react when I tell you."

"Try me," replied Greg. He sipped his coffee. "Take a seat."

"So, when I was younger, I got into a few adventures of which I am not particularly proud. Like many people, I have a past but I'm not going over that. As you realize, Ian Bennett and I have met before. The reason why Bennett thinks I'm a criminal is essentially guilt by association. A number of my friends, particularly those of former years, have had rest periods at the government's expense. Bennett believes that I committed several robberies, jewel robberies by the way, that he was investigating. We had discussions over each one. I had alibis and Bennett couldn't break them. I believe the robberies remain unsolved to this day."

Brent visibly relaxed in his chair.

"As a consequence of this, Bennett seems to have acquired the mental habit of connecting any unsolved robbery case with yours truly. I may be overstating Bennett's position slightly but that is the gist of the matter."

"I see," said Greg slowly. "I looked you up... just to see if you had a record. I didn't find anything, although one person, not

Bennett, told me that your name used to be connected with quite a few incidents. Some of them quite daring, if I may say."

"Oh, um... what conclusion have you arrived at?"

"I look at it like this. I'm in Homicide, Bennett's in Robbery. All the stories are years old, and we've got a lot of work to do. Besides, although Bennett is a good detective, good at his job anyway, his personality is... I'll put it this way, if I bump into him in the corridor about once a month, that's good enough for me."

"I'm relieved to hear this. I was concerned you would take it to heart about this cloud over my past."

"You know what you did or didn't do and I have no need to be told. There is one thing I *would* like to know, where did you get this coffee from? It's really good."

An hour later, when two desks had been littered with documents as the investigators sifted through the information, the two men began to approach something like a consensus of opinion.

"You've shown me about thirty files and I'm beginning to be bewildered," said Brent.

"Thirty-three where an ordinary, household knife was used. Twenty-four of them are closed. In five of them, the knife was left at the scene of the crime. Six cases have the murderer on a bicycle. Two cases have a knife left behind *and* a bicycle was the means of approach and escape but, in one, the murderer was convicted. The other is open and is five months old. This one is a potential only, with no video, so we're guessing."

"Then why have you shown me all the closed ones?"

"To find a pattern." Greg rubbed his forehead with the tips of his fingers as he explained matters. It was proving to be a habit of his. "We have to look at all the cases we can. The cyclist-murderer may belong to a gang where they've decided that's how they do it. I looked at motorcycle, moped, and scooter attacks but all of those were quite different in nature. Not that there were very many of them. One of the guys who was on a moped got a life sentence. He could have been the killer except he was behind bars at the time."

"I got that. He left the knife in the wound, too. Right age, right height but that was five years ago."

"Hey, he could be the older brother. You're looking for a murderer. I'm looking for a template that possibly fits across *several* murders or assaults."

"I apologize for having a block of wood for a head," said Brent. "Did you have time to look at assaults?"

"I did, as it happens. Eliminating everything but the most similar incidents, I found four that made sense to me. In one assault, the perpetrator didn't even get off the bike and just slashed at the victim before taking off. That was a year ago. I'm doubtful about that one.

"The next took place in August last year. The young man got off his bike and tried to stab the victim who happened to be a small-time drug dealer known to the police. The victim pulled a pistol and shot at his attacker and, with seven shots fired, managed to miss his target as he fled the scene on his bike. The case didn't go anywhere as the victim was uncooperative.

"The third took place in September. The cyclist stabbed and slashed at a man walking along the street around seven p.m. The man ran away, shouting for help. He kept running and didn't wait for the police. Several witnesses saw it happen and one of them called in the emergency services. The victim never reported the matter afterwards and, although wounded, has kept quiet about it. I suspect it was a situation where the victim was already in trouble with the police and didn't want to be investigated.

"The fourth assault took place in December. Hooded assailant on a bike rides quickly towards a gang member selling drugs on a street corner. Jumps off and stabs him in the stomach with a kitchen knife before cycling away. The victim survived but declined to say very much. The officer in charge of the case wrote a note to say she was sure the victim knew his attacker but wouldn't say who it was."

"Greg, I'm sure you've noticed that there seems to be a maturing process in the nature of these assaults. Do you think it's the same person? By the way, I'm truly impressed with your encyclopaedic mind."

Greg smiled. "I have a near-photographic memory. It's a possibility that the same person was involved in all the assaults. The evidence is too sketchy to say anything with certainty."

"That murderer who left the knife behind, the open case, that occurred when? January?"

"Early February. The victim was a woman, aged twenty-six, the sister of a highly placed gang member. She was stabbed five times."

"You're the expert. Does this constitute a pattern in your opinion?" asked Brent.

"Oh, yes. At least, I feel we have a starting point."

"What I don't understand is the use of a knife. Wouldn't a pistol be preferable to an assassin?"

"Normally, it is. Some countries have severe problems with knife-related crimes. In this country, one would typically associate the use of a knife with youth crime although there are very many exceptions to that statement. What you said when we first met, still holds true. The knife had been prepared as a form of ritual. I don't know what the basis for the ritual might be." Greg rubbed his forehead again.

"I have a hazy picture of a young man," said Brent, "not particularly intelligent, but possessing a degree of cunning and inventiveness. He believes himself to be very clever and feels secure in his mind that no one will ever catch up with him."

"You don't happen to know his name, do you?"

"Wish I did. From what you said, it's possible three people might know him."

"Two. The one who shot at the cyclist died in a car accident. What we do have as a common thread is that this person on a bike is some kind of enforcer for a gang who deals in drugs."

"He wouldn't be working for a guy named Toussaint?"

"Him? No, I doubt it. All these incidents occurred downtown or in the East District. Toussaint is in the North and everything between there and Belton."

"Now, I'm truly impressed."

"I shouldn't tell you this but we have a map of the city divided up by gang activities. It's updated continuously. Here, I'll show it to you."

Brent followed Greg to a computer.

"Why is it kept secret?"

"Imagine this in a newspaper, 'Police know where the gangs are but are powerless to do anything.' No one seems to realize how hard it is to get evidence. A sting operation or an infiltration can take months to set up and then not come to anything. It takes time and a good deal of work to get anything to stick and the big players rarely get caught. There it is. What do you think?"

"Impressive... So many? There are about forty-five different gangs!"

"There are four main outfits. Most of the others are affiliates... the pink shades are associated with the deep red, the pale blues with the dark blue, and so on. There are only a few independent operators. There's Toussaint. Only two affiliates and see, he's the smallest of the four main gangs."

"I see. Where did the assaults and the one murder happen?"

"Around here and, as you can see, that's border territory between three different factions. Can't tell which of them might be behind them."

"What about a freelancer? The cyclist, I mean."

"Possible."

"Let's say, for a few thousand, our cyclist says he will harm or kill someone. Who would employ him?"

"Most of these would do their own dirty work. We'd need to talk to someone on the Gang Task Force who could explain the current situation."

"How about this. The cyclist has three or four failed attempts at killing men but two successes at killing women. Despite his failures, this person persists in a career of using a knife and riding a bike. Slowly, his gruesome mode of operation improves. But why would he have continued with something that hadn't seemed to be working very well?"

"Beats me," said Greg."

"Wait... I have it. I think I have it. Our man loves riding a bike. He takes the time to perfect a technique employing a bike and he uses a knife because he wants to see the victim's face. This means he is addicted to the idea of killing. He randomly selects people to attack and no one is employing him to do so at this stage. He chooses targets that could cause a fuss among the gangs and stir them up to a war so that then he will get plenty of paying business by being employed by one side or another for retaliatory reasons. He chooses a border section between factions and attacks low-level dealers."

Brent sat forward in his chair.

"Then, he finally kills someone and enjoys it. This marks a change in the nature of his actions. He now begins to perfect his technique and maybe develop a trademark method to gain for himself renown and a dubious kind of respect in his very shady world."

"Brent, this is not a movie. It doesn't work like that. You're building up a picture on conjecture alone."

"That's what I do."

"Oh. I suppose it is. I haven't got used to your style yet. I mean, I put together scenarios but you seem to live in them." He looked up at Brent. "Then answer me this, how has he usually killed his targets?"

"In the most efficient ways - with a sniper rifle or a pistol with a silencer."

"We've had a couple of unsolved cases in the last year where a silencer was used. I'll pull them up. There was another where a garotte was the murder weapon. I worked on that one."

"That sounds grim."

"Let me tell you, Brent, they're all grim."

The detective and the investigator worked through three files. These led to another eleven including a shoot-out between rival gang members in which there were two deaths and three wounded - one of them an innocent bystander. By two-thirty, they had a picture of a man, as yet unnamed, with at least five murders to his credit and another two possibles besides Sheila Babbington. There was nothing else they could think to look at.

"I think we're done here," said Greg.

"We haven't considered how he got out to the vineyard. In everything we looked through, there's no mention of a vehicle. The bike attacks form one category; the rest seem to have him on foot."

"So, he doesn't drive. Maybe he rented a vehicle."

"Yes. A bike is fairly bulky... you have to put it on a rack... unless the vehicle is big enough to put it inside, like a van."

"I suppose so. Why go to all that trouble? It doesn't make sense."

"Let's say he had to have the bike because it was..."

"What?"

"I was hoping you'd fill in the blank."

"I'm too tired to think of anything." Greg followed this up with a yawn.

"Yes, me, too." Brent put his head right back and stared at the ceiling. Then, slowly, he came back to a normal sitting position. He searched among a stack of files and retrieved the Babbington case from the bottom. He looked through, found what he was looking for, and then turned the page round for Greg to see. Pointing at a name, he said, "That's how he got there and that's the reason why he took the bike. Not a great decision on his part but it makes sense from his point of view. It also gets our unknown assailant close to Sheila without her being alarmed."

Greg took the page and stared at it for about a minute. "Couldn't you have spotted this five hours ago? Do you know what it's like waking up a judge in the middle of the night to get a warrant?"

"Really? You're going to get it tonight?"

"No, just kidding you. It can wait until tomorrow. I'd need back up and I'm sorry, Brent, but you don't count. Also, I'd want Jennifer and Damian present when we make the search and the arrest."

Chapter Twenty-six

Time for action

At 8:00 a.m. Friday, Luke Valinho was arrested by Jennifer Allen and Greg Darrow. Valinho was handcuffed and escorted from the Now Courier Company's depot to a waiting car, protesting his innocence all the while by proclaiming a lack of knowledge about anything and everything. Once he was inside the back of the car, he became silent. He looked morose - a staring, bleak face, looking out of the window but seeing nothing. He had been arrested because Brent had suggested that Valinho, the driver of the courier van, had transported the killer.

Concurrent with the apprehension of Valinho, two uniformed officers, accompanied by Damian Field, were searching the driver's apartment. Among other things, a laptop and a gaming computer rig were seized for removal to police headquarters.

Outside the apartment block in his old Jeep, Brent was annoyed at being left out of all these activities because of the cautious nature of the three detectives. He had been expressly forbidden to go to the courier company. As a poor second, he had gone to Valinho's apartment. All three officers there were deaf to his requests for admittance so that he could take a brief look inside. While he could agree with their prudence, he strongly disagreed with the patronizing attitude he thought they displayed towards him.

Brent vividly remembered saying he would be an auxiliary of the team - would not presume to cause offence in any way. Now, when the team had requested he stay out of critical police processes, Brent felt aggrieved and disappointed. He was irritable, mildly irritable, but enough that he could barely sit still in his seat. Also, they seemed to be taking a long time in Valinho's apartment and he did not know what to do with himself while he waited.

After twenty minutes, Brent thought he might be better employed if he reviewed some files. He reached over to the back seat to grab his bag and, as he was doing so, he noticed a man on a bike coming to a stop at the apartment building entrance. Not thinking much of such a frequent summer sight, he opened his ring binder.

Turning over a few pages, a thought came to mind. He looked up but the man had disappeared. Brent got out of his Jeep and walked over to where half a dozen bicycles were locked into a rack. In the middle was an expensive-looking bike. The front wheel had been removed and two locks, one u-lock and a chain lock were securing it and the bike frame to the rack. The frame was metallic purple with yellow lettering - close to the colouring in Kevin Finch's drawing.

Brent crouched to examine the machine. The tires were thick and the heavy tread was slightly worn. There were scratches on the paintwork but nothing significant. The bicycle was in good working condition and looked to have been cleaned recently. He got out his phone and took a few photographs. When he had finished, he walked into the apartment block to find Damian.

He found himself in a small vestibule, the locked inner door of which led into the foyer where the elevators and a staircase were located. As he was looking through the long rows of buttons for the right intercom to press for Valinho's apartment, someone came hurrying through the inner door behind him. Brent quickly turned to catch the handle to enter before the door closed. Now he need not buzz the detectives in the apartment. As he pulled the door back, he caught a glimpse of the person who had just exited. It was the cyclist. It took Brent a second to react. Then he went after him.

"Hey, stop!" shouted Brent, from the front door, as soon as he saw the man beginning to unlock the purple bike. They looked at each other making eye contact. Immediately, the man reached behind him and, from under his shirt, pulled out an automatic pistol. Brent ducked down and back inside as the man fired. He was trapped and locked in the vestibule. A bullet shattered glass in the front door and another punched a hole in the glass wall behind him. He pressed as many buttons as he could until a third bullet struck the panel just above his head. Brent dived to the floor. Two more chance shots followed. They ricocheted off the wall and floor to smash more glass.

The inner door opened seconds later. Brent scrabbled through as quickly as he could, blessing the individual who had blithely let in an unknown visitor. The noise of shooting and breaking glass stopped. Sounds of distant traffic returned.

He waited for nearly a minute, then, with a heavily pounding heart, propped the inner door open and cautiously moved forward to peer into the street outside. The man had gone but the bike remained. A few people, curiosity-driven because of the gunshots, were beginning to venture forth from cars and the houses opposite the apartment building. Brent returned inside to survey the damage that had been wrought.

The elevator doors opened. Damian and the two city police officers had arrived.

"Hey, Brent... Whoa! Look what happened here. You okay?"

"Yes, I'm fine, I think. It was him. The cyclist," said Brent. "He got away."

"Really? Did you return fire?"

"I never carry a weapon," said Brent. "For once, I wish I did."

"Okay. Stand still a moment. You've got glass in your hair. Shut your eyes and shake your head."

"Have I?"

Brent did as he was told. When he had finished brushing his hair and picking a few shards off his shirt, he discovered his hands were shaking.

It took nearly an hour for the uniformed officer, named Justin Schlegel, to take down Brent's statement. The reason it took so long was the over-excited Brent kept asking Damian what he had found in the apartment.

Luke Valinho's home, a two-bedroom unit, was not particularly tidy or clean. Valinho's few possessions and basic furniture were of the run of the mill kind, ordinary and without mystery. It was hoped the computers would yield better results. The second bedroom had little more than a double bed, a nightstand, and a built-in wardrobe. Someone had used it recently, the bed was unmade, and he had left a few clothes in the closet. Nothing else remained to help identify the occupant.

Several other officers arrived because of the shooting. They spent most of their time outside, measuring distances, making chalk marks on the ground, and interviewing other residents and potential witnesses.

"You didn't see him, then?" asked Brent as he, Damian, and officer Justin Schlegel sat in Valinho's living room.

"We had the door shut," replied Damian.

"I'm sure he came up here, heard voices he didn't recognize, and then went downstairs again."

"Yeah... but we don't know for certain... not until the prints and DNA are analysed."

"You've got to leave the bike where it is. I know he'll come back for it."

"So you said. He loves his bike. But I have no jurisdiction here. Maybe Greg hasn't, either. You'll have to tell it to the officer in charge."

"Do you know who that would be?" Brent put the question to officer Schlegel.

"Probably Lieutenant Rio. He should be here soon. There's something I'm not understanding here. How did you know this man was the one you're looking for?"

"I didn't," answered Brent. I had no thought of seeing him and no real description of what he looks like. It was the colour of the bike. It looked a shiny purple with a yellow flash - they proved to be letters up close. It reminded me of Kevin's drawing. He's a five-year-old who drew a crayon picture of a bike he may have seen on the day Sheila Babbington was murdered. He used the same colours. I thought I'd take a closer look. Then, when the guy comes running out and I saw his face, I just knew it was him."

"Well," said Schlegel, "even if the perpetrator isn't the same guy, he's wanted for attempted murder now. He's on the CCTV so we've got a view of his face."

"Should be easy to get his ID from Valinho," said Damian. "About now, Jen should be asking him for his roommate's name."

"Justin, do you need any more?" asked Brent. "I've got a whole lot I need to do."

"No, I don't think so... didn't you want to wait for Rio? Your idea might work."

"Yes, I'll wait for him but I need some fresh air and to think quietly. As soon as I've seen him I've got to go."

Lieutenant Rio proved to be a surly, older man whose even, raspy voice and dismissive manner suggested he had pretty much seen it all. He listened to Brent and shook his head with something like a sneer on his face. He gave much the same response to Damian. Only after Greg Darrow asked him by phone to stake out the bike, in case the shooter returned, did he begin to see any merit in the suggestion. He said he would try it for today and tonight but wasn't going to tie up three or four officers any longer than that.

Valinho was not talking and had no record. He was adhering to a code of silence common among people who sympathize with gangs. The basis of this position is that if they tell what they know they will wind up dead.

"I'm glad to see you're still with us," said Greg, seated behind his desk, as Brent walked towards him in the homicide department. Jennifer Allen was with Detective Darrow. The office was active now with almost every workstation occupied by someone hard at work.

"I'm glad to be here. Hi, Jen. Do you see what can happen when you're not looking out for me?"

"You had a very lucky escape. Are you okay?"

"Yes, except all my teenage notions of being a full-fledged action hero are finally laid to rest."

"He didn't finish you off," said Greg, "because he thought you were a police officer. That would draw a lot of heat if he had killed you and he had enough sense just to make you keep your head down while he made a run for it."

"Seriously? I thought he was just a lousy shot. I don't think I can agree with that. He only missed me by two inches. I thought he ran because I might start shooting back."

"Maybe," said Greg, who clearly liked his theory better. "Rio's a pain," he added, by way of changing the subject. "That bike's worth about two grand new. I'm with you. The guy's a city boy and probably wants his bike back."

"They left it covered in fingerprint powder," said Brent. "I had to clean it up. The guy could spot it from twenty feet and they'd miss him if he turned around and walked away. Also, I had to go to a hardware store to buy a bolt cutter and another chain lock. I removed the existing chain lock and replaced it with a new one. It's a simple delaying tactic that might prove useful. Jen, how do I submit receipts for reimbursement?"

"You have to fill in a form and I get my supervisor to approve it," she replied.

"I see. Here are the keys for the lock. The bolt cutter is in my car."

No one seemed anxious to go anywhere, so Brent found a spare chair and sat down.

"I can't stay long. What are we waiting for?" asked Brent.

"Print analysis and a name. Guy's got to have a record," said Greg.

"Then what do we do?"

"We go find him. I want to get him before Rio does," said Greg. "I hate being number two to Rio. He's so slow."

"Where is it you're going?" asked Jennifer.

"Bartlett's, Forbes, or the Richards - one of them hired a killer and I hope to find out which one."

"How? You can't just go off on your own. You were hired to help with the case not to conduct your own investigation."

"Then it's time to show my hand... at least a little bit. Do either of you know where any of the three parties we are interested in happen to be while we're sitting here?"

"Go on," said Greg.

"Flint is in his office two hundred miles away. Gaudin is visiting a retail wine store not two blocks from here. Arlene Richards is at her regular hairdresser's. She always sees

Monique there who says that Arlene has a slight problem with alopecia. Stuart Richards is stoned at a friend's house while ostensibly looking after a Great Dane named Thomas à Beckett. The friend, by the way, is a television personality and is away on a film set. Forbes is at home. He's probably watching the clock and hoping to hear if his offer on the Songbird Estate has been accepted. Who delivered said offer? Stefan Badowski, that's who. It was drawn up yesterday and is accompanied by a certified cheque for half a million although I don't know the value of the offer.

"Now, you want to know what I'm going to do. One of these people hired the assassin I met earlier. I'm pretty sure I know which one it is but I'm not a hundred per cent certain which is why I'm keeping tabs on all of them. So, there are six names on my list, although I might not have to see them all. Yet, if I have to, I will see all six either today or tomorrow, even if I have to get a last-minute flight for Oscar's sake."

"That's interesting about Badowski and Forbes. How are you affording this surveillance?" asked Greg.

"Obviously not by the amounts I expect to receive for my own work from the Belton police. I'll simply say, I have no need of a job."

"Then why are you doing this? Because of that murder you told me about?" asked Jennifer.

"Precisely. Let me fill you in, Greg."

"No need. Remember, I said I looked you up. I heard about Danny Gould and Percy Smith and how you went after them when the case was cold. I'm interested in that because I've come up against Gould before. It's like a brick wall. Nobody talks and there's never any evidence."

"Jen, Gould is like a Mafia boss working in the city here and Smith is a hitman. They killed my friend, Bob Rowan, for no good reason as far as I could ever find out."

"And here you are, working on a case with a hired killer in the middle of it," said Jennifer.

"Yes, a strange coincidence. Brings back memories and makes me all the more determined to get it right this time."

"Correct. We can't get this wrong, Brent," said Greg. "The fact that you're doing all this work... well, I don't know what to say. It's our job, really. But if you have ways of getting information without disturbing any of our suspects... What's your opinion, Jennifer?"

"I think I have to pretend I never heard any of this. I only have two options: to let Brent work the case or to take him off it. That's it. What happens if I take him off? Look at him, it won't stop him doing these things anyway. At least we get the benefit of what he finds out *and* we can control him a little."

"Yeah, very little. I've trained detectives in the past who thought they knew it all but he's not like them. He actually produces and it's not a pride thing."

"No, he's full of himself but I wouldn't say he was proud," said Jennifer.

"Have you finished dissecting my character? It's making me feel very uncomfortable."

"You bring it on yourself," said Greg. "Good, here's the email. He has a record... all minors and all old. Graham Clarke, with an e, aged twenty-three. Last known address, 153 Belvedere, apartment number 1406... that's in the south-east near Colling Park. Known gang affiliations - none. This may not be current but it does look like he's a freelancer, then. His mother is dead but his father lives at the same address. We've got some photographs here. Nice looking boy at about seventeen... what happened to you, son? I'll forward all this to both of you."

"Okay, Brent, what are you waiting for?" asked Jennifer.

Greg smiled and stared at him with raised eyebrows.

"You both have beautiful souls," said Brent. "Talk to you later and good luck in finding Clarke."

Chapter Twenty-seven

The big dog's house

T he television celebrity's house was in the best part of the right neighbourhood. At ten years old, the large, custom-built home had all the amenities one expected. It had lost that raw, just-finished building look, and the trees and shrubs had matured to the point where they provided an attractive, manicured setting.

The old Jeep looked out of place in front of the house on the scrupulously clean interlocking paved driveway. When Brent emerged from his vehicle, he felt glad he had finally got the oil leak fixed a few weeks earlier. He could not stop himself from counting the number and position of all the security cameras and then determining where the blind spots were. This was an old habit of his and one that he had developed in his old trade. Ian Bennett had accused Brent of being a jewel thief. Detective Bennett was right but then he only knew a fraction of the story.

Brent Umber had a conscience that had grown over the years. That conscience had been absent when he had first turned to crime as a morose teenager who had burgled houses and small businesses. He now hated the thought of those early years. He hated himself for what he had done and his dreams were still troubled from time to time.

His conscience grew as he realized the distress he was causing the people he robbed so he set his sights higher, away from those who could ill-afford financial loss - towards wealthier people. It did not take long for him to realize that wealth does not bring peace of mind to a homeowner when their house has been invaded and valuables removed. As a consequence, the thief had turned to purely commercial ventures and organizations that could afford the losses or had insurance coverage.

This change in attitude to his criminal trade progressed as his education progressed. As a young orphan, he had hated school. As a teenager, he began to wish he had paid attention in class and avoided trouble with authority. As a young man, he did something about rectifying the situation and his prospects. First, he finished the schooling he had once neglected. Then, without taking time off from his criminal activities, he gained a History degree by day while his night-time studies alternated with breaking into warehouses and jewellery stores, this latter being a particular favourite of his. Along with this, Brent started investing some of his extraordinary income in stock markets. He had a lucky break early on with a gold-mining company. This particular company was a penny stock when he bought it but was soon proven to be in possession of a significantly valuable goldfield. The stock went crazy and Brent got out near the top with a profit of over two million. Realizing that it was luck and not his own skill in picking stock, he prudently invested his profits in companies that paid dividends, were undervalued, or showed great promise.

Eight years earlier, Brent had left housebreaking completely. As his mind expanded beyond its own selfish horizons, he became more interested in other people; more sympathetic to their circumstances and feelings. These changes in attitude came slowly and without way-markers pointing to when the changes occurred. His outlook, character, and ways of thinking metamorphosed into something very different to the hard, young man who had begun the process. He became open, friendly, and gregarious. This continued until his friend, Bob Rowan, was murdered. Then everything came to a halt for Brent. Depression, introspection, and a brief period of guilt and self-judgment hit him.

His way out of this dark period was to begin pouring his efforts into finding his friend's murderers. He discovered who they were yet, ultimately, he failed to achieve his object, although he was ever hopeful that, eventually, he would get the evidence needed to convict the killers. Accompanying this new activity of his, a deep remorse set in concerning his criminal past, and Brent ceased from crime of any sort. He held this uncomfortable secret in his heart, agonizing over it, occasionally to the point where his face flushed with shame.

It was this secret shame which made serious, intimate relations with a woman impossible for Brent. His ever-strengthening code of honour equated intimacy with honesty and how could he be honest with such a past as his? He was, therefore, talkative and open with most people but, as soon as he found himself attracted to someone, he closed down and became nervous and sullen - the reverse of his usual self. This annoyed him intensely.

Even now, standing in front of this door, Brent had already assessed the security systems of the house. He did not rate them very highly. He knew how easy it was for him to get past even the most supposedly secure systems, let alone the incomplete system of this expensive property. Brent's peculiar skills included lock-picking and defeating electronic alarm or locking systems; he kept them honed and up to date, deeming them useful in his new profession.

In the past, he had been contracted by other criminals to get them into a secure building solely on the basis of his skill set. However, many times Brent had found a faster way to get in and kept himself in shape as though he might need to use this method at a moment's notice. He simply climbed the exterior of a building and entered through a second or third-floor window. Even though that activity was firmly in the past, it did not stop him from thinking about his old habits and the excitement that came with them as he rang the doorbell now in front of him. How would he gain entry to this place if no one answered? Brent had seen a way. He was mildly disappointed when the maid opened the door.

"Hello, I'm Brent Umber." He smiled, looking most honest and trustworthy.

"Hello," replied the maid.

"I'm here to see Stuart Richards."

"Uh, please come in and wait here. I'll see if he's... um, available."

Brent stepped into the oversized hallway with its cathedral ceiling. He saw immediately that money had been spent to construct and decorate the house but nothing appealed to Brent in the choices of form, colour, or style.

"I know about Stuart's habits. If you would kindly show me where he is, I won't be a bother to you."

"It's no problem, sir. Come with me but you must first let me see if he's awake."

"Lead on, kind lady, and I will await your word."

The maid ushered Brent into an enormous room that spanned the width of the house and had a twelve-foot ceiling. Floor to ceiling windows with very thin frames gave a view of a well-kept but rather featureless garden consisting of an extensive lawn with a surrounding perimeter of shrubs. To the left of the lawn, and immediately in front of Brent, was a small but inviting swimming pool, looking very blue in the sunlight.

This living room had, at its centre, a sunken level before a large gas fireplace insert that was flush to its marble surround. Minimalist sofas and chairs were placed against the low walls forming the other three sides of the sunken square. In the middle was a long, low glass table which stood on a faux-fur rug that was too white to be natural. Above the gas-fire insert was a tall and impressive hammered copper hood - it served no purpose other than being decorative.

Brent had to walk down into the sunken area and up again to reach the man he sought. The alternative was to go around the fire pit which meant a lot of extra steps, navigating past other tables and chairs.

The back of Stuart Richard's head and shoulders could be seen above the backrest of an L-shaped, sectional sofa. His dark hair looked well-groomed. Brent could now see what was holding the man's attention. Built into the wall opposite was a massive salt-water fish tank with coral growing in it. There was plenty of space within for the violet and yellow fish that glided slowly in the upper reaches of the blue depths. Several smaller fish hid among the rocks and corals while three clownfish swam, darted, and played together in all parts of the tank. Brent sat down next to Stuart who turned an expressionless face to him before resuming his study of the aquarium. Neither man spoke for a minute.

"Do you know why I'm here?" asked Brent.

"You're the... uh, police guy." Stuart continued watching the fish.

"That's right. You and your mom put on an act for me. I think it was because you were expecting to buy the Songbird Estate and then you pulled out. The act was to make sure I didn't think you wanted Sheila Babbington killed."

"Uh, yeah. I thought you might see through our charade. Mother and I didn't want you suspecting we had anything to do with the deal."

"Did you back out because of the murder?"

"Yes... Clive was very annoyed about that. And he and Mother have had words."

"I see. I suppose he wanted your mom to finance the purchase and when it was sold later, you and he would get your cut."

"Yeah... and I missed out on half a million."

"What was that for?"

"For having persuaded Mother to go in. She was reluctant at first, thinking Clive might get in trouble. But then I explained how it worked... with the dam raising the water level. She got quite excited when she understood it. Then she didn't want anything to do with the vineyard as soon as she heard the owner was killed."

"You can't blame her for that."

"No, I don't. There's a little shark in the tank but he almost never comes out."

"Is that your favourite?"

"I like all of them... could watch them for hours."

"I thought you were looking after Thomas à Beckett? A Great Dane, isn't he?"

"We call him Tab. He's upstairs asleep in his room. Do you want to meet him?"

"Sure, I like dogs."

"Hey, Tab!" yelled Stuart, without getting up. There quickly followed some dull thudding from somewhere overhead. Noises on the staircase followed. The maker of the noises entered the room and stopped. The smoky-grey dog had a white patch on his chest. Tab proceeded to stretch his huge body and yawn widely with satisfaction. Upon seeing the two men on the other side of the room, he began to lope towards them, leaping in and then out of the fireplace area.

"No running in the house, you great mutt," said Stuart, half-seriously.

The dog responded with a low, throaty, rumbling bark as if to say, 'You're a mutt, too'. Tab came around the end of the sofa and shoved his huge head to within inches of Stuart's face. He pushed it away.

"Why can't you behave?" said Stuart. Receiving this response, the dog went and sat on Brent's feet, leaning heavily against his legs.

"What a weight you are," said Brent who began scratching Tab's head. This friendly attention soon developed into the dog rolling over, waving ungainly legs in the air, and having his stomach scratched.

"Come on, Stuart. The fish aren't going anywhere. Let's go outside and exercise the dog."

"Take the dog outside? What, immediately?"

"Yes. That's the reason you're here, remember? To take care of the dog's needs."

Stuart did not reply but, in answer, got up. He swayed a little, as though unused to using his legs, and then walked to the glass sliding door which led to the garden. The dog swivelled instantly and got up to follow Stuart.

"Do we have a ball or something?" asked Brent as he followed, too.

"There's a box of his toys outside. You do realize, *we're* going to get more exercise than the dog does. He's hopeless at bringing anything back."

"That will do us some good, too, then."

Once outside, the huge dog bounded about as though on springs; more so, when Stuart went towards a wooden locker.

For fifteen minutes, less a couple when Stuart was fiddling with his phone, the two men worked hard to get the dog to chase a thrown ball, frisbee, or rope toy and, hopefully, retrieve it. Not once had the dog successfully brought the object back to the person who threw it. The garden was now littered with the bright plastic objects the dog had scattered, shaken, or playfully savaged.

"You were right," said Brent, as the two men watched the dog toss something in the air at the end of the long garden. "Tab has done everything except bring anything back."

"That dog's smart. He can do it, I've seen him. He just chooses not to. He wants you to get all his toys out so he can make the whole garden his own space."

"Very devious of him. What's he like as a guard dog?"

"Useless. If someone broke in he might wake up and get interested enough to watch them steal everything or he might just go back to sleep."

"You were expecting me, weren't you? Why's that?"

"I thought you might be trouble. You didn't ask the usual questions... the one's the police keep asking. It meant you looked at what we said differently. I saw a stranger watching our place. He didn't look like a cop. You came to mind. How did you find me here?"

"Surveillance. I've had someone following you."

"What are you after? Just the murder or is it the hydroelectric project?"

"The murder only. I'm only interested in the dam in so far as it might be a reason to murder."

"Do you think my brother, Clive, will be arrested?"

"Very likely but the charges might not stick. It depends on who else he gave the information to. Can you help me out there? I solemnly swear I will not tell the police anything you tell me. As I said, I'm after the murderer and no one else."

"Clive's not the murderer. That's not the way he does things. I doubt he'd even *think* of it as a solution to anything, let alone do it or have it done."

"Do you know a man named Stan Forbes?"

"Can't say that I do. Mind if I smoke?"

"What if I said no?"

"I was only being polite. Some people don't like the smell of marijuana." He lit up and began to inhale, holding the smoke in until he almost squeaked when he spoke. "Calms my nerves."

"What about the other things you take... and sell to your acquaintances? You have a solid reputation that way."

"You know about that? Yeah, well, I'm getting tired of all that stuff. I need to do something different."

"Like what?"

"I think I'd like to do carpentry. I used to be good at it at school."

"What's stopping you?"

"My life... want some?"

"No, thanks. Surely, you can just start. Buy a few tools and some wood and just do it."

"You'd think it would be that easy. It's what I want to do but it's not where my mind's at. I feel clamped down all the time. Like, I can make choices and decisions but I can never follow through on them. Like, I really, really get paranoid about doing anything different. You know what I'm saying?"

"Breaking a habit... I know something about that. To do something different you have to start thinking differently. To think differently your circumstances have to break apart. Sometimes some external event causes it to happen or sometimes you have to do it yourself by deliberately tearing things down. That's what you need to do... pull away all the crutches you rely upon. Then it becomes sink or swim but you do need a plan and a clearly defined set of goals to aim for."

"That's deep."

"No, it isn't deep; it's what has to happen when you need to get out of the circumstances you find yourself in. The big thing to remember is to never give up if it gets tough, and that change can be very messy and challenging."

"Yeah... I'll think about it. I really will. Hey, that dog is, like, so cool."

"Come here, Tab! Come!" called Brent.

The dog on hearing its name, obediently and enthusiastically came but left its battered, yellow frisbee at the far end of the garden.

"That dog will never learn," said Stuart. "I got to get something to eat."

He turned away abruptly, going into the house and leaving Brent to play with the dog. When he arrived in the airy, blue and white tiled kitchen, he was momentarily surprised to find someone else already peering into the stainless steel fridge. It was Shawna, the wife of the television celebrity. She looked to be about forty.

"Hi, you got my text message?" asked Stuart.

"Obviously. Is that him, playing with my dog?"

"Yes. He's not the police. He's a private investigator. He knows about the hydroelectric project. I'm really hungry. I've got to eat."

"Help yourself. There's nachos in the cupboard there and some dip in the fridge. So, what did he say?"

"My brother could get in trouble over it. You were wise not to go in."

"You got my stuff?"

"I put it in the freezer in the garage like you said. Price is probably going up next time. That's what I was told."

"What! It's too high already! I can't stand this. I can't stand that guy being here, either. Can't we get rid of him?"

"I'm a suspect in a murder case so I can't do it. At least, I think I'm a suspect. You could throw him out, though he's pretty chill, actually. Easy to get along with and didn't seem like he minded me pulling a stunt with mother to, like, not be suspected as being involved in the deal."

"What stunt was that?"

"We acted like we were *really* weird. Mother was pretending she needed help all the time, like she was an invalid or something. It was so funny, you should have seen her. She was, like, demented." He crunched loudly and sloppily on his nachos and then spoke with his mouth partly full. "I had a blast, too. I pretended I was a druggy and like, 'how dare you speak to me'. I deliberately hadn't washed for days before I went to see the police."

"That's gross. The things you have to do. Why can't they leave people alone?"

"Yeah, it was sort of gross. But it's *a-mazing* how much extra time you get by not washing."

"Look at that," remarked Shawna, looking out of the window. "He's got Tab bringing back the ball."

"Where?"

They both silently watched as Brent threw the ball a short distance, Tab retrieved it, dropped the ball at Brent's feet, and then sat down to receive a brief tickle under the chin.

"I don't believe my eyes. That's three times in a row," said Stuart.

"Why doesn't he do that for me?"

"Who, Tab?"

"Of course, Tab. You've smoked too much and that guy's leaving right now."

"Don't involve me in that," said Stuart.

Brent, smiling, turned around at the sound of the door opening and expected to see Stuart returning. Instead, he saw an expensively dressed woman, striding towards him with a scowl on her face.

"Hello," said Brent. "This must be your dog. He's fantastic. If ever you think of selling him please let me know."

"Not for sale. What are you doing here?"

"I'll tell you, if you tell me what *you're* doing here?"

"I live here. This is *my* house."

"Oh, I guessed that much. More to the point, you've come home when you left Tab in Stuart's care. That means he contacted you. He would only contact you about my presence if he thought it mattered to you. Putting it together, it means you are involved in a fraud. The fraud, and the conspiracies associated with it, are definitely connected and inextricably woven into a woman's murder case. As you seem to be a new player you need to speak to me nicely before the police come round. I'm duty-bound to call them in. Now, that would give the neighbours something to talk about."

"You can't come into *my* house and threaten *me*. I'm going to complain about your behaviour and have you fired." Shawna started back to the house to get her phone.

"It wouldn't be the end of the world for me if you did. As soon as you've made your call, I'll make mine. Here, Tab. Fetch!" Brent threw the ball and the Great Dane went lumbering after it.

"Look, will you leave my dog *a-lone*." Shawna angrily hissed out her words yet she had stopped and even retraced a few steps.

"Very well. One thing, though. Will you tickle him or shall I? He's learning but he needs encouragement."

Tab came back and stood between them and, when nobody reached for the ball, dropped it on the grass and sat down.

"Good boy," said Brent. "You've probably had enough for one session." To the woman, he then said, "Are you going to make your call or are you going to talk to me? I need to know one way or another because I'm very busy today. Just so you know, if you are involved in the conspiracy to defraud, I will never let it be known unless you are also involved in the conspiracy to commit murder. I don't know if that helps you at all."

She stood for a moment and then advanced a step or two closer with a changed demeanour. "Okay, I'll buy it. What do you want to know?"

"The Richards family, particularly Clive, has involved itself in a lucrative but a less-than-legal deal. I'm sure I do not need to explain it to you. First, was your husband involved in any way?"

"No. At least, not at first. I spoke to him about putting some money into the deal but he was busy and said he would need his accountant to see the figures. It wasn't that kind of a situation so I left it at that. Then, Stuart was persistent about our getting in on it. I knew he wanted to get his cut when the property was sold."

"Was this after his mom backed out?"

"Yeah… on account of that woman dying… only he forgot to tell me about that."

"Oh, did he?"

"Too right he did. I found out myself and that ended it all for me. The funny thing is, as soon as I didn't want to be involved anymore, then my husband wanted to know all about it."

"And are you still mad at Stuart over that?"

"I get over things easily."

"So, it wasn't because you thought he or his brother, Clive, or both of them together, had killed Sheila Babbington?"

"Oh, no way. No way. Stuart's a baby over practically everything. I don't know Clive very well but if you saw him, you'd see he's the least likely person to do anything exciting."

"Yet, he's conspiring to defraud. Some might call that excitement. There are serious trust issues and culpable self-interest wrapped up in that little bundle. Maybe he got desperate and hired someone to kill the owner."

"No, I don't think so. That's just not him. Besides, I understand he's well set up. He doesn't need to have someone murdered."

"Thanks, that's helped me sort a few things out. You know, you're well set up here, too. I know Stuart gets your drugs for you. You should give them up."

"We're not talking about that… What did that rat say?"

"Nothing. I can see the hunger in your face. Does your husband know?"

"This is none of your business. Just keep out of it."

"Tell him you're going to stay with a friend and check into a detox centre. Why waste yourself for a few hours' escape now and then?"

"You don't know what I've been through."

"No, I don't. I presume it was bad enough to hurt you severely. Don't think I'm being judgmental - I had to kick a habit that was worse than yours because it hurt other people so I'm not saying all this to condemn you at all but to help you. I know where you're going to end up if you don't quit taking drugs. No one likes getting unsolicited advice but do yourself a favour and at least think about it."

Brent reached down and patted the dog.

"Thomas à Beckett here learned a trick today. You could have taught him the same trick very easily any time you chose. Stuart has a similar problem to you. I see both of you as stuck in a mental prison. The walls are made of habit, the ceiling is impossibility, and the door is only opened by imagination but it appears to be rusted shut. It's up to you to find a way out. Either find a key and some oil or blow the door off its hinges. But do something, won't you?"

"Have you finished with the lecture?"

"Yes, I have. Good day to you. 'Bye, Tab."

Brent stroked the dog's head again before walking away. Tab followed him into the house leaving Shawna standing by herself in the garden of discarded toys.

As he sat in his Jeep, Brent checked his text messages. There was one from Charles Babbington, informing Brent that he had received an offer from a company, called Archangel Investments, in the amount of $4.8 million. He called Charles for more details about it and discovered the offer was for three and a half million down with the balance being paid over three years at a 3% interest rate and without penalty for an early payout.

Brent had yet to tell his friend of the changes that were coming to the Songbird Estate through legislation as it might

258

obfuscate matters should knowledge of the vineyard being affected by rising water levels become widely known. All he said, all he *could* say really, was that Charles should not accept any offers because there was some important news Charles needed to know before making a decision. Brent said he was not free at present to tell him what it was exactly. To his pleasant surprise, Charles accepted and trusted implicitly what Brent told him. It did cross the investigator's mind that perhaps Charles was not the right type of person to be dealing with hard-nosed business types and their sometimes tricky offers.

Another message was from Jennifer Allen. The manhunt had begun for Clarke with an e - his details having been distributed nationwide. A third message Brent received was from Damian, asking, 'Who's the guy watching the Richards' family house?'. He responded by text, saying, "He's working for me. Calling him off now."

Chapter Twenty-eight

Tea for four

The Belton townhouse of Stanley Forbes was as surprising as it was imposing. The property had to possess a high value solely because of its location and the double bow-fronted building was undeniably well-constructed. It sat behind a low stone wall topped by iron railings which guarded a small, stone-flagged forecourt. Built just after the First World War, the residence had been constructed on a massive scale on an incongruously small plot of land as if wedged in between an older commercial bank and a late Victorian row of upscale shops with offices overhead.

The two and a half storey building had unfortunately squandered its opportunity to fit in with dignity and decorum. The roof was a heavy, oversized and very wide A-shape, fully containing the half storey but the overhang was large and ponderous and almost touching the buildings on either side. So pronounced a feature was the roof, it gave the impression that it was propping up the neighbouring buildings while crushing the one upon which it sat. The brickwork was red, the woodwork painted cream, and there were no architectural features present to please the eye. It was a big, raw, plain house - impressive in its immensity but little else.

There were seven oversized windows on the façade whereas, proportionally, eleven or twelve smaller ones would have fitted and looked better. Under the square covered porch which sat on two of the largest round wooden pillars Brent had ever seen, the big, beautifully constructed and maintained dark wooden, double doors were suitably sized for a barn. As he rang the bell, Brent wondered if it would be opened by an eight-foot-tall butler. The house had a pronounced 'feel' to it that was neither inviting nor comfortable.

A woman in her forties opened the door. It struck Brent that she could be the housekeeper, for her conservative dark dress suggested that occupation.

"Good morning. My name's Brent Umber. Is it possible for me to see Mr Forbes? or am I too close to lunchtime?"

"Good morning, Mr Umber. Please come in. Mr Forbes is expecting you."

"Ah, is he? That's good."

Brent, puzzled a little by Forbes' certainty that he would make an impromptu call, stepped inside. He thought he might be playing fly to Forbes' spider. The woman left him in the cavernous hall to inform Stan Forbes of Brent's arrival. A large blue and yellow rug of simple design did not go with the dark wood-beamed ceiling. The low light and emptiness of the space contrived to further the unwelcoming, barren feel of the place.

Large paintings from several eras hung on the plain white walls. On his right, a large abstract, in muted, almost dirty reds and blues, shouted across the gulf at a dark, sombre oil painting of a battle scene in which rows of musket-carrying infantry were firing at one another while a rider, seated on a preposterously rearing horse, appeared to be pointing at something by way of explanation for a bewigged and red-faced gentleman wearing a tricorn hat - presumably the field marshal of the winning side.

Next to where Brent was standing was one of the largest and possibly the ugliest Chinese vases he had ever laid eyes on, and he very much appreciated and was familiar with antique Asian ceramics. Worse still, it was one of an identical pair, both set on low, lacquered stands, and flanking the hallway. The inebriated look on the dragons' faces was quite laughable. Brent knew the vases to be nineteen-twenties reproductions of some ancient Temple Vases. The one he examined was well potted and the blue glaze good but the artist had done fourth-rate work - more suited to the quick painting of cheap souvenirs.

The woman soon reappeared at the farther end of the hall, saying,

"If you would come this way, please, Mr Forbes will see you in his study." The hall proved to have a slight echo to it.

The book-lined study at the back of the house was more intimate, of regular proportions, and better decorated, with an old-gold wallpaper that glowed, giving off a cheerful aura. The view through the window was of an asphalted area where cars, including a Mercedes and a Hummer, were parked within a high, gated wall. The house had no garden whatsoever.

"I knew you would come," said Stan Forbes. He plainly looked pleased with himself. "Take a seat."

Forbes sat down behind his heavy desk. A glass protective cover and a modern LED lamp were the only things on its surface. No work was ever done at this desk. Brent surmised that Stan's real den, if he did any work or studying, was somewhere else in the house. As soon as they were both sitting down, Brent again felt resentment building in him towards the man. He could not isolate specifically what it was that caused the feeling other than Stan Forbes' complete and obvious self-assurance.

"Did you? Why's that, I wonder?" replied Brent.

"Don't you know?" Some of the pleasure ebbed from the host's face.

"I'm sorry... know what?" replied Brent, happy to see the change.

"It spoils the effect to have to explain it. I thought you would come because I put in an offer on the Songbird Estate."

"Did you, now? Was it accepted?"

"I'm waiting on a reply. The seller hasn't responded yet."

"Well, that's because he's received several other offers already. He's probably considering them with extreme distaste. Seems people are inordinately hungry for vineyards just now and can't wait a decent amount of time for him to mourn his wife."

"What offers are those?" Forbes' face became serious to the point of appearing annoyed.

"Oh, I don't know. He told me two days ago there were a couple from wine producers; then, I think there was another company. We didn't talk about it much because it's his business and not mine."

Brent waited to see what result his less than truthful responses would produce. Forbes was now seriously irritated, he could plainly read that. Brent thought over the situation. *He had been thinking I would have heard of his offer and come straight away to see him to question him about it. He looked jubilant just now, thinking he had called it correctly. As he said, my not knowing has spoiled the effect he desired.*

"How much was your offer for?" asked Brent.

"Well, I don't think we need discuss it any further," said Forbes, recovering his composure. "Why did you come here, then?"

"One of the offers was for seven million... and in cash, at that. I never knew vineyards to be so valuable."

This news, false though it was, clearly struck home.

"That's impossible. The place is worth nothing like that amount."

"Oh, so you're a day late and a dollar short, I suppose. That must be very annoying. I know I would be annoyed in your place. Perhaps you should increase your offer if you really want it."

"It doesn't matter. I'll do something about it."

"I'm sure you will. The reason for my visit, believe it or not, is that the murderer of Sheila Babbington is still at large. I have yet to lose interest so I'm still working on the case. I was wondering whether you might have any news for me about her murder?"

"Of course not. Why should I?"

"It's the manhunt, you see. I just thought, if you knew Graham Clarke, that's with an e by the way, you might have heard about our search for him and might know where he was."

"Mr Umber, I have never seen or heard of this Clarke person. I have nothing to do with the murder, as you well know. It makes me think there's something wrong with you. Are you in over your head on this case?"

"That's much better, my old Stan. That's the Forbes spirit. Push back at my little digs. The trouble is, the other guy who's in custody is singing a different tune to yours. The police didn't ask him the right questions but I did. There's no honour among thieves... although I don't hold to that as being strictly true. But you're a smart guy and know what I mean."

"Somebody has implicated me?"

"It's only a matter of time before the police arrest you. That's my belief. Depends on what I tell them. You see, I've kept a few things back for myself. Some choice things that they wouldn't know how to use unless I showed them. Then, when I show them, the proverbial scales will fall from their eyes. That's when they'll come to see you."

"What do you want?" asked Forbes.

"Oh, the usual, naturally. It's hard to make a living these days."

Forbes stared at Brent who smiled back at him.

"If, hypothetically let's say, I thought you had something worth buying what would the amount be?"

"Oh, that's difficult to say. I do have a figure in mind that could speed up an early retirement. I would prefer for you to come up with a suggestion because I really don't know what value you place on everything you have here versus a life behind bars."

"You'll have to give me some time to think about this." Forbes paused for nearly a minute. "I don't believe you have anything. No, I don't. You've not said anything concrete or given any proof of your accusations, which are necessarily baseless anyway. I have no involvement with Sheila Babbington's murder whatsoever." He paused again. "However, I'm mindful that you could tarnish my reputation. That is something I will not tolerate. I'll pay you a modest sum of money to keep your mouth shut and, should you ever open it, there will be consequences for you, personally. You're accusing me of planning a murder. If that were true, I would be fully capable of planning a second one, even if I should be behind bars. I had nothing to do with it but, if you believe your own reading of events, you should consider yourself in danger."

"Well said, Stan. Well said. My knees are knocking together. Nonetheless, you have to meet my amount, or else. I'll leave it up to you."

Having said that, Brent got up and left the room without any further word or action on either man's part. As soon as Forbes heard the front door close at the end of the echoing hall, he reached into a desk drawer and switched off his digital recorder. He had a rueful smile on his face as he erased the last part of his speech to Brent. Then he took out a prepaid phone from another drawer and made a call to Gaudin.

Outside in the street and safely clear of the Forbes' house, Brent happily switched off *his* recording device. It was the first time he had ever worn a wire and he was pleased, almost joyous, with himself in having been so successful with it. *He* would not erase a single word of what was recorded.

Now, if he could, Brent was going to get into his Jeep and pay Claude Gaudin a visit - if someone would tell him where he was to be found. Gaudin had gone missing during the course of the morning, giving the slip to the woman Andy Fowler had sent to keep Gaudin under surveillance. She asserted she had not been spotted but that her quarry had driven away in his car as *though* deliberately to avoid being followed by someone, anyone, and she had soon become blocked in heavy traffic.

Brent decided to call Jennifer and bring her up to date with his theory.

"Hi, Jen. Any progress?"

"Nothing yet. Valinho still hasn't said much. His lawyer is seeing him now. No news on Clarke."

"I had a thought about Valinho. Couldn't you put me in the cell with him? Maybe I could get him to talk."

"You watch too many movies. It wouldn't work at this stage of the proceedings, anyway."

"Ah, I see. I'm rather hazy about police procedure and dealing with lawyers so it's probably best I don't get involved. I'm only trying to be helpful."

"Right. Of course you are. Brent, I want some written reports from you and I want them today."

"You should go easy on me; I could be suffering from shock from being shot at."

"Are you?"

"I'm not sure. How can I tell?"

"You book yourself off and go to see a doctor."

"No, I'm fine," said Brent quickly.

"As I thought," replied Jennifer. "Have you got anything?"

"I have a finished theory. As far as I'm concerned the painting is complete, although a few final brushstrokes are still needed to perfect it."

"Painting? Oh, yes, your mental picture thing. So?"

"Well, it goes like this…"

Brent explained clearly how he saw the murder and property deal from start to finish. He ended by saying,

"… and I think Oscar Flint should be arrested at the same time."

"You know, that all sort of fits," replied Jennifer after she had considered his recap. "There are some holes, though."

"Don't I know it? That's why I must see Charles Babbington, Gaudin, and, as I'm in the area, I'll drop in first on Arlene Richards. That should tie up everything nicely."

"Okay. I'm coming back to Belton; there's no more I can do here. Remember, you're writing those reports today."

"Yes, Jen, I promise to get them all up to date."

Brent parked on a street simply called, Forbes Hill. There were several cars already parked in the Richards' driveway. This got him thinking as he walked along the pleasant, mature tree-lined street. The garden of the Richards' house was laid out like a small park with a dozen or so tall trees shading the fine green grass. Over an ancient cedar hedge, he could see Locust, Plane, Maple, Oak, and Chestnut trees. At one side towards the back, between the house and a tall, black, sheet-iron fence, was a badminton court laid out - empty, save for the net, at present. Of the several lawn chairs he could see, one was draped with a white cardigan, which gave hope to Brent that its owner was somewhere about and available for questioning.

The house was a full three-story Victorian building. It had orange brickwork with complicated yellow brick designs standing proud over windows and doors. The place had missed the full treatment of towers, turrets, and gingerbread woodwork. However, it was substantial and elegant, with tall narrow windows and doors and a steep slate roof that possessed a decorative band of red and green slates close to the eaves that relieved the blank mass of grey ones. Several ancient lightning rods, with their blue glass balls intact, were posted on the highest ridges.

Instead of going to the front door, Brent went around the side towards the net. As he rounded the corner, he discovered the already large house possessed a substantial, two-storey extension. Extending the length of it was a long, wide veranda. Sitting in the shade of the overhanging roof sat three old ladies. They were almost invisible because in front of the railings were growing tall masses of pink peonies. All he could see were the tops of three coiffed and curled heads in a row, two in varying shades of white and one with a distinct blue tinge to it. The blue tinge was nodding rhythmically and Brent could hear voices but not what was being said.

Not wishing to startle anyone, he called out, "Hello, I hope I'm not intruding?"

"Who's there?" demanded the blue-tinged head. "Advance and be recognized."

Brent walked up the few stairs and presented himself. Smiling, he said, "This is a lovely place."

The three women, who were drinking tea and sitting in cushioned easy chairs before a long, low table, reacted differently. The nearest to Brent was she of the blue rinse. This woman was larger than her companions but, sitting back comfortably, her head was on the same level as the other two. She looked at Brent as though he were a poisonous snake. Next to her, and perched upright on the edge of her chair, was the smallest of the three. She had a pink complexion, looked cherubic, and was wearing several layers of clothing despite the warmth of the day. She smiled at him. The third, at the far end of the table, was Arlene Richards. She blushed so completely, to the roots of her white hair, it gave the effect that she had been too long in the sun and had received a mild burn.

"Battledore and Shuttlecock," said Brent, seeing the badminton rackets. "Do you play in a league?"

"Played since we were girls. Only friendly games. Answer my question, who are you? Do you know him, Arlene?"

"I do," replied Arlene Richards. "This is Mr Brent Umber. He's a detective. These are my two friends, Letitia..." - the lady with the blue rinse nodded - "... and Catherine."

"Being a detective must be so fascinating," said Catherine effusively.

"Nonsense, Cat. It must be just like any other job, boring, but has its ups and downs. What do you say?"

"I say," said Brent, "that you are both right. I became a detective because it is fascinating work. However, a lot of the time it is very mundane. Now I would like to tell you something, in the strictest confidence you understand." Catherine nodded quickly. "I'm working on a murder case and I believe I know who the murderers are."

Catherine had a shocked, open-mouthed look; Letitia's eyebrows furrowed; Arlene's expression was unreadable.

"We're getting very close to making an arrest but there are a few issues standing in the way that I must remove before we can do so."

"You'd better sit yourself down," said Letitia.

"Would you like some tea?" asked Catherine, as she touched the teapot. "The pot's still hot."

"What do you say, Arlene?" asked Brent.

"You may as well join us. My friends and I keep no secrets from one another." She blinked rapidly but nowhere near as bad as she had done at their former meeting.

Brent sat opposite them, with his back to the peonies.

"How do you like your tea?" asked Catherine. "Oh, there's no spare cup. What shall we do?"

270

"Get one," said Letitia. "I'll go." She got up suddenly and proved to be about six feet tall, straight-backed, with vigorous movements belying her apparent age of late seventies to early eighties. Before she went, she wagged a finger, sternly warning Brent, "Don't say a word until I return." She marched into the house.

"Letty can be very decisive," said Catherine to Brent. "She has a heart of gold, though, doesn't she, Arly?"

"Yes, but let's wait for her or she'll fuss."

"This is very kind of you, Arlene, to receive me like this... on such short notice - well, on no notice, actually."

Arlene smiled in reply. They waited the minute or so in silence.

Letitia returned, setting a cup and saucer down before Catherine. "I brought some cookies. You're bound to want some. My husband always did." She resumed her seat and said, "Did I miss anything?"

"Not a thing," said Arlene.

"Good. What's this about secrets and murder cases?"

Without mentioning names, Brent, occasionally sipping tea, told them the story of the conspiracies against Sheila Babbington and her vineyard. Not once did they interrupt, although Letitia came close to it on two occasions. When he had finished, he sat back and observed.

"That was the vineyard you were going to buy, wasn't it?" asked Catherine of Arlene.

"It was. I didn't want anything to do with it at first but both my boys persuaded me. They said it was a very good investment and the land value would go up very soon. Then, when the woman was murdered, I could not imagine having anything more to do with it."

She turned towards Brent and looked very sincere.

"I owe you an apology, Mr Umber, and an explanation to both of my friends here. You see, when I told Clive I wanted to back out of the purchase of the vineyard, he said there might be a difficulty about that. He said we all might look suspi-cious... as though we had a motive to murder that woman to go after her property. I didn't understand that because I was no longer in the slightest bit interested in her property so, how *could* it look suspicious?"

"That seems back to front," said Letitia. "What could the boy be thinking of?"

"Exactly my point. So I told him again that under no cir-cumstances would I contribute to the purchase. Stuart tried to get me to change my mind but when he saw that I was firm, he gave up and said I was quite right in being so."

"He knows which way the wind blows," said Letitia emphat-ically.

"I suppose *he* would have made a profit out of it, too," said Catherine. "Am I right in thinking that?"

"Yes, Cat, you are. But that is all beside the point now. You see, I got very worried about the police investigation."

"It would give me palpitations," said Catherine.

"Stuart came up with an idea and, looking back on it now, I can't imagine how I ever came to say yes..."

"You have always been too soft where Stuart is concerned," said Letitia.

"You're right, of course. As you have frequently said, I've over-indulged him since he was an infant. Too late for me to change now."

"But what did he get you to do, dear?" asked Catherine.

"I'm coming to that. He got me to pretend, to put on an act in front of the police... he did it as well... we pretended that we were both not quite all there. And, we made up a little play to hint that we were both having a problem with Clive."

"Not the amateur dramatics!" bellowed Letitia. "You weren't blinking your way through the performance, were you?"

"I'm not sure, Letty. Was I, Mr Umber?"

"Yes, just a little."

"I think you're being diplomatic," said Letitia. "That thing you do, Arly, is very off-putting."

"You see, Mr Umber," said Catherine, "when we were younger, we all did amateur dramatics and oh, how we loved it. The dressing up, the make-up, the actor jargon, and learning the lines together. There were more of us then. It was so romantic. But Arly has a nervous tic. The bigger the part she played, the worse the tic became until none of us could remember what to say because she was blinking so uncontrollably."

"Worst distraction you could imagine," said Letitia. "We had to banish her to non-speaking parts to get through the production."

"Not always," said Arlene quickly. "I had many speaking parts and I carried them off quite well, I thought."

"Yes, you did, dear," said Catherine. "But as soon as you had a couple of lines together, off you'd go. Nerves, Mr Umber. Arly is *very* sensitive to stress."

"Then I'm surprised you agreed to put yourself through such a performance," said Brent.

"I am, too," said Arlene. "But, don't you see? It was the chance for me to play a really big important part. Half of me *wanted* to do it."

"Absolutely ridiculous at your age. At any age. Good grief, Arly, a woman has been murdered. You said you met her. Didn't that count for anything? And as for wasting the time and resources of the police. Well, I just don't know what to say."

"I know you're right, Letty. Am I in trouble, Mr Umber?"

"Not as far as I'm concerned. In fact," Brent leaned forward in his chair and became very confidential, "I have to tell you that your performance was superb and had me completely fooled."

Arlene clasped her hands together in an approved but dated, dramatic fashion while smiling broadly. Catherine leaned over and gave her friend an affectionate pat on the shoulder.

"So, you won't be arresting her?" said Letitia, before laughing out loud.

"No. She has got away with it," said Brent.

"Oh, please don't, Mr Umber. I'm very sorry my thoughtlessness has caused you such trouble."

"Dear lady, we shall not mention it again," replied Brent. "There is something I would like to know, though. I noticed that your house is on Forbes Hill. That being the case, and this house being probably the oldest in the area, I wondered if the house ever belonged to the Forbes family?"

"I'm a Forbes," said Arlene. "My married name is Richards but I inherited this house. My great-grandfather built it in 1876 and the street is named after him."

"That is fascinating and I'd certainly love to hear about the family history at another time. But, as you can well appreciate, I'm working on a case and I have much to do today. I wonder, though, after what you've just told me, do you know Stanley Forbes?"

"I do - at least if it's the same person I know. He's a relation of mine, a second cousin, once removed. I haven't seen him in, oh, I should think thirty years. There was a family rift in my grandfather's day, between him and his brother."

"I think he must be twice removed," said Catherine.

"Once, surely?"

"I think you're forgetting about Edwina. She wasn't a Forbes, although she was treated as though she were a blood relation."

"Do you know, I always forget that fact. She was such an adorable, sweet woman, Mr Umber. Catherine is correct. She remembers my family history better than I do myself."

"It's good to clear up these important points," said Brent. "Would it surprise you to know that he was present on the day you visited the vineyard?"

"Yes, it does. Very much so. I certainly didn't recognize him."

"Would you have spoken to him if you had?"

"Oh, yes. I believe I would."

"I wouldn't have," said Letitia. "There's bad blood on that side. You mark my words, it will come out one day."

"I'm very curious to find out what makes you say that."

"I'm afraid it's something I do not wish to speak about." She held a deep frown on her face and then suddenly released it. "Are you investigating him?"

"I am, as it happens. I came on purpose to ask Arlene if she knew him… and to clear up the other matter." Out of the corner of his eye, he saw Arlene smile briefly. "To find three observant ladies willing to help is such a bonus for me."

"Ooh, he has a soft tongue," said Letitia. "My family had its own trouble with Stanley Forbes' family. I'll just say that Stanley's grandfather on his mother's side, he was not a Forbes of course, cheated my grandmother out of a valuable building lot here in Belton." She crossed her arms, clearly determined to say no more.

Brent had an idea. "It wouldn't have been that downtown property with the big house crammed onto it. The redbrick with the oversized roof?"

"It's a monstrosity. Serves them right - making such a mess of it. Though, I cannot imagine how you guessed the right place. There must be hidden depths to you, Mr Umber. Hidden depths."

"It was just a lucky guess. I happened to visit the place today to speak to Stan Forbes."

All three women stared at him. The veranda went quiet and only the distant noise of traffic filtered through to break the silence.

"And?" said Letitia.

"What was it like inside?" asked Catherine.

"I'll put the kettle on for more tea," said Arlene, as she got up.

Brent stayed much longer than he had intended and did not escape without giving a complete description of everything relating to Stanley Forbes, his house, his life, and something of how he was implicated in the case. All three women were very satisfied with his reportage and, as he finally stood to leave, said he must be sure to call again soon.

Chapter Twenty-nine

All that glitters is not gold

As Brent approached the Songbird Estate he saw a bright yellow Corvette parked in front of the house. He could not think immediately what Gaudin could be doing there except to see Charles in an effort to persuade him to sell the vineyard.

He knocked on the door and waited. A dishevelled, red-eyed Charles Babbington opened the door.

"Oh, it's you, Brent. Um, could you come back later?"

"I know Gaudin is here; I couldn't possibly miss the car. You should let me in because it's important I talk to both him and you."

"Yes, I suppose you must. I'm sorry. I didn't mean to be rude. I'm very distressed at the moment and I hardly know what I'm doing."

They went to the living room at the back with its view over the vineyard. Several vine-dressers were working their way along different rows. With his back to this view, Gaudin sat in a chair with his head in his hands. He looked up at the sounds of approach. He, too, had red eyes plus a tear-stained face.

"I see," said Brent. "You've been telling Charles some of your story."

"Did they send you to take me in?" said Gaudin.

"Uh, no. Is that right, Charles? The police are on their way?"

"Yes. Claude thinks it best. He told me about the package in his car and how he's been an unwitting accomplice in Sheila's death. He wants to go into protective custody. I think that's what they call it. He says that Oscar Flint or perhaps some other person will have him killed to stop him from testifying."

"Why did you come here, Claude?"

"To say I'm sorry for the part I've played in this whole mess. I had no idea... *no idea* they would go as far as murder. It's horrible."

"That's right," said Brent. "It is horrible. Now that I'm here, I have questions I need to ask both of you. As Claude will be leaving soon, I think I'll put my questions to him first."

"Sure, anything you like."

"Where did the money come from to pay Graham Clarke? That's the name of the hired killer, Charles."

"Flint sent it. You know that. It came in the package. He even put it on the courier account under my name as though I was the sender and the recipient."

"That's crazy. It looks so false," said Brent. "Let me phrase this another way. How does Flint know Clarke? How was that contact set up?"

"I don't know. I thought about that. Flint knows some shady characters. Probably through one of them. I'll give some names to the police. As soon as he's arrested they can get it out of him."

"You're pinning a lot of hope on him confessing. Do you really think he will?"

"He's got to. I know enough to force him to do it, don't I?"

"You possibly do. It will probably work out the way you're thinking. Do you know Stan Forbes?"

"Forbes? Yeah, I know who you mean. Met him a couple of times."

"Before or after you met him here?"

"Oh, before. What is this?"

"I have a suspicious mind and suspect everybody. I'm just trying to get Forbes out of the way as a candidate."

"Uh, like I said, I've met him but I don't know anything about him."

"Did Charles tell you that Forbes has put in an offer on the estate?"

"No. I only came here to apologize and explain things."

"Charles? Do you think we might have a cup of coffee? I've hardly stopped all day and haven't had one since this morning."

"Oh, yes, of course. I should have offered you something. Sheila would not have been so remiss." Charles went out of the room.

"Where were we?" said Brent when Charles had gone into the kitchen. "Ah, yes. Charles received an offer from a company Forbes controls. It was for seven million in cash."

"What! Like what!" Gaudin took to swearing loudly before he mastered himself.

"It came as a surprise to me. It seems the estate is a very desirable property but I had no idea of its value. Now, I have one last question. What was your cut going to be?"

"Flint was going to pay off my gambling debts and I was to get ten per cent commission on wine sales from the Songbird for the next three years. After that, it would be three per cent."

"So, it was an incentive for you to maximize the wine sales from the vineyard. You were not to get anything from the appropriation of the land for the hydroelectric project?"

"What are you talking about?"

279

"You've been kept in the dark. It's probably not my place to tell you about it but, since you've been open with me, I'll tell you this much. What I heard was that part of the estate was to be appropriated because of the dam going in and the payout to the owners was to be forty-three million."

Claude Gaudin was about ready to explode but there came a knock at the front door. As it was probably the police, his anger subsided quickly. For the second time that day, Brent, surreptitiously and with satisfaction, switched off his recording device.

Charles answered the door and soon Damian and a uniformed officer entered the living room.

"Hey, what are *you* doing here?" asked Damian as soon as he saw Brent.

"My visit is purely coincidental. I came to see Charles and was then told that the police had been called in."

"Hmm, I find that hard to believe. Anyway, Mr Gaudin, this officer will ride in your car with you and you'll follow me to police headquarters where we will take down whatever it is you want to add to your former statement concerning the Sheila Babbington murder case. Now, you've got to tell me, what immediate danger do you believe you're facing?"

"I think there will be an attempt on my life at any moment. I believe Oscar Flint and his cronies will try and get to me because you guys are getting too close to him and my testimony might be the only evidence you have against him."

"Okay. Let's get you to HQ where you'll be safe. If you will come this way, sir, we'll go now."

The officer left the room with Gaudin. As Damian turned to go, Brent touched him on the arm and whispered, "Don't lose him. Ask Jennifer for details."

Damian nodded and left the house, sending a text message as he did so.

Charles returned with five coffees.

"They've all gone. That was very quick. I imagined they would question him here. Here's yours, anyway."

"I'm very sorry, Charles, but three charming ladies plied me with so much tea earlier that it almost amounted to torture."

"Then why did you ask for a coffee?"

"To get you out of the room so that I could ask Gaudin a few questions that might have been awkward with you present."

"Oh," said Charles, still standing.

"I'll tell you something, Charles. It's been worrying me. You are such an honest person that I have difficulty imagining you dealing with the Gaudins and Flints of the world. Not everyone is like that, of course, but there are enough of them out there."

"You think I'm naïve? I know I am but I'm not exactly stupid. Besides, I've sort of decided to bring in a manager and I have the marketing aspect sorted out. Patti is going to take over all those duties. What I would like to know is why did he come here and put on that show? The whole time he was here I kept telling myself that it was all too silly. It upset me because it brought everything to mind again. But him... he looked all wrong."

"So he is, Charles, and I'm glad to hear you have a handle on things. If you sit down, I'll explain the case to you, only you must promise me you'll not breathe a word of this to anyone, especially the police."

"Right you are. Not a word to another person."

Brent could see the eagerness in the man's face. He wanted to know something concrete to ease his weary mind.

The investigator began with an explanation of the hydro-electric project and the consequent appropriation of about half the vineyard. It came as a thunderbolt to Charles, who sat speechless, shaking his head in near disbelief. Brent could see that he wanted to relay this news back to Sheila - to tell her all about it - to hear her reaction.

"I have to ask you one question. Sheila was in an accident in December. Who was at fault? She or Forbes?"

"Well, it was a strange thing. Sheila swears that he crossed the centre line and hit her vehicle. Sheila told me that Forbes maintained it was her fault and that she crossed the line. However, he was very amicable about it all and paid for everything so that it didn't go through the insurance. We didn't file a police report or an insurance claim. We thought he had changed his mind and realized his error, so we left it at that."

"Ah, good. Good! Now I can tell you how everything was worked. There are two or three parts I have no knowledge about yet but they should be filled in eventually.

"Stan Forbes got hold of the information about the increase in the value of the Songbird Estate. He got it first and I believe he got it from a man named Clive Richards, who was the person who had calculated the compensation figures for the county. These numbers have been reviewed and it seems they are quite fair. Richards wanted Forbes to buy the property and pay him whatever his cut would be out of the proceeds. At some point, very early on, Forbes declined the deal. However, being the rat he is, Forbes set about making the deal his own. Forbes planned everything and it is a rather convoluted scheme.

"First of all, he decides he will operate alone and have all the profits for himself. He sets up the minor car accident and then pays for everything. This allows him to get on friendly terms with both Sheila and you. From then on, he starts his campaign of wooing Sheila. Don't jump to any wrong conclusions." Charles had moved in his chair and was about to take on an outraged look. "Sheila did not encourage him in the slightest, and Forbes was discreet and only friendly. Behind the scenes, Forbes hires private investigators to make inquiries into your family and the wine business. Somewhere along the line, he discovers he has a potential competitor for the estate in the form of Bartlett's Beverage Company and, as we know, Gaudin is the frontman for the company.

"Forbes has two choices. Compete with Bartlett's or join with Bartlett's. He chooses the latter but does so in the most economical way. He enlists the help of Gaudin, who, he discovers, is drowning in debt, particularly gambling debts. Bartlett's, the company, is now out of the picture.

"Gaudin then becomes his own player. It could be that he approaches his boss, Oscar Flint, and tells him of the Songbird deal. That would mean Gaudin is acting as a double agent. This avenue will be explored when Oscar Flint is arrested and interviewed. According to Gaudin, he is the fall guy and Flint is the mastermind. It would be extraordinary bad luck for him to get entangled with two such wicked individuals. My guess is that Gaudin is lying and Flint is not involved in the murder.

"Time marches on and Clive Richards decides that his own mother should now finance his deal. It takes time to persuade her. During that period, he sounds out a few other potential backers. All his work fails when Sheila is murdered. His mother, Arlene, who is a charming woman, by the way, had been coerced by her two not-so-charming sons. She wants nothing more to do with the deal as soon as she hears of Sheila's death. His other backers also distance themselves.

"Arlene Richards and her son, Stuart, tour the vineyard on the day of Sheila's death. So does Gaudin and, entirely separate from him, Forbes is also present. What is remarkable is that the Forbes and Richards families are distant relations and they did not recognize one another, although Arlene and Forbes had last met some thirty years ago.

"Forbes brought a real estate agent along. His name is Stefan Badowski. He brings his wife, Martha. All this elaborate incognito cover is for two competing parties - Forbes and his satellites and the Richards family - both equally unaware of each other's presence on the day in question. As I have said, the Richards family backs out. This leaves Forbes alone, yet possibly having a Flint affiliation. The backdrop is complete.

"Now for the foreground and we come to the motive for murder. Literally, only a few days prior to the tour, the approvals were finalized for the re-worked hydroelectric project. Standing in the way of the Forbes' and Richards' machinations is Sheila's steadfast refusal to sell the Songbird Estate. For the vineyard to be acquired she must be removed. That would leave you, Charles, in possession of a vineyard that you no longer want because of its associations and with a business in an industry to which you are an outsider. I'm sure there is a steepish sort of learning curve to running this place and you would not be emotionally in a position to want to learn. Easy pickings for the circling vultures. You could be expected to sell quickly, as soon as you came to terms with the idea.

"There are only three names that could potentially matter in the planning of the murder - Forbes, Gaudin, and Flint. Two of them have money - Forbes and Flint. One of them hired a contract killer and paid him a substantial amount of cash. This is another uncertain aspect of the story. I have not found evidence to link one name above another in the hiring of the killer. I will tell you about that miserable wretch in a minute.

"According to Gaudin, Flint sent him a package from head office using Gaudin's own name as the sender *and* the recipient, which is weird, to say the least. The story goes that Flint instructed Gaudin verbally to leave the package in his unlocked car on the day of the tour. Gaudin says he does not know who took the package but subsequently presumed it to be the killer.

"The problem with this story is that Gaudin only remembers it all once the investigation starts intensifying. Remember, this is from his perspective. He is suffering under the strain of being questioned and, perhaps, he panics and so makes the mistake of introducing this motif of Flint's involvement, thinking it will get him out of his difficulties.

"Now, look at it this way. If Flint is not involved then it is only when Gaudin decides to implicate him as the mastermind behind the scheme that blame can shift from him to his boss. The whole sending the package to himself-charade was done with malice aforethought in case it became necessary to pass the buck to Flint. However, as a plan, it was inherently weak.

"Let's look at this from Flint's perspective and we'll see how weak it is. Flint and Gaudin saw each other regularly at Head Office. Flint could have delivered the money package personally to Gaudin without arousing any suspicions and without leaving any kind of a trail. Why, then, would Flint so stupidly send a traceable package to a location that Gaudin rarely visits and where the arrival of such a package would be very remarkable? It would make a kind of sense if Flint deliberately, as Gaudin says, wanted to pin everything on him. But then, in the same gesture, Flint would be exposing himself and his company to investigation. That, surely, is the last thing in the world he would want. Flint would not create a trail that implicates himself. The story about Flint is an ill-conceived invention and, whether Gaudin's or Flint's, it will be proved to be so one way or another.

"I say Flint is not involved - at least, not in any way that I can see at the moment. Therefore, the money must come from Forbes, because Gaudin has none. Gaudin really does send himself an empty dummy package from Head Office so that he has the option to implicate Flint if he needs to.

"But Gaudin has not finished with packages just yet. He sets up in advance, hours before the tour begins, his story to Sheila involving the delivery of a lab kit. The critical moment is now looming.

"Before we get to that point, however, there are another person's actions to consider, which occurred during the afternoon of the tour. They are those of Forbes when he was sitting alone in his car in the parking area. Forbes told me it was then that he was rethinking his position regarding Sheila. He told me he had loved her and had wanted to invest in the Estate to help her business expand. When, according to him, she did not meet him as planned, he says he began to have second thoughts.

"He sits in his car listening to music to calm himself because he is thwarted in his schemes. During this meditative time, what does he witness? Nothing, except he hears someone going to a nearby car. Why does he tell me this? He tells me because he wants Gaudin out of the way. Forbes feels the man has now become a liability and that the questions being posed are getting too close for his own continuing comfort. I am quite certain that Forbes entertained no real affection for Sheila and his sitting in his car was not to recover his equanimity but rather to keep a watchful eye over the money package. I have to tell you, I took an instant dislike to Forbes. I shouldn't have but I did. It made me more belligerent in the questions I put to him.

"It was soon after my questioning of Forbes that he must have contacted Gaudin and told him now to admit to the pay-off package having been in his car. If Forbes knows of the pay-off package, it's likely he also knew of the dummy package, in which case he may well have been the one who had advised Gaudin to send it the way he did so that Flint could be implicated."

"Brent, just a moment. Are there three packages, then?" asked Charles.

"That's right. The pay-off package with Forbes' money in it; the dummy package used to implicate Flint; and only the story of a third package from a lab. That last one doesn't exist, Charles. It's pure invention. I'll explain it soon."

"Ah, I see. How devious it all is. Go on."

"Where was I? Yes... Gaudin, believing Flint will now take the heat because of the package of money story, might only be unwittingly implementing Forbes' own backup plan. Forbes can appear innocent while the duped and panicky Gaudin can flounder in his contradictory statements which proclaim that Flint is the mastermind and he only the dupe of Flint. Gaudin, clearly desperate for money, is not a thoughtful guy. He did not see that Forbes was using him this way. The promise of pay-offs or commissions was enough to dazzle him in any event.

"I'm sorry, Charles, but now the whole situation gets even more complicated. Unilaterally, Gaudin has done one of two possible things. Either he has actually suggested to Flint that Bartlett's should buy the Songbird Estate or Gaudin has put in a spurious offer as though it came from Bartlett's. The latter choice makes no sense to me at all. The Bartlett offer, as you know, is also better than the one Forbes subsequently makes. Forbes, therefore, has to be unaware of the Bartlett offer. This development can only mean that Gaudin is playing his own game through all of this and had decided to stick with Bartlett's and Oscar Flint to preserve his career by cutting out Forbes from the deal. Gaudin is fully prepared to pursue this course until the moment when he panics under questioning. Of course, this then means that Flint knows enough of the offer to purchase deal to make him look as though he is guilty of conspiracy to murder also, but, as I said, I doubt that he is involved in it. Possibly, Flint wanted to acquire the estate in its own right and more so when he was told of the land appropriation settlement. I think he was willing to let Gaudin have a crack at getting it but, I believe, that was the full extent of his involvement.

"Who hired the killer? Gaudin did. How do I know? Because the killer was given nothing in advance. Flint or Forbes could and would have paid a deposit or the full sum. I say Forbes sent or gave the money to Gaudin because the killer or the killer's intermediary would not work without first being paid. In other words, Gaudin's cash and credit are commonly known to be at zero and his contact would only go as far as arranging the work but would not follow through without full payment in hand. Had there been no money for the assassin in Gaudin's car, Sheila would not have been killed. I'm so sorry about this, Charles. I can stop if you wish me to."

"But he was sitting right here... only a few minutes ago... crying!?"

"I know, Charles. I know he was. He was selling his story and he did look very convincing. He *may* even be remorseful about Sheila. I have half an idea that he has been threatened with serious harm over his gambling debts. This could prove to be the true motivator for him to undertake the scheme in the first place and has made him a desperate and dangerous man... Do you want me to continue?"

"Give me a moment, please. I want to hear it to the end." Charles Babbington was crying freely - his face was wet and he had placed a finger and thumb on his eyelids as if to staunch the flow.

"Anything I can get you?" asked Brent.

"No. Keep going."

"I will. Now we come to the killing team itself. These individuals are not the brightest but they are cunning. The killer's name is Graham Clarke. He has killed quite a few people. He seems to be a heartless and ruthless young man who kills on contract and for pleasure. I believe he developed a method of killing people with a knife while still sitting on his bike, something that requires accuracy yet gives him immediate means of escape. He also uses firearms and I know this for a fact because he took a few shots at me today."

"He shot at you?"

"Yes, and caused a lot of damage to the lobby of an apartment building! But to continue... Clarke is addicted to his bike. He is an urban thug and his method of getting around the city is on his expensive bike. This man has an accomplice who, I suspect, was coerced into the thing. I don't doubt he was paid for the part he played. Luke Valinho is a courier driver. He brings Clarke out to the Estate and drops him off with his bike. Valinho is on his legitimate route and it is that which probably suggested to Clarke his inclusion in the plan. Clarke has been rooming in Valinho's apartment for some time. I'm not sure why that has been the case and it seems to have been a temporary arrangement. Perhaps Clarke was keeping an eye on his associate in case he decided to talk. Valinho could hardly throw an assassin out of his apartment so he put up with his unwanted lodger.

"Valinho, Clarke and the bike are in the courier van. Clarke wants to arrive earlier than planned with Gaudin. There are two reasons for this. First, Clarke has to be sure of being paid. He wants that money as soon as possible. Second, Valinho's courier route has to go off according to schedule so that there should be no red flags raised about him being missing or late. Anyway, Clarke is on site. He hides for a while. Being essentially stupid he gets bored and so rides around on his bike, waiting for the parking lot to be empty so he can get the payment from Gaudin's car. At some point, he does retrieve the money and this may be the moment that Forbes says he heard a car door being closed, unless, of course, he's lying about that.

"With the money safely stashed upon his person, he cycles up the hill to hide in some bushes at the very top of the vineyard. He's ready. I can imagine that he's wearing a courier company hat under his hoody. He thinks of his hoody as camouflage. What works in a city in November doesn't quite cut it in the countryside on a hot day in May. He obviously looked out of place and was seen by a total of four people, including master Kevin Finch, age five, who, for someone his age, drew a good likeness of the bike.

"There has to have been an inducement to get Sheila to go up to the top of the vineyard, hide her car on a track, and walk into the section of vineyard where she was to meet someone or receive something. Just to receive something makes no sense. She could do that easily at the house. No courier company usually delivers to a field. That was never part of Forbes' plan. Indeed, he was probably unaware of it because it is purely the method employed by the killer who need not tell how he will achieve his objective.

"In advance of the attack, Sheila was never directly contacted by the killers. That leaves only two possibilities - Forbes or Gaudin. Even if Flint were involved, he is remote, and his only agent on the spot is Gaudin, who has damned himself whichever way this all falls out. Forbes could have persuaded Sheila by suggesting a clandestine romantic meeting. Is that possible, Charles?"

"What? No, no... you said yourself she was only friendly towards him. I would have noticed if she had changed towards me. She never did."

"That's what I thought. I cannot imagine that of Sheila. Everything I've heard about her is that she was a good and constant person, who loved her family, was consistent in her friendships, and who devoted her energies to making a success of the vineyard. Money may have been important to Sheila but it was never of prime importance. She would no more sell this vineyard than her children. She invested time and energy in it and she wanted to make you proud of her. She achieved that goal. Sheila would not sell. Forbes could never get her to agree to go up to the end of the vineyard to talk about his buying the place. She would have terminated the friendship on the spot if she thought he had such an ulterior motive.

"That leaves one person who could persuade her to go up there and that is Gaudin. What persuasive reason could he cite? My guess is, he told her, late in the day, just before she's leaving on her trip, that she needs to meet him immediately at the top of the vineyard so that he can show her something about her vines. He also suggests she keep the meeting quiet. There is only one matter I can think of that could galvanize her into action and cause her to comply with his suggestions. He told her that he had seen a diseased plant or two - something like Leafroll. He says he will show her where it is. Perhaps he goes as far as saying he's already ordered some equipment to send samples to a lab for testing, and a kit was to be delivered that same day, too.

"So, Sheila is alone in the vineyard. She's looking among her most precious vines for signs of infestation. So far, she has found nothing or she has taken a few samples. Anyway, there she is at the appointed time in the appointed place. She looks up because she hears a noise. It is Clarke on his bike. Perhaps he is wearing a courier's cap and his hood down. He has a package - the package of money - under his arm. He rides quickly down the track to where Sheila is standing. He puts his bike flat on the ground. He probably speaks, to say he has a package for her. He conceals the knife beneath the parcel as he carries it towards her. As she reaches to take it, Clarke stabs her. Mercifully, it takes only a single, killing blow to end her life - which may have been a first for Clarke. She slumps down and dies among her vines.

"Clarke shows no emotion. He gets back on his bike and heads to the pick-up point where he will soon meet Valinho. The van pulls up to the pre-arranged place, possibly by the bridge. Once inside, Clarke and Valinho return to the depot in Belton. Clarke gets out beforehand. At the end of Valinho's shift, and with the bike strapped to Valinho's car, the two men return home to Newhampton, about an hour's drive away.

"From then on it becomes a waiting game for Forbes and Gaudin. Gaudin puts in an offer for the Songbird Estate. Gaudin's offer is unusual. For a company the size of Bartlett's to be negotiating the deal through a salesman is not at all usual. A lawyer, representing senior management, would be the normal conduit. Why does Gaudin act as the agent of the Bartlett offer? Firstly, it gives validity to his being present at the estate on so many occasions. He furthers this by talking with staff and by making them job offers. But, secondly, and more importantly, I see Flint, once alerted to the increasing value of the property and wishing to act quickly and quietly, himself asked Gaudin to take charge of the offer and expedite matters.

"As you can see, Charles, I have guessed at some things. There still remain a few mysterious elements. The main thing is that the police will now have to get evidence on all these points so that charges can be laid against the conspirators. I'm sure Flint's statements will tear apart Gaudin's lies. When Gaudin goes down, Forbes will go with him. As for Valinho, he is in custody as we speak, and Clarke is the subject of a man-hunt." Charles was shaking his head in confused disbelief.

"Um, that's all I have so far. It's a lot to take in, though, isn't it? Let me summarize it for you. Forbes and Gaudin are equal-ly guilty of murder. The sole objective of the conspirators was to get the Songbird Estate before the compensation payout was announced publicly. They implemented their plan and hired an assassin. As the inquiry came closer to them person-ally they began to panic and make mistakes. They belatedly took to blaming other people - Forbes took action to shift the blame to Gaudin and Gaudin blamed Flint. They made enough mismatched statements for me to see what they were doing and to arrive as close to the truth as I have. I am so, so sorry, Charles."

Chapter Thirty

A near miss

B efore starting off back to town, Brent checked his text messages. One had come in from Martha Badowski. It read, 'Please call me. Seller will accept a lower offer.'

Brent made the call immediately.

"Hello, Martha. What have you got?"

"Well, hello, Brent. Thank you so much for returning my call. Now, there are a few things I need to explain to you..."

"How much and no gushing, please."

"Oh, right. We had that conversation, didn't we? Well, they'll come down but they won't move below six hundred and seventy-five thousand and the big window does need replacing. The seals are gone and there's some kind of green sludge between the glazing. What do you want to do?"

"Can't we take six-seventy-five as the benchmark and deduct half the estimated repair cost so we put in an offer for six-twenty-five?"

"Oh. I don't think they'll accept that but, as I always say, you never know. I'll get an offer drawn up for that amount and you'll need to come in and sign it. I'll add an additional clause making the offer conditional upon the building inspection report. Brent, you really need to go see it. It's better in person than in the photographs. There's a lot of potential there and the garden space is fabulous. It backs onto a park, so you only have the neighbours either side. Nice and quiet... just what you wanted."

"Well, you're a very good salesperson. When can we go?"

"Any time you like. I can get the keys and we can show ourselves around because the listing agent doesn't seem to mind. They've had it on their books for nearly three months."

"Then it was overpriced according to the market, wouldn't you say?"

"True, but it's not overpriced according to what the seller thinks it's worth. That's a big difference right there. The property is part of an estate sale. None of the family wants to live in it. They just want it gone but they're not giving it away. Do you want to go this evening while there's still enough daylight?"

"Yes, I would. I'm in Belton and I have a stop to make but then, I'm on my way to meet you."

"I'll be in the office late anyway so it doesn't matter to me. Are we set, then?"

"Yes, we are. Bye."

Brent drove down towards the bridge. First, he thought over his meeting with Charles. Brent was glad to have had the chance to lay it all out. He hoped he was substantially right because, despite his outward self-confidence, he was prone to inward self-doubt once he had come to a conclusion.

Next, he thought that Stefan Badowski's bark was worse than his bite. After all, it was natural enough for Badowski to have thought, 'a commission is a commission'. That, or the Badowski marital status was still sinking like a stone. He dare not ask Martha about this because she'd take at least an hour telling him. Thinking of Martha, as he crossed over the bridge with his windows open, he thought it a pity she would miss out on her five thousand dollar bonus. He knew he would do something for her even if she *had* failed to get him the place for six-fifty. He had already taken possession of the house in his mind without yet seeing it. 'Ridiculous', he thought, and then smiled to himself.

He was now on the long stretch of road by the river. Traffic was light. He was considering how he could get Jennifer to give him a one-day extension on the reports. As he saw it, the case was pretty much over for him.

The road ahead was empty now and the sports car that had been following behind Brent decided to pass. It pulled into the opposite lane and then seemed to hesitate, causing Brent to glance towards the driver to see what he was doing. As he looked, he saw a pistol pointing towards him. A shot was fired. It passed through the open window just above his arm and went through the windshield. Brent reacted by slamming on the brakes causing the other car to overshoot. Brent started to turn his Jeep around but saw immediately and with a sinking heart that the driver of the sports car had some skills because he was drifting the car around in a controlled skid. Another shot was fired, punching a hole in Brent's passenger door, but it missed him.

With nowhere to go and no one in sight, Brent did the only thing he could. In reverse, he took the Jeep through a screen of brush on the side of the road and bumped heavily down a steep embankment, heading towards the river. At least the car was not able to follow him, even if its occupants could on foot.

At the bottom of the fifteen-foot slope, Brent discovered he was on the flat, open tongue of land around which the river looped. Going forwards now, he skirted a small stand of willow trees and found he was trapped. Not only was the ground marshy towards the river but a raised pipeline cut him off completely. Both upstream and down, the river cut back right up against the embankment. He brought the Jeep to a halt and looked over his shoulder. Two men were coming down the slope as fast as they could and were already on the flat ground. Even if he abandoned the Jeep and ran, he would be trapped in the marsh where they could take pot-shots at him until they were successful.

He had no idea what to do so he took out his phone. Another shot was fired but it was lost in the trees somewhere. If he called the police, they would surely arrive in under ten minutes and, just as surely, he would be dead by then.

"Twice in one day," he muttered to himself. He got out of the Jeep to shelter behind it. The only weapons he had were his phone and a taped screwdriver he used when the driver's window got stuck partially open in the winter.

He looked up and now the men were right in among the trees, one at each end of the stand of willows. Then he noticed something familiar about one of them. He could not think for the moment what it was.

"Excuse me!" called out Brent. "I think I know you." Brent bobbed up and down to see what they were doing. "If you hold on a minute it will come to me. You on the left. I'm sure I know you!" One of them put his hand up. "Not you, the one on my left...! Yes, you... Got it. You're Titus, Archie Banks' son. Haven't seen you in a few years. How are you doing!" To himself, he said, "Please be Titus. Please be Titus."

"How does this guy know you?" said the man on the right who was still pointing his automatic at their quarry.

"I've got a really bad feeling," said the other. "This is bad, bad. Old, blue Jeep, right? Yeah, I know him." He put his head up and called out, "Hello, Uncle Brent."

"Thank God," Brent muttered under his breath before shouting out, "Titus, may I ask why you are shooting at me!?"

For Brent, a long silence followed while a whispered discussion was going on behind the trees.

"You do know him, then?"

"Right. You know my catcher's mitt with the original Sam Mayfield signature on it? He got it for me. He and Dad used to play baseball with me. He used to take care of us when Dad did his stretch. Brought us food, clothes, you name it. He's not my real uncle but I'm finished here."

"You know, I always thought that mitt was a fake. I mean, no one got a Sam Mayfield signature. You say he gave that to you and it's legit?"

"Uh-huh. Uncle Brent can get anything done."

"This is so over."

"Titus, I can't hear you! I have your dad's number all lined up and I'm ready to tell him what you're doing today!"

"Please don't do that, Uncle Brent! Look, we're putting our guns down and coming out with our hands up. Don't make that call. See, we're coming out."

The two men came out from behind the trees. Titus was the shorter and younger of the two at about twenty years of age.

"I'm very disappointed in you," said Brent to Titus, as they approached.

He said nothing and hung his head in shame.

"Did you call the police?" asked the other man.

"What do you think?" replied Brent.

"My name's Neil, by the way. Nice to meet you. But I really think we should be going now."

"I'll let you go if you answer my questions. Has a contract been put out on me by a guy named Gaudin?"

"Er, Godang? No, don't know that name," said Neil. "We were told there was a big bounty to shoot the dude in the blue Jeep coming out of the vineyard. The word was, you'd messed up some woman and that you'd gotta go. We got a call... er, from a friend, and we were in the area, you know, enjoying the countryside and some beats."

"Messed up what...! That Gaudin's got a nerve, I must say. Okay, is this your first... attempted hit, Titus?"

"Ah, yes."

"And you, Neil?"

"Yeah."

"We'll leave the driver out of this. Right, this is what is going to happen. Neither of you is going to do anything like this ever again. I'm confiscating your weapons. Now, who shot a hole in my door?"

"That was me," said Titus.

"Very well. You owe me three hundred to fix it. It was scuffed and needed painting anyway so three hundred should cover the damage you did. It was a pity you didn't shoot the driver's door which sticks, but no matter. The windshield I'm not so worried about because it had a crack in it already. Good job I didn't have it replaced earlier. Titus, do you have that sum of money on you?"

"Yes, I do. Here you are." Titus quickly gave Brent the money.

"Good. As far as I'm concerned this is now over. If I hear of any more violent nonsense like this coming from either of you, then you are both in serious trouble. I'll hand you over to the police and I'll do it with Archie's blessing because I will tell him. Do we have an understanding here?"

"Yessir," said Neil.

"Thank you, Uncle Brent."

"Right. Off you go and leave the guns where they are."

The two young men ran off quickly. As they did so, Brent suddenly realized he might have difficulty getting up the embankment. He had forgotten to add the clause of reimbursement for towing charges - if required.

He selected a low gear and started back towards the embankment. His trusty Jeep did not fail him and, although there was some tense slipping and sliding near the top, he was soon once more out on the road. As he drove, he held up a hand from the steering wheel and saw it was trembling badly again.

Chapter Thirty-one

Journey's end

I t had all come to an end. Brent's services were no longer required. He had the weekend off and, although his back had been patted by Peter Wilson and his hand vigorously shaken by Commander Baker, the loss of his comrades in arms hit him hard. He decided he liked Jennifer the best and Greg the least. This was solely based on personalities and not competence.

Valinho had finally given up some information and Clarke's world shrank, his friends becoming fewer in number. Oscar Flint, while in custody, maintained he knew nothing about any of Gaudin's activities. His assertions were being verified.

Clarke had indeed been seen near his bike obviously hoping to retrieve it but had escaped the sleepy officers who had erroneously assumed he would be a no-show. His bike was afterwards impounded and the Belton police lost a new lock and chain to the Newhampton City police. Greg Darrow was highly confident that Clarke would be brought in eventually. The public was now becoming aware of the change in the dynamics of the case and saw Clarke's photo and an artist's drawing of Clarke's face on its televisions and phones.

To Brent's mind, the most significant developments were when both Forbes and Gaudin had been arrested for conspiracy to murder, among a number of lesser charges. Of a more minor importance to Brent was that Clive Richards had also been arrested and only because it caused him to think of the sadness and shame visiting Arlene Richards about now. He wondered how the badminton set was taking the news and resolved to see them again.

Suddenly it struck him, 'What of Gaudin's family?' It was then that he sank into a depression, entirely forgetting he had bought for himself a delightful house, albeit in need of repairs, and that he owed Martha her bonus because she had got the price down after all. The catalogues he had so enthusiastically acquired from different garden centres were to remain untouched while the fit was upon him.

On Tuesday of the following week, Brent went to see Greg in his office. He had sufficiently recovered from his melancholy and had decided that more work would be a useful antidote, especially work involving murder cases or other serious crimes. He decided to pitch the idea of his being employed by the Newhampton police to Greg, to test the waters so to speak.

"How's your workload at present?" asked Brent as he sat in front of Greg's desk.

"Hungry for work, are you? Let me give you an idea. That pile next to you. There are about fifteen files and they're all open with leads being followed up. You see those twenty or so behind me - they're working their way through the courts. These three I have in front of me are cold cases and I'm getting them off my desk today. Why? Because of the six new cases that started over the weekend and have been dumped on me, because my time at Belton has ended."

"Surely you're not working on all those at once?"

"Nearly three weeks away caused a backlog but I can hand off some of them. However, come the first of next month, I can assign a lot more. I'm getting promoted."

"Congratulations. Do you get a new desk?"

"I get a new office. That's a minor benefit, though. The big change is that I get to review other people's work with next to no running around unless I want to do it. I'll have fourteen detectives to supervise and they'll be doing all the heavy lifting. What a nice change that will be. Life is so sweet, sometimes."

"I'm sure you paid your dues."

"That I have. You're here looking for work, then?"

"I am. I found the case to be quite exhilarating - sometimes more than I liked."

"I can't give you anything, not even when I'm a lieutenant. We have a strong union here and the brass would have to give the okay first. They were surprisingly progressive in Belton and I'd say you did a good job there and earned your keep. I'm not against you helping in an investigation. But to be honest, Brent, I can't see where you'd fit in at present and even if there arose 'a situation' it would be a hard sell all around."

"This is not what I wanted to hear today. I'll have to line up at the soup kitchen by the end of the week."

"What about your PI work?"

"I've gone off it. Too slow and much too boring most of the time. I can't get enthusiastic anymore."

"I get that. I couldn't go back to doing patrols. The wasted hours - necessary - but it's a lot of time just waiting for something to happen. Then, boom, there are four things happening at once. Traffic duty was okay. I kind of liked that because the paperwork was so easy compared to everything else. Now that you've seen the high life, what will you do?"

"I know! I'll become one of those amateur sleuths who is always ahead of the plodding police and solves every case."

Greg fixed a cold stare on Brent with his pale blue eyes. "Don't you dare," he said quietly.

"Would that annoy you?"

"I'd arrest you the first opportunity I had. Wait a minute, though, that is an idea. What would a judge make of you? It would be an interesting summing up. There's a couple I know who would tear you to pieces and very much enjoy it."

"Although I normally relish a challenge, the odds are too severely stacked against me if it's as you describe it. Seriously, I've got no idea what to do. I have a few other interests to keep me busy. I'll immerse myself in those for the time being."

"Sorry. The best I can do is keep you in mind and if a case sets up the right way, I'll bring your name forward at a meeting."

"That's decent of you. Seeing as you're so busy I should get out of your way. Oh, what about Clarke - any news?"

"Last I heard we were up to thirty sightings in four different cities. We have one old gentleman, comes in as regular as clockwork, and he swears he's seen every fugitive we've had over the last ten years. He says he saw Clarke on a red and black bike with very fat tires, hood up, pedalling like crazy just around the corner from where the old gentleman lives."

"Isn't that funny? I would take that seriously. Supposing your old gentleman actually had a real sighting for the first time in his career and you didn't follow up?"

"No, it is not funny. Right there is the difference between the overworked paid professional and the amateur with time on his hands. Go and interview him, if you like. You'll both enjoy yourselves."

"Ah, you caught me once like that. I'm beginning to know you, Greg. You have a twisted sense of humour."

"Yes. And you should see my twisted sense of anger. Get out of here and let me get something done, will you?"

302

"I'm going but I shall return from time to time to make sure you keep your promise of getting me some work."

"Did I promise?"

"You gave your word while being serious and I trust you implicitly. Therefore, it is as a promise to me."

"Goodbye, Brent."

"Goodbye. Say hello to Bennett for me if you bump into him. That should upset the rest of his day."

Greg watched Brent walking between the desks, heading for the elevators. When he had gone, he opened a newly arrived file and began to read over the horrific details of a violent and unnecessary crime.

On Wednesday afternoon, Brent kept his appointment in Belton and was having his hair cut by Erica Stevens, the long-time friend of Sheila Babbington. He had forgotten what type of salon she owned and discovered that a male in the place was something of a rarity unless he were aged twelve or under.

There were nine women of various ages present. One of them was having something inscrutable done to her hair for she was wearing something Brent could only think of as an alien space helmet on a stand. Her hair also gave off a faintly acrid smell that permeated the salon.

"What is that lady having done to her?" he whispered quietly as he and Erica looked at each other in the mirror.

"She's having a perm. The dryer is setting it."

"Oh, a dryer. I see."

After that, he took to studying a nearby display of creams and lotions in upmarket mauve and purple boxes signed by someone whose name he could not decipher. Madame

Aesthete was the name of the line. He saw a price tag for eighty-nine dollars.

"Erica, in all seriousness, is that stuff worth that price?"

In all seriousness, Erica replied, "Yes. It makes the hair supple again by repairing damage. It is a very, very good product. That is our mid-range line."

"Damage? From what?"

"Everyday abuse, blow-drying, perms, that kind of thing."

Brent was quiet after that. His mind was making nonsense thoughts out of the term 'everyday abuse'. He found the salon to be a baffling place. Then the news came on the radio that was playing in the background. Graham Clarke had been captured.

To the astonishment of the peaceful salon, Brent tore his cape off and jumped up, shouting, "Yes! Yes!" He then briefly hugged Erica, his hairstylist, and sat down again.

"At least that's over," she said.

"Yes. You can begin to find some relief now. It won't be an uphill climb for us anymore. Ah, are you okay to finish my haircut? "

"Oh, yes."

The salon settled down once more into its usual routine and the customers returned to their isolated and dignified demeanour - as dignified as permanent waves and semi-public hair washing will permit. From time to time, several ladies did give quick, sideways glances, possibly hoping to witness another outbreak from the only male in the place. Undoubtedly, their curiosity was eventually relieved through the confidences of their own, personal hairstylists.

Chapter Thirty-two

EPILOGUE

Paul Blake and Brent Umber had toured the whole Johannes Vermeer art exhibit and had successfully fitted in as the media types they were pretending to be. They were standing before a small, twelve by twelve oil painting hanging in a wide, heavily carved, wooden frame. Over it, the caption read, 'Is this a Vermeer? - You decide'. Ballot papers and a ballot box stood on a small table close to the picture.

Paul Blake, taller and burlier than Brent, had the habit of putting his head sideways to view a painting. He was doing so now.

"Security is very lax," he said as he studied the small oil. "I say we take The Dancers, my favourite, Visit to the Tomb, your favourite, and this here piece because it's the cutest painting I've ever seen."

"Agreed," said Brent. "We'd need a diversion if we were to do it now. I say this is a Vermeer."

"I do, too. I could feign a heart attack or something."

"Difficult. I couldn't snatch three paintings in one go on my own."

"What about we get some smock things like the gallery staff wear? We could put a couple on ice and take the paintings at the end of the night."

"We could." Brent's tone of voice suggested he was not convinced. "The risk would be our two strange faces with no verifiable story."

"I know. I was just thinking out loud. This is one of his few outdoor scenes. That barn looks so natural it's like it grew out of the ground."

"You know what I like? The scene is devoid of humans and animals but yet it is so alive as if something is about to happen at any moment."

"True... true. We'd have to come back, then. Did you see the alarms?"

"Yes. No camera blind spots. Motion sensors only on the doorways. I didn't see anything else. I should imagine two guards overnight. Then there are the building systems. They are dated. An hour to get in and get the guards comfy, I should say. The paintings will be wired to the wall."

"What are our chances?"

"We can get the paintings easily enough. About zero after that, unless we are investigated by five-year-olds, in which case we should do it."

"Excuse me, may I get to the ballot box?" A lady in her late sixties was smiling at them when they turned around.

"I'm so sorry," said Paul Blake. "That painting got us talking about old times."

"It is lovely, isn't it? I quite understand."

As they both stepped back to allow her to pass, Brent said,

"I know the ballot box is a private affair, but we're voting for Johannes."

The lady turned to them, cupped a conspiratorial hand over her mouth and whispered loudly,

"Don't tell anyone but so am I." She, Brent and Paul laughed together.

"Your discernment is excellent," said Brent. "That's at least three for Johannes."

"Yes. And now, I'm heading back to the wine and cheese table. It's really very good this time. Have you tried some?"

"We did, thank you," said Paul.

The lady smiled, gave a little wave and walked away. The two friends returned their attention to the picture.

"We can't do it, can we?" said Paul.

"No," said Brent. "But it was nice thinking about it."

Brent enjoyed the remodelling of the front of his house because he did not have to live through it and in it. He had an architect draw up plans and, instead of the large expanses of glass at the front, a dark grey stone with a subtle hint of purple was used to build out the entrance and enlarge the vestibule. The stone both complemented and slightly contrasted with the existing grey walls. The entrance and the front façade in general were vastly improved. It cost Brent a small fortune and he had yet to begin on the garden.

The garden now seemed a huge project by itself. Brent quickly discovered a world of difference between looking at pretty plant photos online or dreamily flipping through enticing seed catalogues and actually beginning a garden from scratch. He did not know where to start. He visited a garden centre seeking therapy for his condition and advice as to which direction he should take. Undoubtedly, he reasoned, a professional landscaper would be needed. It was here that he met Eric.

"Excuse me, do you work here?" Brent spoke to a tall, upright senior who possessed tanned, gnarled hands and was wearing a green work shirt over a pair of work pants of a different green. The man was standing near the cash register.

"Who me? No," said Eric.

"I need to talk to someone about my garden."

"Someone'll be along soon."

"Where did they all go? Can't be lunch, it's too early in the morning."

"Hmm," said Eric. "Waste of time is what it is. I'm only here for sheep manure and they moved it on me."

"Sheep manure? What do you use that for?"

Eric turned and stared at Brent, looking him up and down.

"Soil amendment."

"Oh… What's soil amendment?"

"If the soil's not good you have to improve the structure and add organic material. Manure adds nutrients."

"I get it. I thought nutrients came in granules or liquids."

"Ha, ha, ha-uh." Eric's laugh sounded like a deep, rumbling hiccup.

"I know," said Brent. "I really haven't a clue about gardening except what I've read online. That's why I'm here. I need to find a landscape designer. I'm starting a garden from scratch."

"Well, it's none o' my business, but you don't sound like you know enough to do that. You see, with a designer, you have to tell 'em what you want or they'll put in what *they* want. That will cost you more 'an you bargained for."

"What should I do?"

"Have a clear plan of what you want. Decide where the compost heap, sheds, and greenhouse goes. Put in yer trees, shrubs and perennials according to yer plan. Get yer beds set up for flowers and vegetables. Make sure you have good sightlines so that it all looks pretty. Layout yer walkways, irrigation and such, improve yer soil where needed, and always be mindful of light levels."

"If you don't mind my asking, could you come and take a look at my place?"

"Look at it? Why, I just told you what needs doing."

"I thought you could help me draw up my plans. I'd pay you for your time."

"Hmm." Eric scratched the slight stubble on his chin. "S'pose I could do that. Where's yer place?" Brent told him. "That's good. We're practically neighbours. One thing we has to do an' that's stop by my place. We need beer to draw up gardening plans 'cos I find it to be dry, thirsty work, I do. You like beer?"

"Once in a while."

"That's good, 'cos I make some very nice homebrew, even though I say it myself."

On hearing this, Brent was less certain about his fortuitous find. However, it turned out well. Eric got his manure and Brent got an experienced gardening genius at a reasonable rate.

An afternoon and evening of Eric's homebrew, which proved to be excellent especially when augmented by a delivery of Chinese food, got the plans sorted out perfectly. One relationship dynamic was established very early on. In all matters pertaining to the garden, Eric was master and Brent merely the servant who paid for everything.

Although Brent would have worked with them again in an instant, Jennifer and Damian disappeared off his radar. He recognized that, when the case ended, their common interest ended also because no time had been spent, or could have been spent, in developing deeper friendships. As a consequence, the detectives' celebration dinner never did materialize.

The expenses of the new house continued with redecoration and furnishings. Patricia Epstein's tropical beach scene was given the most prominent place in the living room. Technically, it was a better-executed piece than the much earlier, original one. However, somewhere in the intervening years, an elusive, indescribable nuance had been lost between original and copy. She had been in love for the first and she was not for the second.

The harvest of Pinot Noir came in at the Songbird Estate. It was an excellent vintage and declared to be such by a beaming and effusive Sergio Calabrese.

Brent visited the estate about once a month now. He was good friends with Charles, got on with the children, whom he had finally met, and was accepted as a welcome regular by the staff. Sheila's legacy was in good hands.

As he had insisted, Brent paid full price for one case of the highly prized wine. Charles slipped a second case into Brent's Jeep without his knowing. Both men had preserved their honour and dignity. Charles did not appear to be quite so naïve as he had once seemed.

Out of such an abundance, Brent dispatched gifts of two bottles each to Jennifer, Damian, and Greg. He hoped they would appreciate it. Their replies of thank you suggested that they did.

That was in December. Before then, however, another matter arose.

Chapter Thirty-three

EPI-PROLOGUE

The romantic life of a clever, entertaining, sometimes silly, trustworthy-ish, early thirties, modestly wealthy young man should be a matter of plain sailing. On paper, Brent looked to be a relatively sound investment. In person, it was a different matter, mainly because of his own behaviour. Undoubtedly, he could have formed an alliance that would have ended badly for one reason or another. That was not his goal, though he never thought in those terms. All he knew was that he had yet to find 'her', the woman who was a match for him or, at least, 'she' who could put up with him and still love him. The young man had an extraordinarily wide circle of friends. Some of Brent's most trusted friends haled from his criminal past and were of long-standing. They had shared memories, experiences, figurative trials, and legal trials, although Brent had escaped the latter. His friends chided him on his charmed existence.

Brent had many acquaintances - people he knew to talk to and be glad to see in order to be brought up to date with news of all their doings but he was also content not to see them for another year or two or five.

After his criminal career ended, new friends came into being but these were of a more superficial nature. No fire had forged the bonds and these friendships were more of a social nature.

One such set was forever trying new restaurants. For the most part, Brent was happy to go along with them and sample the culinary delights, although he found this could become tedious if indulged too often.

Among this set, on one convivial evening, Brent pledged himself if not to a blind date, certainly to a myopic one. He had met his date-to-be beforehand. In fact, they were sitting on opposite sides of the table when they both were ensnared in the scheme of the others.

"You're the only two not married at this table!" went up the cry. "You should go on a date!" followed. "Date, date, date!" was the incessant chant until they both capitulated to save face.

Brent wondered if he was suitable for quiet Linda Roberts. She, also, wondered if Brent was a suitable match for her. On this uncertain basis, a table for two was booked in a restaurant called 'Garlands', situated in the very expensive 'Shepherd's Luxury Hotel'. There was nothing of the sheepherder about the place. It attracted almost exclusively both the idle and the industrious rich.

The restaurant was its own entity with its own reputation. Garland's was widely known as a place that was chic, à la mode, and either hot or cool which, for some people, perversely amounts to the same thing. It was one of the places to be seen. The food was often experimental to the point of weirdness but solid, standard fare was also available. Everything was priced accordingly. It was the sort of place that if one happened to mention one had been to Garland's, eyebrows would be raised. They would be raised not because of one's implied culinary expertise but by the hearer's thought that you either must be loaded or someone important, or both. Brent, impeccably dressed, chose to take Linda to the restaurant in his near-vintage and pristine Porsche Boxster instead of the Jeep.

The dinner at the quiet, corner table was not an immediate success. It consisted of one long silence sprinkled with sporadic, unrelated discussions.

"So, you're a private investigator, then? Isn't that kind of shady?" asked Linda.

"Uh... you could say that," replied Brent, slightly taken aback. "There are definitely some aspects to the business that are not quite decent by usual standards. But I'm not one anymore. Private investigator, I mean. Unless an interesting case comes up."

"Oh."

Forks clicked on plates as they sat, eating in silence. The rest of the dining room was having a fine time. A continuous hubbub of conversation, punctuated with laughter and exclamations, ebbed and flowed. The cozily lit room was animated and convivial with faint scents blending together from different tantalizing dishes to give the atmosphere a unique character.

"What do you think of the food?" asked Brent.

"It's nice but I'd try something else next time."

"You can have another entrée if you like."

"Oh, no. I don't seem to be hungry anymore."

"Um... do you like gardening?"

"Not really. You mean, like cutting the lawn?"

"More like growing flowers and vegetables. Making your own private space beautiful with lovely plants. It could be for others to see and enjoy or become one's own garden of delight."

"Sounds like a lot of work."

"Oh, well, I suppose it is, really. But it's worth the effort... not that I'm very good at it, yet."

"Brent? Why did you give up being a private investigator?"

"Ah, well, yes. You should find this very interesting. I did some work for someone and that led me to being invited in on a murder case..."

"Oh, stop! Don't tell me anything horrible. I hate murders."

They ate on in silence.

"What *do* you like?"

"Most of all, I would say, I love my family. Holidays are my favourite when we all get together. I see my brothers and sisters and all the little ones. They make fun of me because I'm late marrying but I don't mind. My great-grandmother, Nana Bet I call her, right from when I was only three years old, she's such a darling..."

Linda waxed lyrical about her family, near and distant, for some time. Only the desserts being placed on the table brought her discourse to a halt. Brent had learned much about people that he had decided he would never meet. He could not help wanting to yawn when she was speaking.

"What about *your* family?" asked Linda.

"I don't actually have one that functions as a family as such. To put it in a nutshell, my father disappeared and my mother fell ill during which time I was put up for adoption. Then she died. Adoption never happened and turned into a series of foster homes. The relatives I know about can't seem to be bothered with me. To tell the truth, there's no love lost between us. That's about it for my family."

"That's awful. You don't have a family? I can't wrap my head around it."

"You really don't have to try to do that. I was pretty young when it all happened and I got used to the situation. It doesn't bother me."

"You were adopted, I mean, fostered, whatever? I don't think anything like that has ever happened in *my* family. There was only uncle Simon who got caught stealing a car when he was a teenager. That's about it."

Brent thought of several things to say but, looking at Linda, he decided not to expend the energy. He was about ready to call it quits for the night.

"Is there anything else you would care for?" asked Brent.

Three sharp explosions shattered the restaurant's atmosphere. Chairs overturned, patrons threw themselves to the floor or crouched down, things shattered or crashed. For a moment there was silence before the screaming started. A wide gap had formed around a table near the centre of the room as people had backed away from it. Linda started screaming in a piercing, high-register wail. Brent left her to it.

With his eyes darting everywhere and ready to dive for cover, Brent went forward as quickly as he could. He made his way around tables with cowering people behind them and stepped over living prostrate forms. He was heading for the leper table.

As he drew closer, Brent noticed a gun on the floor. A few steps further and he reached the table. Glass and cutlery had been swept off and lay haphazardly on the thick carpet. Lying on the far side of the table, still in his overturned chair, was a man, his body twisted slightly, with arms at awkward angles, and his head to one side. His dark jacket lay open to reveal what should have been a white shirt except it was now mostly wet and red with two obvious holes in the chest area. Brent saw him and went cold, the sight bringing him to a standstill for some seconds.

A large man approached as Brent was staring at the body. Brent looked towards the newcomer who was holding a pistol with both hands down by his side.

"Are you police?" asked the man, in a deep, low voice. There was no look of the killer upon him.

"Not really," answered Brent. "Have you called them?"

"Yep." The man scanned the room and said over his shoulder, "Know him?"

"No... I think I saw the murder weapon. I'm going to secure it. If you can stay by the... body."

"Sure."

Brent found the weapon again and stood by it. He saw some people starting to leave the room so he shouted out,

"Attention, please! The danger is over! If everyone can stay where they are until the police arrive it would be a help to them!"

Most of them stopped but a few escaped to safety. Brent took a video of them with his phone as they left.

"Please, stay where you are! I know this is awful and frightening but we must all do what we can to help the authorities! Try to remain in your places! The danger has passed!"

The flow of departures halted. Brent could not blame the ones who had left. They did not want to stay and answer questions all night and some were clearly distraught, scared. He called a number.

"Hello, Brent," said Greg Darrow. "Haven't heard from you in a while."

"I'm at Garland's restaurant. There's been a murder. It happened about two minutes ago. You should get over here now."

"On my way. Try not to let anyone leave."

After disconnecting the call, with his hand shaking slightly, Brent quietly said to himself, "What a way to get a job."

Also By G J Bellamy

If you liked this book please help us by leaving a good review.

BOOK 2 Death in a Restaurant is available now on Amazon in the US
https://www.amazon.com/dp/B097FCMKZ7
Amazon in the UK
https://www.amazon.co.uk/dp/B097FCMKZ7

FREE STORY CYCLE If you liked this story, a great choice is to sign up for the **monthly newsletter** to learn about upcoming new releases and to join the **Free Story Cycle**.
https://gjbellamy.com/newsletter-landing-page/

The current cycle of novella-length stories is entitled:

The Village of the Sevenfold Curse
- Murder Mystery through the ages

This new series of seven unpublished stories are free - exclusive only to newsletter subscribers.
But it doesn't stop there.
When one **Story Cycle** ends... another begins.

OTHER TITLES IN THE BRENT UMBER SERIES
Death in a Restaurant
Death of a Detective
Death at Hill Hall
Death on the Slopes
Plus more coming soon

Printed in Great Britain
by Amazon

33436288R00184